HEALING LOVE

EASTMONT SERIES
BOOK TWO

BY JAYNE LAWSON

xulon PRESS

Copyright © 2015 by Jayne Lawson

Healing Love
by Jayne Lawson

Printed in the United States of America

ISBN 9781498421423

All rights reserved solely by the author. The author guarantees all contents are original and do not infringe upon the legal rights of any other person or work. No part of this book may be reproduced in any form without the permission of the author. The views expressed in this book are not necessarily those of the publisher.

Unless otherwise indicated, Scripture quotations are taken from the King James Version (KJV) – public domain

www.xulonpress.com

Carla,
The story of Valerie closely parallels my own battle with cancer. I hope it is a blessing to you. Love, Jayne

1 Corinthians 10:31

2019

DEDICATION

This story is for those amazing women in my life who have walked through the "valley of the shadow of death" as they battled cancer themselves or cared for a loved one who did.

Acknowledgements

I am so grateful to my Lord and Savior, Jesus Christ, for His precious gift of salvation and for allowing me to be so wonderfully blessed by traveling through life with the following individuals.

To my beloved husband, John. Facing breast cancer was one of the most difficult times of my life. I cannot imagine how I would have survived it without you by my side. You were my strength when I was weak; you were my song when there was no melody in my heart; you were and always will be my one true love and my very best friend.

To my precious daughter, Samantha. You constantly amaze me! When God blessed me with a daughter, I never dreamed of the joy you would bring me. Your efforts as a wife and mother are a blessing to behold. I love you with all my heart. You may have outgrown my lap, but you'll never outgrow my heart!

To my adorable granddaughters, Ryanna and Bree. Where would I have gathered so much information about emergency room pediatrics if it hadn't been for both of you? Our visits to the ER have been unforgettable! (But no more, okay?)

PROLOGUE

A warm, gentle breeze blew across the rolling green hills of the Lakeside Baptist Church cemetery. Fragrant pink, white, and red azaleas lined the gravel path that wound through the grounds allowing visitors easy access to the final resting places of their loved ones. Dr. Will Garrett walked slowly but deliberately, his deep-set dark brown eyes scanning the stone memorials until he spotted the one for which he sought. As he meandered through the graveyard, he fought to control his emotions. His heart ached with a great emptiness every time he visited the cemetery, and today was no exception. Reaching his destination, his eyes moved slowly over the name etched in stone.

Standing silently, he struggled to comprehend the death of individuals far too young to leave this life, yet resigned himself to the knowledge that that was the way of life. Brushing a lock of thick black hair from his forehead, he stooped down to gaze at the gravesite monument. The hollowness in his heart threatened to overwhelm him, and as he knelt, his fingers moved across the smooth face of the marble stone, hesitating for a moment over the engraved name.

"I wish you were here. I miss you so much." His voice was a grief-stricken whisper that faded in the wind. He stood up slowly, placing his hands in his pockets. The wind suddenly felt cold.

"I never thought I'd lose you when I did. I guess I thought you'd be here forever..." The sun momentarily disappeared behind the clouds, casting shadows reflective of the sorrow in Will's heart.

He sighed deeply, never taking his eyes from the tombstone. "What I'd give for one more day with you. There's so much to tell you." He paused for another moment, looked upward, and then returned his gaze to the stone. "So much has happened since you've been gone. You'd be amazed at who I am today... and proud, too, I hope. I love you..."

~Two Years Earlier~

CHAPTER ONE

"Clear!"

The lifeless body on the bed arched slightly as 250 volts of electrical current passed from one defibrillator paddle to another. Five pairs of eyes focused on the cardiac monitor waiting for any indication of a return to a normal heart rate.

Nurse Valerie Garrett reached over to the defibrillator. "Charging to 300," she said firmly, her hazel eyes focused upon the tall, dark-skinned doctor standing beside her. As he held the paddles in place on the chest of Eastmont Hospital's latest emergency room patient, Dr. Ben Shepherd waited for the head nurse's signal that the paddles were fully charged once more. As soon as Valerie nodded, Dr. Shepherd commanded his staff to stand clear and discharged the paddles. The body of the 36-year-old patient arched once more, and again, all eyes followed the thin white line on the overhead monitor. Suddenly, a small blip appeared, followed by another, and then more in a somewhat irregular pattern, but one that could sustain life.

"We got him back, folks. Now let's keep him," stated Dr. Shepherd. He placed a stethoscope on the patient's chest and listened while the ER staff around him automatically moved to stabilize their patient.

"BP's low, but holding," reported Valerie as she watched a student nurse attempt to establish an intravenous line in the hand of the patient.

"We need that line in now," Dr. Shepherd said brusquely.

"Mrs. Garrett, I don't think I can get this in," whispered the young woman who had just stuck a needle into the hand of the nonresponsive patient.

Valerie saw the student nurse's hand trembling. Resisting the impulse to take the needle from the young girl and do it herself, Valerie spoke reassuringly to her. "Don't retract the needle. Hold it steady and feel for the vein. You know it's there; it just needs an anchor. You can do it, Beth. Once you feel it pop, advance the needle forward a bit and slide the catheter into the vein."

The blonde woman nodded her head and palpated the patient's vein once more. Valerie glanced upward and saw Dr. Shepherd observing Beth intently. His dark brown eyes moved toward Valerie and met hers. Nodding slightly at the doctor, Valerie saw his concerned face relax, and she knew that her small gesture had succeeded in reassuring Ben Shepherd that everything was under control.

"Got it!" Beth announced as soon as she saw the blood flash back into the hub of the catheter. Quickly retracting the needle, she secured the IV tubing to the catheter and taped it in place. Looking up at Valerie, she softly confessed, "I didn't think I was going to get it in. Thank you."

"Get those meds on board," ordered the doctor as he turned his attention to the overhead monitor.

Valerie smiled understandingly. "I know, but you did fine. It's much more difficult with a compromised circulatory system. Those little veins just don't want to be stuck." She quickly administered the drugs ordered by the physician, and then moved slightly to accommodate the electrographic technician preparing to take an EKG.

"Get cardiology in on this, and then let's get this fellow to the cardiac care unit," instructed Dr. Shepherd as he wrote on the ER chart.

"Yes, Dr. Shepherd," responded Beth as she hurriedly exited the room.

"Nicely done, Val," commented Dr. Shepherd as he handed the chart to Valerie. He removed his latex gloves and tossed them into a biohazard bin. "I didn't think she was going to get that line in."

Valerie agreed. "Neither did I."

Ben raised an eyebrow. "Really? I thought that was a look of confidence you shot me, or was it a look of 'Shut up'?"

"It was neither," Valerie laughed. "I didn't want you to say something to scare Beth any more than she was. She's going to be a good nurse one day, Ben. She just needs practice." Valerie raised the side rails on the patient's bed.

"Scare her? Me?" grinned the doctor. "I try not to do that, you know. I happen to be a very nice guy. Just ask me."

Valerie chuckled as he continued.

"I think I'll grab a cup of coffee after I talk to the patient's wife... if she's here. After that, I'll be in the lounge if you need me." He gave her a parting nod as he left to find the young man's family.

Valerie watched Ben leave the room, and then went back to her patient. She did a quick assessment of his vital signs, checked his IV, and made him presentable for his trip to the cardiac care unit.

"How does a 36-year-old man have a massive heart attack?" she muttered softly as she made some notations on his chart.

Valerie took a sip of her lukewarm coffee and sat down at the nurses' station to review the status of the ER. Two possible fractures were awaiting x-rays; one asthmatic was receiving a breathing treatment, and one woman was waiting for an obstetrician to determine if her abdominal cramping was genuine labor or merely the false labor of Braxton Hicks contractions. The waiting area was nearly empty, and Valerie thought this would be a great time for a break.

Walking into the staff lounge, Valerie found it unoccupied. Only the sound of muffled conversation from the hallway disturbed its silence. She emptied her coffee cup in the sink and refilled it with the warmer brew in the coffee maker. More than halfway through her twelve-hour shift, she sighed as she plopped down into an overstuffed recliner. She was looking forward to meeting her husband later and having a romantic dinner as they celebrated their sixth wedding anniversary. She gently fingered her wedding ring. The center diamond glittered softly in the dim lighting of the lounge. The brilliant blue marquis sapphires flanking the half-carat diamond were Valerie's favorite gem, and she fondly remembered the moment Will had presented the ring to her and asked her to be his wife.

She smiled dreamily, closed her eyes, and allowed her memories to transport her to the moment when he had dropped to one knee and made his request in the middle of a crowded restaurant. A hush had fallen upon the patrons surrounding their table, and when Valerie had nodded her consent to his proposal, a burst of applause had erupted in the Italian bistro. As she reflected on that evening nearly seven years ago, the door opened and jarred her back to the present.

"Val, we need you in treatment room four."

Valerie rose to her feet, took one more sip of her coffee, and exited the lounge.

Stepping inside the examination room, Valerie saw an elderly man sitting on the bed. Holding a cloth over his left ear, he kept murmuring to himself. Standing next to him was a woman who appeared not much younger than the man. Valerie quickly perused the couple, noticing the woman's blue-gray eyes darting around the room, and her frail, wrinkled hand gently patting the back of the man.

"Hi, I'm Valerie." She smiled at the woman, and then turned to the patient as she picked up the admittance chart. "What happened to you, Mr. Halwood?"

The old man looked at her, a puzzled expression on his face. "I don't know what happened." He turned to the woman beside him. "Do you know?

The woman's eyes misted over. "He slipped and fell on the sidewalk. Hit his ear, and I think... I think part of it is gone." Her voice wavered a bit. "He... um... he has a hard time remembering things. Do you think you can help him?"

As she put on a pair of latex gloves, Valerie nodded reassuringly to the woman. "Absolutely. We'll take good care of him. You sit right here. Are you his wife?"

The woman's voice trembled. "Yes, we've been married forty-four years. Joseph was my high school sweetheart." She glanced over at her husband.

As she listened to Mrs. Halwood, Valerie gently removed the cloth from Joseph's ear. The outer ear was very difficult to visualize due to the extreme amount of bleeding, but it was evident to Valerie that there was a great deal of tissue damage. As she wiped away some of the blood, she could see that the layers of skin in some places had been abraded down to the cartilage.

"Mr. Halwood, can you hold this on your ear for me?" She placed a thick layer of clean gauze dressings over his ear.

"Sure," he replied, and then added, "I don't know what happened to me. Is it still bleeding?"

"Yes, it is," said Valerie as she turned to his wife. "Mrs. Halwood, there's quite a bit of bleeding from this wound. Is your husband taking a blood thinner?"

The gray-haired woman thought for a moment before answering. "Yes. Yes, he is. He takes one of those pills every day. Plus, he has a heart pill and a gout pill, but his gout hasn't been bothering him lately. Oh, he also takes a water pill."

"Thank you," said Valerie as she jotted down the information. "I'm going to go and get Dr. Shepherd. I think you'll like him very much. He's a very good doctor."

Mrs. Halwood smiled nervously at Valerie. "Thank you, dear."

Valerie walked to the nurses' station and saw Ben Shepherd scribbling in a chart.

"Can you see Mr. Halwood in four? Laceration to the left ear with quite a bit of bleeding. On warfarin, and probably has some dementia. His wife is in there with him," reported Valerie.

Ben looked up. "Sure, Val. No problem. Let me just finish this, and I'll be right there."

Within five minutes, Valerie followed Ben into the treatment room where the Halwoods waited. The doctor quickly donned a pair of latex gloves and began examining the patient. Valerie stood by, ready to carry out his orders.

"Let's see if we can irrigate this a bit, so we can get a better look," he said to Valerie. Then he turned to Joseph. "Mr. Halwood, I'm going to have to rinse out this ear, so I can take a better look inside. Is that okay with you?"

The elderly man nodded his head. "Sure, Doc. Whatever you need to do is fine with me. Hey, what happened to me anyway? I can't remember a thing."

"You had a little fall and hit your ear," replied Ben as he adjusted the overhead lighting.

"He forgets things," interjected Mrs. Halwood. A tear trickled down her cheek.

Valerie handed her a tissue. "Would you like to wait outside?"

Mrs. Halwood hesitated, looked at her husband, and then nodded. "Maybe I better. He will be all right, won't he?"

"We're going to do our best to make sure he is," reassured Valerie as she directed Mrs. Halwood to the waiting area.

As she turned back to the doctor, he stated, "Let's get this irrigated. I need to see what's going on in there."

Valerie quickly opened an irrigation set-up and a bottle of saline. She moved the tray table next to the doctor and opened another bulk package of gauze dressings.

"Now, this is going to feel cold, Mr. Halwood," cautioned Ben as he squirted some of the fluid into the old man's ear.

"Goodness, that's cold!" cried Joseph. He moved his hand toward the injured ear.

"Keep your hands down, Mr. Halwood," ordered Valerie in a soft voice. "Dr. Shepherd is rinsing out your ear."

"My ear? What happened to my ear?"

"You fell down and hurt it," responded Valerie.

"I did? Why, I don't remember doing that. How'd it happen?"

"You slipped and fell, and hit your head on the sidewalk."

Ben maneuvered the overhead light once more to better illuminate the outer ear canal. He frowned as he carefully probed the bloodied lining of the canal.

"Aha!" he said triumphantly. "There's a small bleeder in here. Looks like an arteriole from the way it's pulsating. Let's stitch that up and see if that helps. Let's also get him some vitamin K to counteract the warfarin."

He turned to Mr. Halwood. "Sir, I have to numb your ear a little because it's going to need a few stitches."

"That's just fine, Doc. Is it still bleeding? I just can't remember what I did," repeated Mr. Halwood.

Valerie smiled as Ben patiently explained once more about the fall to Mr. Halwood. She placed a vial of anesthetic on the tray table with a needle and syringe, opened a suture kit, and set it within easy reach of the doctor.

HEALING LOVE

"This is going to sting a little," informed Ben as he began to numb the ear.

"Ow!" cried Joseph, "That sure does hurt my ear, Doc."

"Hang in there, Mr. Halwood. Just a little more."

Ben repeated the numbing procedure a few more times until he was satisfied that the ear was deadened to sensation. He carefully began to suture the torn blood vessel as Valerie stood by, waiting to assist him if needed.

When finished, Ben turned to Valerie. "Let's get a pressure dressing on this and watch him for an hour or so. Once the bleeding is stopped, we'll need a CT scan of his head. I want to make sure there isn't any intracranial hemorrhaging. If that's okay, we can let him go to be followed up by his regular doctor." He removed his gloves and tossed them on the tray. "Thanks for your help."

"No problem, Dr. Shepherd," replied Valerie as she deposited the used needle and syringe into the sharps container. She turned to Mr. Halwood. "Joseph, don't touch the bandages on your ear. I'm going to go and find your wife."

"What's this on my ear for?"

Valerie smiled slightly and reiterated, "You had a fall…"

It was nearly eight o'clock when Valerie had finished giving her patient report to the oncoming nurses. Now, with her shift ended, she leisurely entered the staff lounge, walked over to her locker, and opened it. After stifling a yawn, she removed the stethoscope from around her neck and carefully draped it over a hook inside the locker.

"Long day?"

Startled, Valerie jumped and turned, coming face to face with a handsome, dark-haired oncologist.

"Will Garrett, you scared the life out of me!" scolded Valerie as her husband leaned forward and kissed her on the forehead.

"Sorry, sweetheart, I didn't mean to. I thought you heard me come in," apologized Will. "Forgive me?" He cocked his head and gave her a lopsided grin.

"Always," replied Valerie, her tone quite a bit softer. She put her arms around his neck and kissed him firmly. "Happy anniversary!"

"Happy anniversary to you too, sweetheart. Still feel up to dinner?"

"Definitely! I have been looking forward to this all day."

"Me, too." He took Valerie in his arms once more just as the door to the lounge opened, and one of the nurses poked her head in.

"Oops, sorry, but... Val, where's the silver nitrate? Dr. Shepherd says he needs it for Halwood. Apparently the bleeding hasn't completely stopped, and he wants to try that."

Valerie sighed as Will released her. "I'll meet you at the car?"

He nodded. "No problem. I'll pick you up at the ER entrance." He kissed her lightly again on the forehead and walked out of the lounge.

Valerie watched him go, and then hurried to assist Dr. Shepherd.

CHAPTER TWO

"You look a million miles away." Valerie retrieved her stethoscope from her locker and hung it around her neck. She closed the locker's door and turned around to face Dr. Maggie Devereaux.

"Oh, Mags..." Her hazel eyes twinkled as her smile grew. "You've got the best brother in the whole world!"

Maggie's eyebrows raised and a mock frown appeared on her face. "Will? You've got to be kidding. What did he do?"

"Last night, he took me to the same restaurant where he proposed to me. It was so romantic, Maggie. I fell in love all over again."

Maggie rolled her eyes. "Oh, spare me the details." She chuckled as she fastened her long auburn hair into a ponytail. "Seriously, congratulations! I can't believe it's been six years already."

Valerie nodded. "Six of the most wonderful years of my life! Look what he gave me." She pulled a small heart shaped diamond pendant out from under her blouse. Cradling it carefully, she held it up so Maggie could see it more clearly. It sparkled in the soft lighting of the lounge.

Maggie squinted her eyes, looking over the rim of her glasses. "Oh, Valerie, it's beautiful!"

"Thanks, Maggie. I may never take it off!" She giggled, then tucked the pendant back under her blouse. "He's taking me to the theater this weekend, too!"

Maggie's eyes opened in surprise. "The theater? What did you do? Brainwash him?"

As Valerie started to reply, the lounge door opened, and another nurse stuck her head in.

"Dr. Devereaux, we need you in treatment room one."

Maggie nodded. "I'll be right there." She turned toward Valerie and hugged her. "I am so very happy for you, Val... for both of you." As they exited the lounge together, Valerie turned toward the nursing station, while Maggie headed in the opposite direction.

Maggie straightened her lab coat as she strode toward the treatment room. Upon entering, her eyes rapidly scanned the pale young man sitting on the side of the bed holding a blood-stained towel around his wrist. His sleeveless t-shirt, peppered with bloodstains, did little to hide his athletic frame. Sawdust flecks adorned his well-worn jeans. His tousled blonde hair, streaked with natural highlights and his deeply tanned face indicated he spent hours in the California sun.

"I'm Dr. Devereaux." After donning a pair of latex gloves, she picked up the admittance chart hooked on the end of the bed and glanced at his name. "Evan, lie back and tell me what happened." The muscles of his arms were well defined, and despite the use of only one, he easily moved his body lengthwise on the bed. His deep-set blue eyes watched her intently, and as she began to unwrap the towel, the blood began to ooze as soon as the pressure on the wound lessened. Maggie firmly grasped his wrist, pressed the bandage tightly against his arm, and held it up above the level of his heart.

As she held on to Evan's wrist, she leaned toward a cabinet to get a handful of gauze; it was just out of her reach. "I need some help in here!"

In seconds, a slender Hispanic nurse entered the room. Assessing the situation before Maggie uttered another word, she quickly moved to the cabinet and removed a large pack of gauze dressings. She opened them deftly, offered them to Maggie, and then turned to the cabinet after Maggie grabbed a handful of the sterile compresses.

"Thanks, Claire." Maggie added several more dressings to the man's wrist and held them tightly. "Can you get me a cold pack, too?" She turned her attention back to the young man as Claire reached for a cold pack and popped the inner bag. Receiving the compress from the nurse, Maggie carefully removed a few of the dressings she had just applied, then placed the compress atop the rest, and secured it tightly with another bandage. "I'm sorry, Evan, let's start again. Tell me what happened." Her eyes studied her patient one more time.

Still pale, but alert. That's good.

The young man frowned and shook his head slightly. "It all happened so fast, Doc. I was removing a plate glass window-- it had this chip in it. That's why I was removing it-- to put in a new one. The next thing I knew, it broke! Right at the chip, and the top section slipped out of my hand and took a slice right out of my arm. Slipped right outta my fingers! I was holding the top and bottom edges like this." He pantomimed holding the glass with his good arm. "Then the glass broke. Sliced right down the side here. Man, it never would've happened if I'd used suction cups like the glass guys do." He shook his head once more and sighed. "I'm gonna be okay, right, Doc?"

"Let's hope so," Maggie responded. "Once the bleeding has stopped, I can clean you up and stitch up the wound. However, before I do that, I need to make sure there's no nerve damage. You're a construction worker?"

"Yeah. Working on this movie star's home in Malibu. Really fancy place. Been working there off and on for about a year. He always wants something remodeled. The glass was huge. It was for his Jacuzzi room. They're kind of particular, y'know, these celebrities and all."

"So I've been told." Maggie smiled to herself. "Other than the cut, how are you feeling? Any pain?"

"No, just a little lightheaded, I guess. Otherwise, not too bad."

Claire moved to elevate the lower part of the bed. Maggie nodded at the nurse, repositioned Evan's arm, and depressed the fingernails of his injured arm. She watched the blanched nails become pink immediately upon her release of pressure. Satisfied that the blood flow was unrestricted to his hand, Maggie stood up and made a quick notation on the bedside chart.

"I want to keep this compress on for about fifteen minutes, Evan. It will help some of those blood vessels constrict, and the blood flow should slow down quite a bit. I'll be able to take a better look then. Meanwhile, you need to keep that arm up on these pillows." Maggie stepped back while Claire arranged two large pillows under Evan's left arm, elevating it above his chest.

"If you need anything before I come back..." Maggie handed him the call button, "you press this, and one of us will come right in."

He gave a nod of acknowledgement. "Thanks, Doc. I really appreciate it."

Forty-five minutes later, Evan's wound was stitched, and he was resting comfortably. Maggie removed her gloves and tossed them into a biohazard receptacle. "You should be fine, Evan. We're going to discharge you shortly, but you'll need to see your regular doctor to remove those sutures in about five to seven days."

Evan nodded. "Sure, no problem, Doc. When will I be able to go back to work?"

Maggie shook her head. "Not until those stitches are out, I'm afraid."

"Seriously? Oh, man... no work, no pay, Doc. You sure it can't be sooner?"

"If the sutures rip out prematurely, Evan, the bleeding could start again, and you'll end up right back here for a longer period of recuperation."

Evan frowned. "Okay, I get it. No work until I get 'em out. That ought to thrill the guy I'm working for. He's pretty demanding." He looked at his bandaged wrist, then up at Maggie. "Oh well, I guess it could've been worse, huh?"

"Without question." Maggie crossed her arms. "You were lucky. You could've lost your entire hand."

"I know, Doc. Thanks again."

Maggie left the room, carrying Evan's chart. Before she had an opportunity to write her final notes, the ambulance bay doors opened, and two paramedics were rapidly wheeling in a patient on a gurney. A third firefighter was doing single-handed compressions on a patient Maggie couldn't see. She handed the chart to the clerk and fell in step with the firefighters.

"Seven-year-old female found unconscious in the family swimming pool by her mother. Her name's Kami. Don't know how long she was in there. A neighbor started CPR right after Mom called 911, but no response. We've been on it for..." He glanced at his watch. "27 minutes." They maneuvered the gurney next to the bed. "On my count. One... two... three. "

The men moved the lifeless girl to the bed in one single movement without interrupting the cardiac compressions. Valerie had entered the room quickly behind the gurney, and now moved to connect the child to the cardiac monitor, which only confirmed the rhythmic artificial compressions of the paramedic.

"Let's get epi on board. What's her weight?" Maggie glanced up at a paramedic.

"Approximately 22 kilos."

Maggie positioned her stethoscope on the child's chest. "Stop compressions," she ordered as she listened carefully. Nothing. She shined a light into the girl's pupils. No reaction. "Continue compressions." A respiratory technician took over for the firefighter.

"Give her .2 mg of epinephrine. BP?"

"Low, but holding."

I could use a little help, Lord.

"Epi's on board, Dr. D."

"C'mon, c'mon, Kami, stay with me." *What else can I do?*

Ben Shepherd walked in and crossed the room in three strides. Pulling on a pair of latex gloves, he moved to the bedside opposite Maggie. "Nothing?" He watched as Maggie placed her stethoscope once more on the child's chest.

She shook her head. "Not yet."

"Dr. Devereaux, it's been almost 35 minutes."

"I'm not calling it. Not yet." Maggie's voice was stern and determined with a hint of frustration. Her eyes focused on the cardiac monitor. No one spoke another word of opposition, but continued working as a cohesive team fighting together to save one young life.

Please, Lord. Help me. Show me what to do. Help me save this little girl.

"Pressure's dropping!"

"Get the bicarb on board! C'mon, Kami..."

The team fought valiantly to save the little girl's life, but nothing they did produced the results they wanted. Precious minutes ticked by, and still no response from the girl on the bed.

"Maggie..."

She felt a hand on her arm and looked up into the compassionate eyes of Ben Shepherd. "Maggie, there's nothing more we can do."

Maggie stared into Ben's eyes and started to argue, but then hesitated and nodded. She stood up slowly, pulled off her gloves, and reluctantly looked up at the clock on the wall.

"Time of death nine-thirty-one." She glanced over at the small still form on the table.

Why? Why couldn't we save her, Lord?

"Val, is the mother here?" The frustrated sadness in Maggie's voice reflected the sorrow on the faces of the ER staff.

"Yes," replied Valerie softly. She moved closer to Kami. "I'll get her ready." She turned off the cardiac monitor and removed the IV as she began to make the little girl presentable to her soon-to-be grieving family.

"I'll go tell her mother," offered Ben as he moved toward the treatment room door.

"You sure, Ben? I--"

"No problem, Maggie. It's never--"

A slight movement of the top sheet caught the attention of both physicians.

"Did you see--?" Maggie yanked her stethoscope from her pocket and placed it on the child's still chest.

Ben returned to the bed quickly and shined his penlight into the eyes of the little girl. The black circles sluggishly shrunk to small dark spots. "I don't believe it... I've got pupillary action!" His voice escalated.

Valerie spun around from the monitor and stared at Maggie, as Ben bent over the girl reassessing her status. Turning toward the open door, Valerie called out, "We need some help in here ... NOW!" Her voice was the catalyst for action. Suddenly, the room sprang to life once more in a frenzied attempt of ER personnel to save the life of a little girl who had just been pronounced clinically dead.

"Get her on that monitor," ordered Ben as he felt for a carotid pulse. "Faint and slow, but it's there."

Maggie glanced up at the monitor when she heard the first blip, validating what she heard through her stethoscope.

"C'mon, baby, don't quit on me," Maggie urged. She glanced up at the cardiac monitor once more, just as the small body quivered and coughed. Water spewed from her mouth and down her face. Another cough, and then a gasp for air.

"We've got her back!" Ben nearly shouted.

"C'mon, Kami, fight, baby, fight," coaxed Maggie as she continued listening to the heartbeat. Its rate and rhythm continued to increase. "I need that line in, Valerie." The urgency in Maggie's voice was both an order and a plea.

In response, Valerie continued to palpate the girl's hand for a suitable vein in which to restart an intravenous line. She shook her head and scowled, as she continued feeling for a patent vein. Her slender fingers finally felt a tiny blood vessel, and she stuck the point of a small butterfly needle into the little girl's skin. The needle resisted entry, but Valerie persisted. "Got it! I'm in!" she exclaimed. "Normal saline running."

"Good job," Maggie commended. "What's her pressure?"

"Eighty-five over forty, but going up."

"Let's get her stabilized and up to the PCCU. Val, get Dr. Markham for me, please. He'll need to follow her there—and McEverett."

Valerie nodded and scurried to the nurses' station to notify the cardiologist and pediatrician of their newest patient.

Thirty minutes later, Kami was transported to the pediatric cardiac care unit, awake, stabilized, and asking for her mother.

Maggie watched her go, and then turned to Ben. "I can't believe what just happened."

Ben rubbed his fingers on his chin. "I've never seen anything like that before, Maggie."

"She was gone, Ben."

He nodded his head. "I know." He glanced upward. "Guess He had different plans." He returned his gaze to Maggie. "No wonder they call Him 'The Great Physician.'"

She cast her eyes toward the ceiling and allowed herself to smile. "He certainly is one for drama, isn't He?"

"What just happened?" asked Valerie as she met Maggie at the nurses' station.

Maggie shook her head. "I can't even begin to explain it, Val. That child was dead. There was no pulse, no respiration, no nothing. It was..." She thought for a moment, and then stated confidently, "... a miracle."

Valerie looked at her sister-in-law skeptically. "Maybe you missed something--" She stopped abruptly when her eyes met those of Maggie's. The doctor's eyes were narrowed and focused on the nurse. The irritation was impossible to miss.

"I didn't *miss* anything." Maggie crossed her arms. Her lips were set in a hard line.

"I didn't mean *you* missed something, I meant... maybe there was something we didn't know... you know, some underlying condition or event... or something."

"It *was* an event, Valerie. It was a supernatural event." Maggie's authoritative voice was unwavering.

"Are you trying to tell me that God raised her from the dead, Mags? That doesn't happen these days."

"How do you know?"

"Because I know."

"Look, Val, I can't explain everything that God does, but I know He *can* do it. He did it before, right?"

"Well, yes, but that was in Bible times, and besides, most of those miracles can be explained by science. This is the twenty-first century, Mags. If God really did those miracles, why doesn't He do them still today? Don't you think we'd see a whole lot more miracles?"

"We do, Val," Maggie affirmed quietly. "Every day in this ER. Every single day. Now if you'll excuse me, I need a cup of coffee... a very strong cup of coffee."

Valerie sighed as she watched her sister-in-law disappear into the staff lounge. "Seriously?" she muttered. "You're a doctor, Mags. You can't really believe that." She shook her head and frowned.

"You talking to yourself these days?"

Valerie looked up into the amused eyes of Ben Shepherd and felt her cheeks warm. "No, I wasn't talking to myself, well, yes, I guess I was. I just don't always understand my sister-in-law, especially when she talks religion."

Ben chuckled as he walked away. "We Christians are an odd bunch, aren't we?"

Valerie glared at him good-naturedly. "More than you'll ever know, I'm afraid." She watched him enter the elevator and shook her dark curls. "But I still love you both," she whispered under her breath as she picked up a fresh chart and headed for treatment room two.

CHAPTER THREE

Maggie entered the staff lounge, walked over to the coffee maker, and poured a cup of coffee. Taking her first sip, she glanced around the room. Seeing no one, she stood for a moment, and then impulsively retrieved her cell phone from her locker, and plopped down on the sofa. In moments, she heard a familiar voice on the other end.

"Hi, love. What's going on?"

"Morning, Colin," she said. "I hope I'm not interrupting something important."

"There's nothing more important to me than you, love. And, it's evening here," he replied, chuckling.

Maggie grimaced. She always forgot about the eight-hour time difference between Los Angeles and London, England.

"Am I interrupting dinner?"

"A call from my fiancée is never an interruption. And no, you're not interrupting dinner. I'm just working on a song. Something wrong? You don't sound like yourself."

Maggie smiled. Although the two of them had only been together as a couple for a few months, Colin Grant could easily read her.

"No, nothing's wrong, in fact, barring my inability to remember the time difference between London and L.A., everything is fine. I called to tell you about something amazing that to face Maggie. She handed her a chart, hesitating a moment before speaking.

"Mags, I hope I didn't offend you earlier. I didn't mean to imply--"

"No apology necessary," Maggie responded as she opened the chart. She jotted a few notes and then scribbled her signature.

"It's just that, well, I know we're not on the same page when it comes to religion, but..."

Maggie glanced over at her sister-in-law, closed the chart, and then set it on the counter. "Don't worry. I don't think God will strike you down with a bolt of lightning."

Valerie looked at Maggie through dark lashes moistened with the hint of tears and managed a small smile. "I would just die if anything happened between us. I didn't really think before I spoke, and I, well... I just was so afraid I'd hurt your feelings."

Upon realizing the seriousness of Valerie's apology, Maggie tilted her head slightly and focused her total attention on her sister-in-law. "Val, it's fine. *We're* fine. I'm not mad, honest. Maybe I was a little defensive at first, but if you and I can't talk openly and honestly with each other, then we would have a real problem, right?"

The nurse pressed her lips together tightly and nodded, and then jumped up and hugged the doctor. "You're the best, Mags!"

Maggie pulled back and held Valerie at arm's length. She stared into the warm eyes of her sister-in-law. "I promise you, if I am ever mad at you, I will take you aside, and we'll work it out. That's what families do. Besides, I, uh..." Maggie quickly scanned the area around them. Seeing no one, she continued, but this time her voice was barely audible as she whispered into Valerie's ear. "I could never be mad at my matron of honor."

Valerie's mouth opened, but no sound came out. Her hazel eyes widened as she stared at Maggie.

"Matron of honor? You mean it? Colin asked you to marry him? Oh, my!"

Maggie nodded, her smile wide. "Well, will you?"
Valerie's hand shot up, covering her mouth. "Of course! I'd be honored!" She impulsively grabbed Maggie and hugged her again, but this time more tightly. "Oh, Mags! I am so excited for you!" Releasing her grip, she stepped back and asked, "Does Will know?"

"No, I haven't told him yet. I was kind of waiting. I wanted Colin to be here, but, well, this seemed like the right moment... for us."

"I knew it! I knew he was the one for you!" She embraced her sister-in-law once more. "I am so happy for you, Mags! You are perfect for each other! When? When are you getting married? Is he going to ask Will for your hand?"

"Technically, my hand isn't Will's to give away, but we'd both like Will's blessing. We knew we had yours the moment you met Colin." Maggie paused for a moment. "I would like to tell Will when Colin is here. Do you think you can keep it a secret until then?"

Valerie's eyes twinkled. "Me? Of course, I can! Maybe you two can come over for dinner when Colin gets here, and you could tell Will then. I'd love to see my husband's face when he finds out you're actually going to marry a rock star!"

Maggie scowled playfully. "He's not a rock star, Val."

"He was, Mags. One of the most popular ones ever! Where are you going to get married? Here or England? Do you have a dress picked out yet? What about the music-- oh, that's a silly question. You're probably going to use his songs, right? How about--"

"Valerie, slow down! You're making my head spin," laughed Maggie. It was so easy to be enveloped by Valerie's enthusiasm for life.

Valerie continued as if she hadn't heard Maggie's plea. "Remember how much Will was against you two dating? I'll never forget that night we came over for dinner. I thought Will was never going to be okay with you and Colin."

"It was a tense evening to say the least."

"I just can't believe it!" Valerie wrapped her arms around Maggie and squeezed her once more. "I am so happy for you!" She stood back, and her eyes brimmed with tears, but this time the reason was joyous. A wide grin filled her face.

"Hey, what's going on, you two?"

They both turned to face Ben Shepherd. He held a steaming cup of coffee and took a sip from it before leaning on the counter.

"Nothing special, Ben, just sister-to-sister bonding time," replied Maggie vaguely. She gave Valerie a quick wink. "I think I'll grab a bite to eat. See you both in a bit. Remember, Val, just me and you."

"Got it!" She watched Maggie disappear around the corner.

"Got what?" Ben leaned farther over the counter. He raised his eyebrows as he waited for a reply.

"Nothing, Dr. Shepherd. Absolutely nothing!" said Valerie, mustering up as much innocence as she could. She made a motion as if zipping her lips together. "I need to go check my supplies. Call me if you need me!" She walked briskly toward the supply cart, leaving Ben Shepherd alone at the counter, smiling and shaking his head.

Valerie walked away from the paramedic relay room into the nurses' station. She glanced toward the waiting room and frowned at the gathering of patients before turning toward Claire and one other nurse.

"MVA on its way in. Car versus motorcycle. Let's put it in treatment room two. Who's available?"

"Shepherd's in three on a possible overdose. Devereaux's in one with a hot appy. It's probably headed to the O.R. for an appendectomy," responded Claire as Valerie wrote M-V-A on the triage board indicating the room in which the motor vehicle accident patient would go.

Less than ten minutes later, the ambulance bay doors opened. Three paramedics wheeled in the gurney bearing the young motorcycle driver. Valerie joined them and listened carefully to the report from Josh Grainger, the paramedic who, nearly two years ago, was engaged in his own fight for life. He had sustained third degree burns on his face and hands as well as smoke inhalation when he had rescued a young child in a fire. Now, he was fine, but often when he saw Maggie or Valerie, he would thank them again for all they had done to help him through those dark days of recovery.

"Her name's Diana Littleton. We stabilized her in the field with the C-collar, and her vitals are within normal limits right now. She's complaining of left arm pain, but no sensation from mid-thorax down. No outward signs of serious injury. Helmet's scratched all on the left side. No meds given in the field due to possible head trauma," Josh reported.

"What happened?" asked Val as they moved the young woman to an examination table.

"Eyewitnesses said that a car in front of her slammed on its brakes to avoid a dog. Diana hit the back of the car and sailed across the roof, landing on the pavement in front of the car."

Valerie grimaced.

"She's been in and out of consciousness, but when she's with us, she's oriented times three."

Valerie nodded. She knew that the proper responses to questions at the scene of an accident reveal a lot to the first responders. Diana's ability to answer correctly to who she was, where she was, and the current date were key indicators of mental status.

She connected Diana to the cardiac monitor and checked the intravenous line for patency. Valerie then crossed the room to the cabinets and retrieved the equipment she knew a doctor would need to examine the patient. As she set up the tray table, Maggie entered the room and picked up the patient's chart.

Valerie quickly relayed the information that Josh had given her and moved to one side of the bed, giving Maggie full access to the young girl.

"Diana? Diana? Can you hear me?" Maggie gently cut away some of the clothing to allow better visualization of the injuries.

"Yeah, I can hear you." Her voice was weak. She opened her glazed eyes slowly and tried to look at Maggie but was prohibited by the cervical collar she wore.

"Don't try to move," ordered Maggie gently. "I'm Dr. Devereaux, and I need to examine you. You've had a pretty nasty accident, but we're going to do our best to patch you up."

"I... I can't feel my legs..." Tears ran down Diana's cheeks. "Am I paralyzed?" The fear in her voice intensified.

Stopping her examination for a moment, Maggie looked into the young girl's frightened eyes.

"Let's not jump to conclusions, Diana. You've had a major accident, possibly with some spinal cord trauma. It could be permanent, but it could also be temporary. If there's a lot of swelling around the spinal cord, sensations are affected, but often when the swelling is relieved, sensation returns. I promise you, you'll get the best care possible."

Diana's fearful wide-eyed gaze never left Maggie's face. "Okay." Her voice trembled. "What about the people in the car? Did anyone else get hurt bad?"

"Not that I know of, Diana, but let's concentrate on you right now."

Maggie continued her assessment while Valerie stood by, ready to assist if needed.

"Val, can you see who's on for neuro and get them down here?"

Valerie nodded and left for the nurses' station. She perused the physician schedule and made the call for Dr. Edward Sorenson, knowing that Diana would have difficult days ahead of her. Glancing up at the triage board, she made a quick mental note of who was where and then returned to assist Maggie.

"Claire's paging Dr. Sorenson," said Valerie, as she noted that information on the patient chart.

Maggie nodded. "Thank you. Let's get a head and neck CT scan, x-rays of the chest and back, pelvis, and lower extremities, EKG, and CBC to start." She turned to Diana. "We're going to do some tests, Diana. After that, I'll know more. I've asked Dr. Sorenson to come and see you. He's one of our neurologists, and he's the one who will be able to determine more about the loss of feeling in your legs."

As Diana closed her eyes, silent tears trickled down her cheeks. Maggie took hold of her patient's hand and held it for a brief moment, and although it was almost imperceptible, Valerie noticed Maggie's lips moving ever so slightly before the doctor released Diana's hand.

"I'll be right outside, Val, if you need me," stated Maggie as she walked out of the room, chart in hand.

Valerie's puzzled gaze followed Maggie as the doctor left the room. *Was she praying?*

CHAPTER FOUR

The California sun was near the horizon, and the sky was changing from its dirty blue haze into a resplendent array of yellows, oranges, and pinks. While the metropolitan Los Angeles area had a bad reputation for its smog-filled skies, the ever-present cloud of pollution was a prime factor in the glorious sunsets that resulted from the smoke and dust particles suspended in the atmosphere.

Eastmont's emergency room was steady with patient flow, and Valerie brushed a wisp of dark brown hair from across her eyes as she wrote the disposition of a patient on the triage board in the nurses' station. From the corner of her eye, she caught a glimpse of a young man standing at the counter waiting, she presumed, for information regarding when his turn would be.

Without turning around, she asked, "May I help you?"

"You look busy, love."

She jerked her head around quickly upon hearing the soft British accent of the man at the counter.

"Colin! Oh, my goodness! When did you get here? Maggie didn't say anything about you being here!"

The blonde singer grinned and held a finger to his mouth. "Shhh... she doesn't know I'm here. I just arrived a bit ago. I was wondering if she was around."

Valerie looked over one shoulder and then over the other. "I think she's with a patient. Want to wait in the staff lounge?"

"Sure, if that's not an imposition. How are you doing?"

"Couldn't be better!" She then lowered her voice. "Congratulations! Maggie just told me a few days ago!"

Colin's smile widened. "Thanks, love. I understand we're supposed to come over to your place for dinner to tell Will?"

Valerie nodded her head. "Yes, yes! Do you want to come over tonight?"

"It's okay with me, but I suppose I'd better square it with Maggie. She might have a date or something." He winked at Valerie.

She laughed. "Or something!"

When Maggie exited her patient's room, Valerie met her with the announcement that she had just brewed a fresh pot of coffee. As Maggie entered the lounge and closed the door behind her, she walked directly to the counter where the coffee maker sat empty. Placing her hands on her hips, she stared at the pot as a familiar voice penetrated the silence of the room.

"Sorry there's no coffee, love. Will I do?"

Maggie whirled around, coming face to face with the man who had captured her reluctant heart and filled her life with so much happiness.

"Colin!"

She fell into his arms and allowed herself to be pulled closely to him.

"I missed you so much, Maggie." His kiss was tender; his hold was strong. He lessened his embrace and tilted her chin up, looking into her cinnamon brown eyes. He kissed her once more and then held her against him without speaking.

Maggie didn't resist. Instead, she closed her eyes and melted into the moment. Finally, as they sat down on the worn sofa, she asked, "What in the world are you doing here?"

"Well, you said you told Valerie about our engagement, and I thought I'd better come and tell Will before Valerie accidentally lets the cat out of the bag. Not that she can't keep a secret, but…"

"She really can't keep a secret!" Maggie laughed softly.

"Besides, it was a wonderful excuse to come visit you a bit prematurely, don't you think?" He held tightly to her hands.

"Of course, I do." Maggie looked directly into his adoring blue eyes and feigned a scolding. "Too bad you don't have telephones in England. You could've called me to say you were coming." Her teasing words were warm with love.

Colin grinned sheepishly. "I like to surprise you. You always seem so serious, and I love to watch your expression when you're caught off guard."

"Is this what life with you is going to be like?"

"I hope so. I love to see you smile, and when you do, your eyes have the most beautiful sparkle in them." He raised her left hand to his lips and kissed it, never taking his eyes away from hers. "Valerie asked if we wanted to have dinner with her and Will tonight… if you're game."

Maggie smiled and shook her head. "Valerie… I'm going to have a word with that woman. She enjoys setting me up. Yes, dinner will be fine, if you're ready to face my brother."

"I'm still on his good side, right? If so, tonight is fine."

"Yes, he thinks you're very good for me," admitted Maggie.

"Now, he does. I still remember when he was ready to cut my heart out." Colin put a protective hand over the middle of his chest. "I believe your comment was that he could've shot me?"

Maggie laughed, remembering the evening when Will met Colin. Believing the singer was toying with Maggie's affections, Will was ready to do battle in order to protect his big sister, and thus, the tension was thick that evening. However, by the end of the night, Will had cautiously accepted the relationship between Colin and Maggie, but not without his own reservations. It wasn't until Will came to understand the depth of Maggie's love for Colin that he gave her his blessing on their growing relationship.

She patted Colin's hand reassuringly. "He's a doctor. Sworn to protect human life, remember?"

Colin rolled his eyes. "Right. He wasn't sworn to protect mine. Not that night, anyway." He paused for a moment and then gently brushed her cheek with his fingers. "But then, if you were my sister, I'd have done exactly the same thing... protect you from anyone who might possibly hurt you."

Maggie's cheeks warmed, and she lowered her eyes. Despite all that she had done to reject his love, Colin had remained patient and faithful, not only waiting for her to find love in her heart for him, but more importantly, he had waited until she had found the forgiving love of God. It was Colin's deep abiding faith that touched Maggie's heart and enabled her to see Christianity in action. His career move from secular music to gospel, his willingness to put God's will above his own, and his sacrificial love for her drew Maggie to him and to Christ.

Her emotions threatened to overwhelm her as she thought about the road they had traveled to get to today, and it was hard for her to speak, but she managed to whisper, "I love you so much, Colin."

He took her in his arms once more and kissed the top of her head just as Valerie poked her head into the lounge.

"Colin, what a surprise!" Her exaggerated exclamation was followed by a stifled giggle as she added, "I really am sorry to interrupt, but we have a possible cardiac in three, Maggie." She smiled apologetically before disappearing as quickly as she had appeared.

Colin stood up and pulled Maggie to her feet. "I'll pick you up at your place? About six?"

Maggie nodded and smiled. "I'll see you then. By the way, you owe me a cup of coffee."

He grinned, kissed her one final time, and then held the door open for her as she walked into the emergency room and to her newest patient.

"When did he get in?"

Valerie turned to face her husband. She set four glasses on their dining room table. "I think he said this morning. He just showed up in the ER to surprise Maggie."

"I'll bet she was thrilled."

"That's an understatement. He was pretty over the moon, too."

Will walked up behind his wife, grabbed her, spun her around, and then kissed her firmly. "Yeah, love does that to people, y'know."

"Will Garrett, how am I supposed to get everything ready if you're always in the way?"

"In the way? You hurt me, wife." He allowed her to squirm from his hold, then called out as she fled to the kitchen. "I remind you, my dear, I am never in the way!"

Valerie's laughter resonated from the kitchen. "Gotta go... don't want to burn dinner!"

Will smiled as he watched his wife disappear into the next room. "Need me to do anything in here?"

"Yes. Would you light the candles? I want it to smell nice like gardenia, not like roast."

"Yes, dear." Will obediently lit the candles just as the doorbell rang. "By the way," he called out, "your roast smells delicious. I'd take a roast scented candle over gardenia any day."

"You're so lucky I'm not in there. Just get the door, husband."

Will chuckled as he opened the door. "Hey, you two!" He gave Maggie a hug, and then extended his hand to the man at her side. "Colin! Good to see you. How's it going?"

"Well. Very well." Colin shook Will's hand vigorously. "How have you been?"

Will gestured for the two of them to enter and then closed the door behind them. "Fine. Keeping busy as usual. C'mon in here." He motioned toward the dining room.

"Val in the kitchen? Does she need any help?" asked Maggie, removing her jacket.

Will shook his head. "I don't think so. She's got everything handled. My job was to light the candles. How did I do?"

Maggie grinned and patted her brother on the back. "You did just fine, Will."

"You two are right on time!" Valerie exclaimed as she entered with a platter containing a tri-tip roast surrounded by carrots and potatoes. "Let's eat!"

"Wow! That looks like a feast," commented Colin. He pulled a chair out for Maggie before sitting down next to her.

Will helped Valerie into her seat and then took his place at the head of the table. He glanced over at Colin, hesitated for a moment, and then asked, "Colin, would you like to say grace?"

"Love to." Colin reached for Maggie's hand and bowed his head. His blessing was short but sincere, and Maggie squeezed his hand after his "amen." He glanced up at her and winked before releasing her fingers.

The evening progressed at a relaxed pace. The light dinner conversation was pleasant, but Maggie found her mind wandering to the possibilities of Will's response when Colin announced their plans to marry. She managed an apologetic smile when she noticed Valerie staring at her. Valerie mouthed 'Don't worry. It will be fine,' and Maggie nodded and forced another small smile.

At the finish of the main meal, Valerie ushered everyone into the living room for the dessert. A carafe of vanilla-flavored coffee was the perfect complement to the strawberry shortcake she served. Finally, there was a lull in the conversation, and Colin set his dessert plate on the coffee table.

"Will, I have something I'd like to discuss with you."

Will finished a mouthful of shortcake before answering. "Sure, Colin. What's on your mind?"

Maggie's eyes darted from Will to Colin, and then back to Will again. Valerie leaned forward in her chair. Colin cleared his throat.

Will studied the three people sitting across from him. His fork was poised in mid-air for a moment, and then he set it back on his plate. "Okay, you all look like the cat that swallowed the canary. What's going on?"

Colin reached out for Maggie's hand. He took a deep breath. "I've asked Maggie to marry me, and she's agreed. I realize you're not her father, but--"

"That's what this is all about?" Will laughed loudly. "You three ought to see yourselves! You look scared to death!" He then turned to Valerie and pointed at her. "You knew, didn't you? You knew, and you didn't tell me." Turning back to Colin and Maggie, he grinned as he stood up and pulled Maggie to her feet. "I am very, very happy for you." He hugged her, kissed her cheek, and then turned to Colin. "Welcome to the family!" The two men shook hands, and Colin visibly relaxed.

"This went a lot better than the first time we met," Colin whispered to Maggie.

She looked at him, smiled, and nodded. "Much better."

The next two weeks passed too quickly for Maggie, and soon she was saying goodbye to Colin. Although she knew his career frequently brought him to the United States, his life was predominantly in England. The depth of her emotions had surprised her the first time they had separated, and she still struggled to maintain her composure each time they had to say goodbye. This time was no different. Trying to mask her feelings was an impossibility, but that didn't stop her from the attempt.

"Thanks for lunch." Her effort at lightheartedness was not lost on Colin.

"You're welcome." Colin's response had a hint of sorrow as he hooked a wisp of hair behind her ear. He took her hand as he led her from his car to her door.

"I hate this," she confessed to Colin as they stood together on her doorstep. His strong arms encircled her, and she closed her eyes, willing her tears to remain unshed.

"I know. Me, too."

"England is so far away."

"I know. I'm sorry I have to leave."

"I do this every time, don't I?" She looked up at him.

Colin smiled at her wistfully. He tightened his hold around her and kissed her forehead. "I'm only a few hours away by plane. If you need me, you just call me."

Maggie nodded but said nothing, her head resting against his chest once more.

"I'll call you when we land, okay?"

She nodded again, and after a very long time, she looked up into his warm eyes.

He tenderly brushed his fingers down her cheek. "No tears?"

Maggie smiled. "Not until you're gone," she admitted honestly.

"I love you."

"I love you, too."

Colin held her to him, inhaling the musky fragrance of her perfume. He finally eased his hold on her, looked into her tear-filled eyes, and kissed her one last time before getting into his car.

As Maggie stood, watching until he drove out of view, her heart ached, and she knew it would not feel whole again until Colin was back with her once more.

CHAPTER FIVE

Although it was her day off, Valerie still had her alarm set for six o'clock in the morning. Deciding to brew a pot of coffee, she glanced over at her sleeping husband. His black hair was tousled from slumber, and his face had the shadow of an overnight beard. Leaning over, she kissed him lightly on the cheek. He stirred slightly and then rolled over on his side without waking. She quietly rose from the bed.

Walking into the kitchen, she opened the window, and along with a cool breeze, the song of a sparrow greeted her. Its chirpy melody augmented Valerie's mood, and she stood for a moment just watching the tiny bird sing out robustly. Smiling, Valerie thought about her life. "I am so lucky," she sighed.

After starting the coffee, Valerie afforded herself the opportunity of a long, hot shower. The citrus smell of her body wash filled the bathroom, and she enjoyed the aroma as she quickly finished soaping up. Remembering that it was the first of the month, Valerie deftly completed a breast self-exam. Ever since her mother had lost her own battle against breast cancer just prior to Valerie's nursing school graduation, Valerie had faithfully checked herself every month.

As she palpated her skin, she paused for a moment, unsure of whether or not she had actually felt something. She carefully pressed down on her skin once more. There it was again... a small, round lump. She checked the area repeatedly. It didn't vary. She tried to remember the previous month. Was it there then? No. She would not have forgotten that. Her mind raced, but one word dominated all of her thoughts... *cancer.*

She quickly toweled off, dressed, and dried her hair. *Should I wake Will? It's probably nothing. He needs his sleep, but what if...?*

Finally, unable to contain her tears any longer, she allowed them to flow freely as she leaned against the bathroom counter. She never heard Will approach.

"Valerie, what's wrong?" Will turned his wife around to face him. His concerned eyes probed hers, and his face tensed as he waited for an answer.

Valerie didn't speak; she only clung to him, her face buried in his chest.

"Valerie, what's wrong?" he asked again, stroking her hair as he held her. His voice was more apprehensive, yet simultaneously compassionate.

She struggled to speak. "I found... I found... a lump."

Will took her by the shoulders and pushed her back. "Where?" His focused eyes stared directly into her frightened ones.

"Here," she whispered, pointing to the location.

He led her back to their bed and sat her on its edge. As the oncologist part of him took over, he reassessed her findings.

Valerie searched Will's face for a hint of what was going on in his mind. *Say something... please...* Her chest tightened with each breath she took.

Finally, Will spoke. "It's probably a cyst. Was it there last month?"

Valerie shook her head. "No," she whispered. "It wasn't there."

Will looked at his wife and spoke tenderly. "It'll be okay, Val, but you know we have to do a work up. We need to see if there's any fluid in this. I can do it this morning in my office."

Valerie nodded her consent. She knew if the lump did turn out to be malignant that early diagnosis and treatment was the best way to a successful ending, but that knowledge did nothing to dispel her fears.

She forced herself to ask what was echoing in her mind. "What if it's not a cyst, Will?" Her voice trembled. "What then?"

Will reached for her hands and held them in his own. "Whatever happens, Valerie, we'll face it together. But right now, let's try not to make any assumptions, okay? This could be nothing."

"But it could be something..."

"Yes, it could be, but..." Will hesitated. "Sweetheart, it'll be fine. I promise you." He moved next to her, wrapped his arms around her, and held her for a very long time.

Valerie sat very still on the thin paper overlay covering the examination table as she waited for Will to extract fluid from the lump in her chest. Her eyes followed every move Will made.

"This is just some lidocaine, Val, so you'll feel a little sting, then the area should be numb for the rest," stated Will. He adeptly injected the anesthetic in several areas around the lump before inserting a larger needle to withdraw some liquid from the mass.

After a few minutes, he set the needle and syringe on the examination tray. He sighed deeply.

"What's wrong?"

"There's no fluid in it, so we need a biopsy to be sure there's no malignancy."

"A biopsy?" Valerie looked at him in disbelief. Her eyes filled with tears. "Oh, Will..."

"I still think there's a good chance it's benign, maybe a fatty tumor, but to be sure, we'll need to examine some of the tissue directly." He took her hands in his and looked directly into her fearful eyes. "Val, it'll be okay. I promise."

"You can't make that promise, Will. I know you want it to be nothing, so do I, but you can't really promise me that, can you?" Valerie took a deep breath. She bit her lower lip, closed her eyes tightly, and allowed Will to wrap his arms around her. Her silent tears fell unrestricted onto his shirt.

"No... no, Val, I guess I can't, but--"

"I know." Valerie swallowed hard. "We both want it to be fine, but it may not be, so... so I want you to do whatever you think we need to do. I trust you, Will... completely."

"I'll talk to Brett Delmonico and see what he's got available. He's the best surgeon I know," Will said softly. "Why don't we go home? I can take the day off and stay with you."

Valerie looked at Will through moist lashes, shook her head, and choked out a reply to her husband. "No, I'll be fine, Will. Really, I will be. You've got patients who need you. Go ahead and make the appointment with the surgeon, and I'll see you at home later... please. We can talk more then. Right now, I think I just need to be alone. I need some time to absorb all this, okay?"

Will nodded, and against his better judgment, he allowed Valerie to leave his office without him by her side. He sat next to the exam table staring at the door Valerie had closed behind her. Finally, he slowly rose from the stool, left the exam room, and entered his private office.

Sitting down behind his large mahogany desk, he took a long, deep breath. The discomfort within him was unsettling. Although outwardly he was calm and confident, inwardly he struggled to control his own fears. He had seen many patients battle cancer, only to lose the fight, and the thought that Valerie might have to go through something similar terrified him.

Pulling his cell phone out from his jacket pocket, he hesitated only a moment before punching in the number for his sister. Less than two years older than him, Maggie had always been close with her brother. Their joint decision to go to medical school had made their bond even tighter, and now Will desperately needed to hear her voice. It seemed like forever before she answered her phone.

"Hi, Will. What's up?" came the cheery voice of his older sister.

"Maggie, where are you?" He struggled to sound as though everything was fine.

"Just about ready to leave the hospital. Why? What's wrong?"

"Can you come up to my office?"

"I'm on my way." The phone connection terminated.

Seven minutes later, Maggie Devereaux walked briskly into her brother's office. Still wearing her lab coat from her latest emergency room shift, the attractive doctor sat opposite her younger brother.

"What's going on?" she asked quickly. Her eyes locked on Will's face.

"It's Val--"

"Val? What's wrong? What happened?"

Will struggled to maintain his composure, but with the appearance of Maggie, he was losing the battle. They had always supported one another, and now he wanted to tell her everything... anything to alleviate the tremendous fear he felt for Valerie... and himself.

"She found a lump." He stammered. "Maggie... I'm so... I can't think straight."

Maggie stared at her brother; her eyes narrowed. She reached across his desk and took his hand in hers. "A lump? Where? Will, tell me what you know."

The oncologist took a deep breath before continuing. "Left breast. It's about one to two centimeters upon direct examination and not fluid-filled. On palpation, it is smooth, round..." His clinical training rescued him from losing control as he described the mass.

Maggie sat quietly as Will continued to describe his findings. "I talked to Brett Delmonico. He'll do the biopsy early next week, and then we'll go from there."

"But it could be nothing, right?"

"It could be, but with her history, there's a good chance it's something," he admitted.

Maggie nodded as she recalled Valerie's description of her mother's exhaustive battle with breast cancer.

"Is Val at home?"

"Yes, I told her I'd go home with her, but she insisted I stay at work." He shook his head in frustration. "I know she's got to be thinking about her mom."

Maggie spoke firmly. "You've got to be strong for Valerie. She's going to need you more than ever, especially if the biopsy is positive."

Will thought for a moment and exhaled slowly. "I know, Maggie. It's just that…" He paused for a moment and shook his head. He looked directly into his sister's concerned eyes. "What if Valerie does have cancer? I can't lose her." He rested his elbows on his desk and dropped his head into his hands. "I just can't." His anguish was unmistakable.

"You don't have to lose her, Will. You know that. What you'll do is face it and deal with it. People don't necessarily die when they have cancer. You know that as well as I do. And Valerie found it early, right? That's definitely in her favor," Maggie reminded him.

Will lifted his head, looked at Maggie, and nodded. "You're right. And there's been a lot of new treatments in the field of oncology. I guess I'm not thinking too clearly right now."

"She's your wife, Will. You're not really supposed to be the clinician when it comes to her," commented Maggie. "And frankly, it's still scary. The 'what ifs' are enough to drive anyone crazy."

"Yeah, you're right, as usual." Will managed a weak smile. "Thanks."

Maggie reached across the desk again and squeezed her brother's hand. "What can I do?"

"She's got to be scared, Maggie. I shouldn't have let her go home alone. Do you think you could drop by and see how she's doing?" Will sighed. Guilt mingled with fear shadowed his handsome face. "Maybe I should go home." He shook his head, rubbing his fingers across his forehead.

"Work is probably good for you today. It'll keep your mind occupied," stated Maggie. "I'll go by and see how she's doing. If she needs you, I'll call. How does that sound?"

Will smiled gratefully. "That sounds good, Maggie. I'll leave as soon as my rounds and appointments are finished. Thanks…thanks a lot. You have no idea how good it is to know that you're here for us." He rose to give her a hug.

"You're welcome, Will. I'll head over to your place right now, and I promise if I need to call you home, I will." She hugged her brother tightly, and then added, "It'll be okay. We'll get through this."

Will sat back in his chair and stared for a long time at the door that Maggie had closed behind her. She had provided the words of comfort he so desperately needed to hear, and he hoped Maggie would be able to do the same for Valerie.

Maggie sat quietly in her car without turning it on. *Cancer.* The very word was frightening to anyone, but to someone in the medical field, that fear escalates with the knowledge of the ins and outs of treatments, side effects, prognoses… all those things only mentioned to patients on a "need to know" basis. As she grappled with the right words to say to her sister-in-law, she pulled her cell phone out of her jacket pocket. In moments, she heard a familiar voice on the other end.

"Hello, love. What an unexpected pleasure."

"Morning, Colin," she said, her voice feigning cheerfulness.

"You've got to work on your math, love. I kindly remind you that it's late afternoon here," he replied, chuckling.

Maggie grimaced.

"However, I will overlook you being arithmetically challenged, since I love hearing your voice. What's going on?"

Maggie took a deep breath before beginning. "I just finished talking with Will," she began slowly. "He told me that Valerie found a lump in her breast. Her mom died from breast cancer a few years ago, so you can imagine what's going through their minds right now."

"Cancer? What... how?" His voice increased in intensity.

"I don't really have any other information than that. She found it this morning. I'm heading over to her place right now. I was trying to think of what I was going to say, when I thought that maybe you'd pray with me first."

"Oh, Maggie... I'm so sorry. Of course, I'll pray with you. Are you okay?"

"Yes, I'm doing okay, but Will's having a very difficult time."

"I can imagine."

"And I'm sure Valerie must be scared right now."

"I understand, love. Let's pray."

Maggie closed her eyes and bowed her head as she listened to her fiancé petition the Lord on behalf of her sister-in-law and brother.

"Father, thank You for loving us so much. Thank You for giving us Your Son, Jesus, so that we could have a relationship with You, one where we can call on You for anything, and more importantly, one where You want us to call on You. Your Word tells us to let our requests be made known unto God, so Lord, this moment we hold Valerie up to You and pray for Your healing hand upon her. Father, we know You already know the outcome of the biopsy. You know if it's cancer or not, and You know how everything is going to turn out for Valerie. We pray that it is not cancer, but if You allow otherwise, give Valerie the strength and courage she needs to face this trial. Guide her doctors and nurses as they minister to her health needs.

"Take care of Will, Lord. Help him to be the support that Valerie needs now. Give him wisdom and guidance as he travels this path with her. And Lord, please help both of them realize how much You love them. May they both find You through this.

"Father, give Maggie strength to go through this as well. Help her have the right words to say that will comfort Valerie and Will and point them to You.

"We know that You control all things and nothing catches You by surprise. Nothing happens that You are not aware of. Your Word tells us that You care for the tiniest sparrow. Not one falls from the sky without Your knowledge, and we know that You care for us much more than those little birds.

"I pray that through this, the cause of Christ will not be hindered, and You will be glorified through it all. I know we can't see how right now, especially if it is cancer, but help us to remember that You are a sovereign God, and even though we don't understand, You do, and You're in control. Help us to trust You in every aspect of this. In Jesus' precious name, I pray. Amen."

Maggie wiped the tears away from her eyes with a tissue as she managed a weak, "Thank you so much."

"Do you need me there? I can be there in no time at all," Colin offered.

"I know," she replied, "but I think... maybe... no, I'm okay, really."

"If you change your mind-- "

"I know."

"Keep me posted?"

"Of course."

"I love you, and I will be praying."

"I know. I love you, too." Maggie ended the call, reached for the key, turned it, and listened as her car sprang to life. As she pulled out of the parking space and into the mainstream of traffic, she continued to offer up her own silent prayers. Once more, she petitioned God for strength, wisdom, and the right words to say that would ease Valerie's fears and give her hope.

CHAPTER SIX

Valerie dried her tears for the umpteenth time. As she tossed another crumpled tissue into a wastebasket, she heard a knock at her door.

No, I don't need any visitors. I don't want to talk to anyone. Not now.

The persistent knocking irritated Valerie as she rose to answer the door. Walking slowly toward it, she straightened her blouse and mentally prepared to shoo away the caller. Her mouth dropped open when she saw her sister-in-law standing there.

"Maggie?"

"Hi, Val. May I come in?"

Valerie regained her composure and nodded. "Of course! I'm sorry, come on in." She gestured for Maggie to enter.

"I talked to Will," Maggie stated straightforwardly as she moved into the living room.

Valerie sighed deeply and stared at her clasped hands.

"Come on, let's sit down." Maggie reached out and took the nurse's hand, leading her to the sofa. "I'm here for you, Val. What can I do?"

Valerie looked up at her sister-in-law and silently shook her head. She hesitated for a moment, looked away from Maggie, and bit her lower lip. "I don't know, Mags… I'm scared. Really scared. I'll never forget how my mom died…" Her voice trailed off.

Maggie sat without talking, simply listening as the petite nurse shared her deepest fears.

"I don't want to have cancer... I don't want to die." Valerie spoke haltingly, her eyes brimming with unshed tears. "It's all I'm thinking about now."

Maggie's gaze lingered on the downcast face of her sister-in-law. "I can only imagine how you must be feeling, Val. I know it has to be hard, but you'll get through this, and so will Will. You don't even know if it is cancer at this point, right?"

Valerie nodded, but her voice was solemn. "I know, Maggie, but I just have this feeling that, well, that it is, and I don't want... I don't want to go through what my mom did, and I... I don't want Will to go through what I went through. It was horrible, Maggie, really horrible. My mom--"

"Whatever lies ahead, you and he will get through it together. No matter what the outcome of the biopsy, you've got each other to hold on to." Maggie stopped for a moment and squeezed Valerie's hand. "And I'm here too. We're family. We get through things like this together."

Valerie began to softly cry. "Oh, Maggie, I can't believe this is happening." She buried her face in her hands and for the first time, heart-wrenching sobs poured forth.

Maggie reached out and pulled Valerie into her arms. She stroked the nurse's dark brown hair and whispered, "It'll be alright, Val. I promise. It has to be."

Valerie's surgery was without complication, and now she fearfully waited for the results of the biopsy. She was expecting Will to be home before dinner when the call came in the late afternoon.

"Valerie, this is Brett Delmonico. I was wondering if you and Will could come and see me tomorrow morning?"

Tomorrow morning? Are you kidding? What doctor calls you at night to arrange for an appointment if it's not bad news? He has to tell me now. I can't wait until tomorrow.

"Please," she begged, "tell me now."

"Is Will there?"

"Not yet, but he'll be here shortly." She paused, and then pleaded, "Please, Dr. Delmonico, please tell me now. I'll be fine, I promise. And Will, he'll be here any moment."

There was a long pause.

"I'd rather--"

"Please..." She heard him sigh deeply.

"Valerie, I'm sorry, but the biopsy came back positive. It is cancer, but I think..." He continued to talk to her, but Valerie heard nothing else he said.

Cancer. Her mind ceased to function after hearing the word. *Cancer... cancer... cancer.* The word echoed in her head.

"Valerie, are you with me? Can you both come in tomorrow morning?"

"I'm sorry. Yes, we'll be there. Nine-thirty. Thank you very much," said Valerie automatically. She set her phone on the table and stared at nothing in particular.

"Will..." she whispered. Time stood still. She sat at the table frozen to her chair, not moving at all. Numbed by the diagnosis, she had no idea how long she had sat at the kitchen table when she heard the key in the side door lock. She sat very still, listening for it to open.

"Will..." she whispered once more almost as if she were in a trance. She stood slowly and faced the door.

It opened, and Will crossed the threshold, shutting the door behind him.

"Hi, Val--" He stopped mid-sentence. "What's wrong?" In two long strides he was next to her, his deep brown eyes focused on her face as she seemed to stare through him.

"The biopsy results came back. It's positive. I have cancer."

The night was long for Valerie. Sleep evaded her, and throughout the dark hours she tossed and turned, not wanting to wake Will, yet in her fear, she reached out to touch him on several occasions, needing to know he was still there.

Why me? What if I have to have a mastectomy? What if my hair falls out? What if I can't do my job during treatment? What if Will doesn't find me attractive? What if... I die?

It was in the early morning hours when Valerie finally fell into a fitful sleep. In her dreams, she was once again beside her beloved mother trying to coax her to drink small sips of broth and then rubbing her back as she bent over the side of the bed violently rejecting what little nourishment Valerie had been able to get into the frail body. In the depths of slumber, Valerie stood by the casket refusing to look upon the still form of her mother lying in repose, and when she finally gained the courage to do so, she found herself staring at her own body resting on the satin cushions. Her screams pierced the darkness of the night.

"Valerie! Val, wake up! You're dreaming, sweetheart! Wake up!"

Valerie felt herself rouse from the shroud of sleep. Her terrified eyes darted around the room and finally focused on the concerned face of her husband.

"Will?" Instinctively, she clung to him. His arms wrapped around her.

"I'm here, Val."

Her body shook as she closed her eyes tightly. The images from her nightmare still tormented her. "It was awful! It was me!

It was my mother at first, and then... then it was me! Oh, Will..." She sobbed in his embrace.

"You're safe, sweetheart," soothed Will. "I'm here. It was just a bad dream. You're safe." He held her protectively and tenderly kissed the top of her head.

Valerie lay next to her husband, and for a time, no words were spoken. Will continued to hold his wife in his arms and gently stroke her hair.

"I know you're scared, Val, but we'll get through this," promised Will softly.

Valerie's voice was shaking when she finally spoke. "My mom died from this, Will, despite the radiation and chemo. We did everything the doctors told us to do, but she still died. It's so hard to believe everything will be okay. It wasn't for her. I still remember how she looked those last few weeks of her life. I hardly recognized her. And at the end, I actually hoped she would pass, just to end her suffering." Her voice broke, but she continued. "I don't want to end up like that."

Will propped himself up on his elbow and turned Valerie's head toward him. The light of dawn illuminated her face. His dark brown eyes met her tortured ones.

"Your mom was stage four, Valerie. She was a smoker, plus a lot has changed in oncology since your mom died. There are new meds all the time. You'll have the best care possible... the best doctors... the best medicines... the best everything. You are not going to end up like your mother," insisted Will.

Valerie's lower lip quivered. "I know you believe that Will, and I love you so much for saying that. It's just hard for me to believe that... and I am so afraid. I try so hard to keep from being scared, but I am. I'm terrified. I keep thinking that I'm a nurse, and I shouldn't be afraid, but I am."

"Wait a second, Val. Being a nurse doesn't mean you can't have fear. That's normal. I'll admit, I'm a little scared too," he confessed. "But I am not going to lose you..." His voice broke off. He reached out and brushed a strand of her hair away from her eyes.

She forced a weak smile of encouragement, but the fear in her eyes betrayed her.

"Promise me you won't give up, Val," begged Will. "You've got to fight this. We've got to fight this together with every fiber of our being." His voice was almost a whisper. "I won't let you die."

Valerie's despair abated slightly as Will continued to speak words of comfort. She brushed her fingers over his lips, never leaving his gaze. "I won't give up, Will, I promise," pledged Valerie. Will pulled her closer to him. She laid her head on his shoulder. *Please be right, Will. If anyone can make this okay, it's you.*

CHAPTER SEVEN

Alone in Dr. Brett Delmonico's office, Valerie fidgeted in the black leather chair opposite a large black desk. *Please, please get here, Will. I don't want to hear this alone.* Her hands were shaking despite her efforts to calm them. The movement of the door handle captured her attention, and she looked up quickly as the door opened. Dr. Delmonico entered the room. Wearing a light blue western shirt and denim jeans encircled by a silver buckled black belt, he looked more like a ranch hand than a physician, but Valerie believed, as Will did, that Brett Delmonico was the best surgeon at Eastmont Hospital.

"Morning, Valerie," he began. "Will not here yet?" He circled to the back of the desk and sat down, placing a chart in front of him.

Valerie shook her head. "Not yet, but he said he'd meet me here."

"How are you doing this morning?" He opened the chart and pulled out a typed report. He looked directly at her when he spoke.

"As well as can be expected, I guess," she answered solemnly.

The doctor nodded as another knock rapped lightly on the door. It opened, and Will entered the room. "Sorry, I'm late." He shook hands with the surgeon before sitting down in a chair next to Valerie. The tension in Valerie's face faded slightly as Will smiled reassuringly at her. His presence stilled her trembling body, and as he reached over and laced his fingers through hers, she allowed herself to pay closer attention to Dr. Delmonico.

"No problem," said the surgeon. "I have the pathology report, and I thought we could go over it together."

Valerie held tightly to Will's hand and nodded. Although she had a decent understanding of oncology and a fair idea of what was ahead of her, she knew she would have difficulty processing all the information that Dr. Delmonico shared. Will's presence was her security blanket, and it enveloped her with a pensive serenity.

"Since the biopsy confirmed the malignancy, we need to remove the tumor. Valerie, there are two options. We can do a lumpectomy, which means that I remove the lump and surrounding tissues until I get clear margins all around, that is, no cancer cells in the surrounding tissues, or I can do a mastectomy, complete removal of the breast and all surrounding tissues. The survival rate for either is very much the same. Should you elect for a lumpectomy, you will need radiation therapy afterwards. None is required with the mastectomy as long as there is no further involvement. To determine that I will need to remove some of the lymph nodes. If the nodes are negative for malignant cells, that's as far as we go. If they're positive, we will need to discuss further options."

Valerie nervously glanced at her husband. "We talked about both options, but I'm still not sure. What do you think, Will?" She struggled to find some clarity in her thoughts, but her fear of making the wrong choice overpowered her ability to process any information.

"Brett, can you give us a few minutes?" asked Will as he stood and moved closer to Valerie.

"Of course. I'll be back in a few minutes. You know, you don't have to make the decision today. If you need to go home and talk about it, that's okay, too." He nodded as he exited the room, closing the door behind him.

"Valerie, sweetheart, what are you thinking? Do you still have questions?" asked Will as he moved a chair directly opposite her. He sat down, leaned forward, and took both of her hands in his.

"I don't know, Will. I don't even know what to ask right now. It's like everything we talked about is a complete blur. What do you think I should do?" Valerie frowned and avoided eye contact with Will.

He took a deep breath. "I probably would recommend taking the least invasive procedure since the outcome is the same."

"Remind me again about what happens during radiation."

"It depends. Sometimes the skin can burn a bit... like a sunburn, sometimes worse. Sometimes nothing happens. You might be fatigued quite a bit."

"But I could still work, right?"

"I don't see why not. Of course, we have to see how you tolerate the radiation treatments, but if there's no problem, you should be able to work. Just adjust your schedule as needed. There would be several weeks of treatments."

"And with the mastectomy?"

"Longer recovery time, but no radiation. And of course, there's the disfigurement of the body to deal with." Will hesitated before continuing. "Valerie, whichever one you choose, I will support you. Do you understand that?"

Valerie nodded and exhaled slowly, blowing her bangs up from her forehead. "What if I choose the mastectomy over the lumpectomy?"

Will tilted her face up and looked directly into his wife's misty eyes. "You need to do what you are comfortable with. I will love you no matter which option you select. I didn't marry you for the outer part of you. I married you because you were-- you *are* a beautiful woman on the inside. You are the sweetest, dearest thing in life to me. Do you understand me?"

She hesitated before responding. "Yes, I just don't want to make the wrong choice."

"There isn't a wrong choice," countered Will, "except to do nothing." He paused for a moment before adding, "Do you want to go home and think about it?"

"No. I want to know—I need to know-- what I'm going to do before we leave today." Her voice broke. "I'm so scared, Will."

"I know, sweetheart. I know." He reached out and took her hands. "What can I do to help you?"

Valerie looked at her husband. The love she felt for him suddenly overwhelmed her. For a moment, she couldn't speak. *If you only knew how much I love you, Will. Your strength, your tenderness, your love.*

She forced a small smile for him. "Just by being here and holding my hand. By listening to me and answering all my questions over and over again, and by telling me that you'll love me no matter what." She wiped away a tear that threatened to fall from her eye. "I can face anything I think, as long as I know I won't lose you." Her voice was barely above a whisper, but she managed another feeble smile for her husband.

Will's strong voice had no hint of hesitation. "You will never lose me, Valerie. I don't care if you have a double mastectomy, lose all your hair, or whatever. I will be with you forever. I love you. We are in this together, sweetheart, and we will face this... you and I *together*."

Valerie smiled halfheartedly through her unshed tears and nodded. After wiping her nose with a tissue, she leaned forward and gave him a kiss. She looked into his eyes and softly said with as much confidence as she could muster, "Let's do the lumpectomy, as long as you think that's a good choice."

"If that's what you want, then it's a good choice. I'll go get Brett."

Will paced quietly in the waiting room, periodically looking at his watch. Maggie sat in a well-worn, faux brown leather chair watching her brother walk back and forth.

"Will, do you want some coffee?"

"No, I don't think so."

"She's in the best hands, you know."

"I know. It's just that… well, it's Val, Maggie. I can't help but worry." He sat beside her. "It's ironic, isn't it? Me being an oncologist, and my wife gets cancer."

"Cancer is no respecter of persons." Maggie stated solemnly. "Val did everything right, Will. Monthly self-exams, regularly scheduled mammograms. Even her blood test was negative for the cancer gene. Sometimes, these things just happen. There's nothing any of us could have done to prevent it. Instead, we have to rely on our training, do what we've been taught to do, and put all our efforts into fighting it."

Will nodded. "I know you're right, but I keep wondering if there was something else I could have done. Was there something I missed?"

Before Maggie had an opportunity to answer, her attention was diverted to another person entering the waiting area. She looked up and gasped, "Colin!" Standing quickly, she stared, unmoving, until she felt his arms surround her. She fell against his chest and held him tightly. Her trembling voice betrayed her outer calm. "I can't believe you're here!"

The tall blonde man kissed Maggie lightly on the lips before responding. "I thought I should be here with both of you." He held her until she relaxed, than slowly released her and walked over to Will, extending his hand. "How are you holding up?"

Will shook his hand and smiled weakly. "I'm hanging in there. Thanks for coming, Colin. I can't tell you how much I appreciate it."

"I've been praying for you all. If you need anything, you just let me know." He moved to sit beside Maggie and took her hand in his. "No news, I take it?"

Maggie shook her head. "Not yet. She's been in for about an hour. Did you get finished with your stuff in London?"

Colin shrugged his shoulders. "Not completely, but it isn't anything that can't wait, and I really wanted to be here to support you."

The nearness of her fiancé brought a tremendous sense of relief to Maggie, and she reached out a hand to stroke his cheek. "Thank you," she whispered. "It's hard for both of us being on this end."

Colin nodded and said quietly to her, "I suppose it must be." He looked directly into her eyes and spoke reassuringly. "Maggie, remember that God is in control. Nothing happens that He is not aware of or that takes Him by surprise. We may not understand why, but we can depend on Him to work through this."

"I wish they knew the Lord," she replied in hushed tones. "I've been praying for that so much, and I just wish I knew what to say."

"There's no special formula, love. Just allow God to work through you; say what's on your heart. It's sincerity that counts, not a particular set of words," reassured Colin, "and if you let Him, He will be faithful to direct you."

"But you always know exactly what to say," maintained Maggie.

Colin grinned. "It only seems that way to you. Remember Santa Molina? I wasn't too confident then."

Maggie thought back to the trip to which he was referring. She had invited Colin to visit the small Mexican community in an effort to share with him her passion for her former brother-in-law's ministry. After the death of her first husband, Maggie had embraced the work that he and his brother had started there by visiting as often as she could to staff a makeshift clinic for the locals.

During her last visit, Maggie had accepted Christ as her Savior, but only after she and Colin had reached an impasse concerning his desire to help in the Santa Molina ministry. That impasse threatened to destroy their relationship and led to a very long night of soul-searching for Maggie. At that time, Colin had believed he had been inadequate in sharing the gospel with Maggie, but God had been faithful and used the words of the British singer to help Maggie find her way to a personal relationship with the Son of God.

As the months had progressed, their love had grown, and after much prayer and seeking of God's will, both were convinced that a future together was in the Lord's plans for them.

"Hey, where are you?" Colin whispered as he squeezed Maggie's hand.

Maggie shook her head and smiled. "Sorry. Just reminiscing." She saw Will sit down and put his head in his hands. She glanced up at Colin.

"I'll go," he whispered, rising to his feet. He walked over to Will and sat down opposite him. He spoke so softly that Maggie couldn't hear the conversation, but she saw Will lift his head to look at Colin. The tears in her brother's eyes broke her heart, and she prayed silently that God would give Colin the right words to say, words that would provide the peace that her brother so desperately needed.

Another hour passed before Dr. Delmonico entered the waiting room. Will stood up immediately and waited for the surgeon to speak.

"Will, I have good news," began Dr. Delmonico. "First, the tumor was small. Approximately one and a half centimeters. Secondly, all margins were clear. Thirdly, and most importantly for Valerie, there was no lymph node involvement."

An audible sigh escaped Will, and relief was evident on his ruggedly handsome face. "How is she doing? Can I see her?"

"She's in recovery right now. She has a small drain that she'll go home with, and I'll see her in about a week to remove it. Other than that, when she's fully awake and able to take some fluids, I'll send her home with you. You will need to make an appointment in oncology for follow up."

Will nodded and shook Dr. Delmonico's hand. "Thanks, Brett. I really appreciate it."

"No problem, Will. Let me take you back to sit with her."

Maggie watched her brother disappear behind the double doors of the recovery room, and then the tears spilled over onto her cheeks.

"Are you okay, love?" inquired Colin, concern washing over his face. He put an arm around her and drew her nearer to him.

"Yes. Yes, I am… I'm just so relieved. It could have been much worse."

"Okay, do me a favor and translate what the doctor said," requested Colin as he handed her a tissue.

"Thank you." Maggie dabbed at her eyes and began. "Let's see, her tumor is small. About an inch in diameter. The tissue all around it was clear of any malignant cells, so that is very good. That indicates the cancer is localized, and the lymph nodes are clear. That means that the cancer, in all likelihood, hasn't spread to any other part of her body."

"So, does that mean she's cured?"

"No, not really. Not yet. She'll still need the radiation treatments… maybe chemotherapy, but that's up to her oncologist, and then she needs to be monitored for several years," explained Maggie.

"Wow, this is just the beginning, isn't it?"

"Yes, but she has a good chance for recovery. However, it's not going to be easy for either of them," confessed Maggie. "Radiation therapy is physically draining, and chemotherapy is worse. So, Val's going to need help. Some days it will be fine, and other days, she'll feel like crawling into a hole and quitting."

"They're going to need a lot of prayer."

"Yes, they will." She slipped her hand into his, and together they bowed their heads and prayed for God's grace and healing touch upon Valerie and Will.

CHAPTER EIGHT

The office of Dr. Renee Sommers was quite unlike that of Dr. Will Garrett. Although they shared specialties, his office was somewhat plain with its perfunctory potted plants and watercolor paintings. In Dr. Sommers' waiting room, vibrant colors from the hot end of the spectrum splashed across the walls. Poster-sized photographs of hot air balloons, stock car racing, and bullfighters hung in random arrangement on the walls. Freshly cut flowers in a crystal vase adorned a small wooden table in a corner illuminated by a multicolored leaded glass fixture hanging from the ceiling.

"Should I put my sunglasses on?" whispered Will when he sat down on a plush orange upholstered chair.

Valerie smiled at her husband as she plopped down in a similar chair with a violet hue. "Shhh... I think it's... well, it's cheery."

"That's an understatement. It's like somebody blew up a rainbow in here."

"I think it's rather nice," grinned Valerie as she linked her fingers with Will's.

Will shook his head and rolled his eyes as the door to the examination rooms opened. A nurse, holding a clipboard, smiled as she called out, "Valerie Garrett?"

Valerie stood, pulled Will to his feet, and followed the nurse into a private room. Much less flamboyant than the waiting area, this room, painted pale blue with colorful butterflies and bees flitting over wildflowers, provided an aura of peace and serenity. Valerie sat quietly on the examination table while Will stood near the window looking toward the outside parking area.

"I'm still kind of nervous about this," admitted Valerie. She fidgeted with a tissue in her lap.

Will turned toward his wife and smiled weakly. "I totally understand, Val. I'm a little nervous, too."

"You are?" Valerie stared at him in disbelief.

"A little. This is a new role for me. Usually, I'm the doctor, not the caregiver. I want to make sure I'm doing everything I can to help you through this as your husband, not just as an oncologist."

Valerie smiled appreciatively. "I don't know how people get through this all by themselves. Without you, I'd be so terrified. Just having you here with me helps so much."

Will looked lovingly at his wife and reached for her hand. "One day, we'll look back on this time as just one bad moment in a lifetime filled with happiness."

A small knock on the door interrupted their tender moment, and it opened before either Will or Valerie could respond. A small, petite blonde woman entered the room, her short, bobbed hairdo framing a heart-shaped face. She held out her hand to Will, and her warm smile relaxed the anxious couple.

"Hi, Will," she said as she clasped his hand. "And you must be Valerie. I'm Renee Sommers. It's good to finally meet you, although I wish the circumstances were different. How are you doing?"

"Okay, I think." Valerie glanced at her husband, who had eased himself into a chair. "It could've been a lot worse."

Dr. Sommers agreed. "Yes, it could have, but your pathology report is very encouraging, and I believe with the proper care and treatment, you will do very well." She sat on a stool and fixed her gaze upon Valerie's skeptical face.

"Valerie, I want you to know something that is very important. You were not handed a death sentence. You will survive this. Your pathology reports show that your cancer was not aggressive, nor was it grossly invasive. There are several options for treatment as Will has probably discussed with you. I'm here to help the two of you make the right decisions about your care and to be with you each step of the way."

The oncologist's words were powerful, and Valerie hung on every one. She listened intently as Renee Sommers outlined the recommended treatment plan.

"Valerie, you're facing something that is very frightening. It doesn't matter if the cancer is stage one or stage four; it is a very fearsome diagnosis, and as a medical professional, you know a lot about cancer and its prognoses. As a previous caregiver, you also know how difficult the road ahead can be.

"Due to the size and location of the tumor, I would officially classify your cancer as stage one. That means that it is localized; it hasn't spread to any surrounding tissues. You elected to have the lumpectomy with radiation, which I think was a very good choice," reassured the doctor. "With the lumpectomy behind you, the next step is radiation. This will involve directing radioactive energy to the area where the lump was. This eradicates any remaining cancer cells that may have strayed from the immediate tumor site. There are thirty-five treatments, and after that, we'll evaluate and decide if any further treatments are necessary."

"We'll start as soon as the wound is healed, right?" asked Will, leaning forward in his seat.

Dr. Sommers rotated on her stool to face him. "Yes. As you know, the surgical wound needs to be completely healed, probably in about four weeks. The drain's out, so let's plan on one month from now." She turned back to Valerie. "How does that sound?"

Valerie cast an uneasy glance at her husband, looked back at Dr. Sommers, and nodded her head. "It's good to know the plan. It feels like I'm more in control now, not the cancer. I--" She hesitated for a moment, but then responded confidently, "*We're* ready to fight this."

Dr. Sommers smiled approvingly. "That's good to hear, Valerie. That positive outlook will definitely help you in the weeks ahead. You are very fortunate that you have such a good support system, and while Will may be able to answer any questions you have, you can also call me for anything, at any time."

They spent the remainder of their time with Renee discussing the radiation process, possible side effects, and expected outcomes. When they finally left the office, Valerie's oppressing burden of fear had been lessened. With Will's arm around her shoulder as they walked, she confided softly to her husband, "I never thought it would really happen to me, Will."

Stopping midstride, he turned to face Valerie. "Me, neither, sweetheart, but we've had nothing but good news. You're going to beat this, Val." He kissed her lightly and hugged her to him.

"I know," agreed Valerie, but her heart still held a small sliver of doubt.

The next four weeks passed by quickly for Valerie. She worked a few half-shifts at the ER, which were uneventful for the most part. It was easy to forget the overwhelming fears of the previous month since her recovery was without incident, and she remained relatively pain-free. Only the residual pink surgical scar hinted of the invasive disease that now became the unspoken focal point of her days.

Today, Valerie was in the oncological radiation center to receive several small markings that would indicate the area in which to direct the radiation. The waiting area was large with many chairs covered in gray and blue tweed-like upholstery. A muted television displayed the local news through closed-captioning, and soft instrumental music filled the room via invisible speakers. The muffled conversations between those who were waiting for treatment and their apparent caregivers were a subdued testimony to the solemnness of the trials ahead.

"Mrs. Garrett?"

Valerie looked up at a young woman wearing a set of green scrubs. Her smile revealed perfect white teeth, and for a moment, Valerie thought she could be a model for a toothpaste commercial.

"Yes?"

"My name is Allison. I'm going to get you set up for the markings. How are you doing this morning?"

"I'm doing okay." Valerie walked through the automatic door into the oncological radiation department as Allison directed her through the hallway.

Allison pointed to a curtained changing room. "Everything off from the waist up. Opening in the front. I'll be right back to take you to the treatment room." She smiled as she handed Valerie a hospital gown.

After changing into the blue and white printed gown, Valerie sat quietly on the dressing room bench. *How did you get through all this, Mom? I feel so alone.*

Within moments, Allison had returned and guided Valerie to the treatment room. They entered through a thick door that closed with a solid thud. Valerie glanced around at the stark room, her eyes widening as she noticed the stainless steel examination table over which hovered a huge mechanical contraption. Her old fears threatened to overwhelm her. *What was I thinking? I should've brought Will with me.* She struggled to regain her composure and confidence.

"This won't take too long, but it's very important that we get the exact locations, so I'm going to ask you to be perfectly still while we position the machine and mark the spots."

"Okay."

Valerie swallowed hard, willed herself to be calm, and followed all the directions the technician gave her. As she lay on the cold, steel treatment table, she stared at the massive machine above her, trying to ignore the individuals in the room as they manipulated and marked her body.

"You all right?" asked Allison as she moved from one side of the table to the other.

"Yes," Valerie lied. *No! No, I'm not okay! I HATE THIS! Why is this happening to me?*

"We're almost finished. When you begin your treatments, this is the room you'll be in. It will only take a few minutes actually. We'll line up this machine, do the treatment, and then you'll be free to go. It will take you longer to check in and get changed than to have the treatment. We'll see you Monday through Friday at the same time every day."

"Do I need to have someone come with me?" *Please say 'yes.' Tell me I shouldn't come alone here.*

Allison shook her head. "Not really, although many people do. The treatments will not adversely affect you at all when you get them, so you can drive yourself. You won't be here longer than 20 minutes at the most."

Valerie nodded and closed her eyes as the final measurements were made.

I can do this. Will could come with me; I know he would. Or maybe Maggie. Maybe at least for the first time.

"We're all through, Mrs. Garrett. Do you have any questions for me?" asked Allison as she helped Valerie sit up on the table.

"No, I don't believe so. Not now, anyway."

Allison guided her back to the changing area. When Valerie entered the draped cubicle, she sighed deeply and leaned against the wall, closing her eyes.

I can do this.

After a few minutes, she slowly reopened her eyes. Taking a deep breath, she held back her tears as she looked down at the small circular markings now imprinted on her body forever. Mesmerized, she reached up and touched each blue-black dot, permanent reminders of the disease that was changing her life forever.

"I can do this," she repeated aloud. "I really can." She took another deep breath, dressed, and left the facility, never looking back.

The first day of Valerie's radiation treatment was a typical southern California summer morning. A cool sea breeze promised to keep the temperature from rising too quickly into the mid-nineties, and the pansies, daisies, and poppies on Valerie's backyard patio opened their petals to receive the warmth of the sun.

Valerie had chosen to wear a lightweight pair of blue sweatpants and a cotton t-shirt with the words "Nurses Call the Shots" lettered on the front of it in bright pink embroidery. Admiring the flowers from her kitchen window, she finished a glass of orange juice. Hearing the doorbell ring, she set her glass on the kitchen counter and moved to answer the door, knowing that it was probably her sister-in-law.

She opened the door widely. "Good morning, Mags!" Valerie tried to sound cheery.

"Morning, Val," replied Maggie as she gave Valerie a small kiss on the cheek. "Are you ready?"

"Yes, I think so. Will said there wasn't much to this. I just lay under this humongous machine for a few seconds, get zapped with the radiation, and then it's over."

"Is he still okay with me going with you and not him?"

Valerie nodded. "Yes. I told him that I wanted our life to be as normal as possible, and therefore he needed to go to work."

Maggie nodded in agreement. "That's a good idea." They walked together toward her car. "Are you scheduled to work today?"

Valerie shook her head. "No. I figured I'd better wait and see how I feel. Even though Will said I wouldn't feel anything today, I decided to take the day off." She hesitated, and then continued as she got into the car. "Do you think I should have gone to work? Am I being silly about this?"

Maggie sat in the driver's seat and reached out to squeeze Valerie's hand. She looked over at her sister-in-law and spoke softly. "No, Val. I don't think so. This isn't easy for anyone. Just because you're a nurse doesn't mean it isn't hard."

"I know, Mags. Even though Will's told me so much-- and believe me, he's given me tons of information-- I still feel like I'm heading into uncharted waters, and it's kind of... well, terrifying."

Maggie maneuvered her silver Lexus into the traffic. "I can imagine. It's so different when it's you... or someone you love. You've been on both ends. This is new to me and Will."

"It's hard going through this, isn't it... for all of us?"

"Yes, it is, but I think we're doing great, especially you."

Grateful for Maggie's encouragement, Valerie smiled, and they finished their ride to the medical center in casual conversation, neither one of them mentioning the radiation treatment to come.

After changing into a pale blue hospital gown, Valerie followed the technician into the same treatment room in which her body had been marked a week earlier. The huge radiation machine still hovered above the long steel table on which she was to lie.

Motioning for her to recline on the table directly below the machine, Allison asked, "How are you doing today, Mrs. Garrett?"

"Fine. Just a little nervous." Valerie positioned herself on the table beneath the monstrous device overhead. The cold steel sent a shiver through her body.

"That's understandable. Do you have any questions that I can answer right now?"

"No," Valerie answered, her breathing more rapid and shallow than before. She turned her head to one side, avoiding eye contact with the massive machine above her. The radiation warning signs were on the walls in bright red and inescapable to anyone who entered the room. They were an ominous reminder of the treatment that was to come. Valerie closed her eyes tightly and tried to imagine a happier place, but the technician's voice brought her back to the reality that loomed before her.

"Mrs. Garrett, I'm going to step out of the room now. Remember that there is a monitor, and we will be aware of what is going on in here every moment. If you need anything, you just need to call out. I need you to be very still for the next few minutes, okay?"

"Okay," Valerie whispered. She felt a tear slip from the corner of her eye and trickle down the side of her face. She gripped the fabric of her gown and waited. Her entire body stiffened and despite her efforts, she could not ease the tension that was building. She heard the heavy door to the room close and latch. *I am all alone.* The enormity of her solitude intensified with each passing moment. Fear gripped her heart.

In seconds, the lighting of the room changed, and Valerie knew the treatment was beginning. Before she had time to consider what was happening, everything stopped. The large door opened, and Allison reentered.

"You're all done, Mrs. Garrett."

"That's it?"

"That's it. It wasn't too bad, was it?"

Valerie shook her head as she rose to a sitting position. "No, not at all. Seems like my imagination is my worst best friend."

Allison smiled. "The unknown is often fearful, but now that you've experienced one treatment, the rest should go very well for you. I look forward to seeing you tomorrow then." She escorted Valerie to the changing room.

As soon as Valerie stepped behind the curtain of her dressing area, she leaned against the wall, and in a tremendous release of tension allowed her tears to silently fall. Finally, she drew in a deep breath and exhaled slowly. She blew her nose and dried her eyes before changing into her own clothes.

When she walked into the waiting area, Maggie stood up.

"That was quick. How did it go?"

Valerie managed a half-hearted smile. "Piece of cake. Exactly like Will and Dr. Sommers said it would be. I guess I was worried for nothing."

Maggie looked compassionately into Valerie's reddened eyes. "You have to stop being so hard on yourself."

"I know. It's just that…" She trailed off as they walked outside the building.

Maggie stopped and turned toward Valerie. "You need to give yourself permission to be you, not what you think others expect you to be," she chastised softly as she gave her sister-in-law a loving embrace.

Valerie clutched Maggie tightly. "Thanks, Mags." As Maggie held her, Valerie felt protected and loved, and at that moment, nothing else seemed to matter.

CHAPTER NINE

It had been a week since Valerie's radiation treatments began, and Will was making his rounds in the hospital when Maggie finally caught up with him.

"How's it going, Dr. Garrett?"

He looked up from a chart and grinned. "Just fine, thanks. Thanks so much for taking Val to her first treatments, Maggie. I know it made her feel good to have you there."

"I was glad I could do it, Will. How are you doing... really?"

He hesitated for a moment. "I'm doing okay, Maggie. I have my moments, but for the most part, I'm handling it."

"Can we talk for a second?"

When he nodded, they both entered the staff lounge as two nurses were leaving.

Choosing a table in the corner, they sat facing each other. Maggie reached out her hand to touch Will's as she spoke. "I love you both so much. I am so sorry you have to go through this."

"I know." He took a deep breath. "I feel so... so... helpless sometimes. It's totally different from being the doctor. Having to face it yourself... or with your loved one, is hard. But I'm not going to let her die."

"You know, Will," began Maggie hesitantly, "sometimes that decision is not up to us."

"What do you mean?"

"God's here if you need Him." She heard Will sigh deeply. "Maybe if--" She shook her head. "I'm not very good at this. I'm sorry."

"No need to apologize, Maggie."

"Will, I want so badly to tell you about God and... and what He's done for me, but I don't know how to do it and not sound like I'm preaching to you," admitted Maggie. "I want you to know that He really does love you, and Valerie, too, but I don't know how. I mean, I was so lost when Scott died, and then Colin came into my life. I needed God so badly, and I didn't even know it. It was hard, really hard. I didn't understand what it meant to trust Christ and be saved, but somewhere along the way, I reached out to Him, or He reached down to me-- whatever it was, and now, I'm learning to trust Him more and more each day-- in everything. It's Christ who's getting me through this, because, honestly, I'm scared, too." She paused for a moment and then sighed, "I wish I knew how to explain it all to you."

Smiling lovingly at her, Will simply stated, "I think you just did."

Maggie looked up at her brother and shook her head. "I don't think I'm doing a very good job. I just know, Will, that if you would let Him, God would help you through all of this."

"Honestly, Maggie, I don't want to hurt your feelings, but right now I don't know what I feel about God. How am I supposed to trust someone who let this happen to Val? I know you and Colin have your faith, and I respect that, but right now, I'm trusting in me and the medical profession, not some deity who doesn't really seem to care about Valerie," said Will straightforwardly.

Maggie sat stunned by her brother's admission. As Maggie listened to her brother, her heart broke. *What am I supposed to say, Lord?*

"I don't want to upset you, Maggie, but..." continued Will, "we've always been honest with each other."

"I know."

"If it helps, Colin talked with me a little about his beliefs, too. I've been thinking about the stuff he shared with me, but right now, I'm not really interested in God," stated Will bluntly. "I need to focus all of my attention on Valerie. I'm here for her now, and frankly, I think I can take pretty good care of her."

Maggie nodded half-heartedly. "I understand." She squeezed his hand. "I'm here if you ever decide you are ready."

"I know." He stood up. "I really do need to get back to my rounds. I'll talk with you later?"

"Of course." She sighed deeply, watching the door close behind him as he left the lounge. *Well, that didn't go the way I thought it would, Lord. I know I couldn't face all of this without You. How's he doing it? And Valerie? You opened my eyes when I was so reluctant to accept Your love. I know You can do the same for them. You're still the God of miracles, right? Could You please do one now?*

CHAPTER TEN

"It's so good seeing you back on the regular schedule!" Claire Donnelly's eyes brightened when she saw Valerie walk into the ER nurses' station. "How are you feeling, Val?"

"Actually, I'm feeling really good," responded Valerie, giving the nurse a warm hug. Joining the emergency room staff at almost the same time, Valerie and Claire had become good friends in the work place, and Valerie greatly respected Claire's abilities as an ER nurse. Having gained the majority of her ER training in her native country of Costa Rica, Claire brought a wealth of experience to Eastmont that she was more than willing to share with her co-workers.

"Treatments going okay?"

"Yes, better than I thought. I'll admit I was very scared at first, but now that I've had a few, I'm doing fine," stated Valerie. "How are things here?" She glanced up at the near empty treatment board. It contained only one name.

"Slow," Claire replied. "Very slow. Shepherd's stitching up a hand on an over-zealous skateboarder in three, and nothing on the wire. You picked a good day to come back."

Valerie grinned. "I guess so."

"So what's the scoop on your tumor?"

Valerie sighed. "If I have to have cancer, this is the one to have. It was about 1.5 centimeters in diameter and with no lymph node involvement; I am officially classified as stage one."

"Oh, Val, honey, I'm so happy for you! Dr. D's been keeping us up-to-date, but it's so good to hear it from you! You're looking great."

"Thanks. I'm doing a lot better than I thought I would. Will's been great. He's been such a rock. I couldn't do this without him." Valerie's eyes shone with admiration.

Claire smiled. "Well, from my perspective, you must be doing great because you look wonderful!" She hugged Valerie once more as a familiar voice interrupted their sweet reunion.

"Now, who's this young lady?"

Valerie looked up to see Ben Shepherd approach. He handed Claire a chart as he simultaneously gave Valerie a one-handed hug. "It is so good to see you, Val. How are you doing?"

"Much better than I expected."

The doctor smiled. "I'm glad to hear that. Will's kept me posted, but it's much better to see you in person looking so well. You're a survivor, Val, and I have no doubt you'll beat this. Been praying for you since I heard. I'm expecting a full recovery."

Valerie smiled warmly. "I really appreciate that, Ben. Thank you so much."

He smiled back at her and nodded. "I think I'll get myself a cup of coffee, ladies. Give me a holler when you need me." With that said, he retreated into the staff lounge.

Claire quickly read Ben's notes on the chart, and then said, "Well, I guess I better go discharge the guy in three. See you in a bit. It's good to have you back."

As Valerie watched her leave, she heard the alert on the paramedic relay. She hesitated for a moment, looked around the emergency room, smiled, and then proceeded to answer the call.

Valerie's schedule became routine with radiation treatments every Monday through Friday, and three twelve-hour shifts per week in the emergency room. She didn't have too much trouble with fatigue, but on those days when she felt overly tired, she spoke with her nursing supervisor, who was extremely supportive and adjusted Valerie's schedule whenever necessary.

The emergency room was quiet for most of this particular shift, but now Valerie was awaiting a stabbing victim from a local college football game. Called in by onsite paramedics, she had alerted both Maggie and Ben of the incoming trauma victim and prepared treatment room two for his arrival.

In less than ten minutes, the ambulance bay doors opened, and Valerie scurried to walk with the paramedics as they wheeled the wounded man to treatment room two.

"Intestinal evisceration due to multiple stab wounds to the abdomen. Pulse is weak and thready, and BP's low but holding." The paramedics assisted Valerie in moving the patient to an examination table just as Maggie entered the room.

"What've we got?" she asked as she donned a pair of latex gloves.

"Intestinal evisceration following a stabbing." Valerie hung the normal saline bag on the bedside pole, and placed electrodes on the man's chest, pulse oximeter on his index finger, and blood pressure cuff around his arm. The cardiac monitor sprang to life; its colored lines providing quick information regarding heart rate, oxygen level, and blood pressure. "Apparently they took their on-field rivalry into the parking lot. This guy must've been on the losing end."

"Let's make sure he's stable, then up to the O.R. to check for any other organ damage." Maggie glanced at the paramedic field chart. "Mr. Drake, can you hear me?"

The man half-opened his eyes, but said nothing.

"Michael... Michael... Tell me what happened to you," urged Maggie as she began her physical exam.

"I… I don't re… remem…" His eyes rolled back into his head, and he slipped into unconsciousness once more.

"BP's dropping, Doctor," reported Valerie.

"Get me two units of O negative," ordered Maggie. As Valerie moved to call the lab for blood, Maggie carefully removed the abdominal dressing administered in the field. The jagged stab wounds exposed glistening pinkish-grey intestine threatening to spill out of the patient's body. She carefully inspected the area for excessive bleeding, but found none.

"We've got to get him into surgery; he's got to be bleeding internally," Maggie muttered to herself as she continued feeling for abnormalities inside the abdominal cavity near the wound site.

"Blood's hanging."

"O.R. four is prepped and ready."

"BP's holding. Breathing's shallow."

Maggie looked up at the cardiac monitor and then placed her stethoscope on the man's chest. Satisfied with what she heard, she ordered, "Let's move him now." She backed up while her team of nurses and technicians rapidly prepared the patient for transport. In less than five minutes, Michael Drake was on his way to the operating room where a surgical team awaited to repair the damage to the young man's body.

Maggie shook her head as she removed her gloves. Tossing them into a biohazard bin, she glanced over at her sister-in-law who stood watching the empty doorway.

"You okay?"

Valerie quickly turned and nodded apologetically. "Yeah, just wondering how a football game can lead to something like this. It doesn't make too much sense, does it? Life is just too precious for that."

They walked together toward the nurses' station. The treatment board was beginning to fill up.

In treatment room one, Ben Shepherd listened intently to the lungs of the eight-year-old girl. With each breath, he heard high-pitched wheezes. The little girl swung her feet back and forth as Ben quickly completed the physical examination.

Wheezes, nasal flaring, retractions with breathing... acute asthma.

He smiled at his patient. "Mallory, you're going to be just fine, but I think you need a breathing treatment, okay?"

"Okay." She continued swinging her feet and clutching a small stuffed horse.

"Do you like horses?" asked Ben, as he made some notations on the chart.

"Yes! I want to be a cowgirl when I grow up and live in Texas!"

"You do?" He smiled, patted her on top of her light brown curls, and then turned to the anxious mother. "I'm going to order a breathing treatment for her, and then we'll see how she's doing. I suspect that'll open up her lungs enough to ease her breathing, but she'll definitely need follow up with her pulmonologist-- her lung doctor."

"Will the coughing stop? She was coughing so much, I thought she was going to throw up," the mother stated, taking notes as Ben spoke.

"It should. Right now, she has a lot of wheezing in her lungs. This means the tubes inside are constricted, making the openings narrow. That's what makes the high-pitched noises. The treatment will open up those tubes, and that will make it easier for the air to get in and out."

"Is there anything else I should have done before bringing her in?"

Ben shook his head. "No. With asthma, it's better to bring her in when she's having problems. You did the right thing." Reassured, the mother visibly relaxed and set her notepad down.

"Thank you, Doctor. I was so worried."

"I understand completely. I'll send the respiratory technician in to start the treatment, and then I'll be back when it's completed to see how Mallory's doing." He took the chart to the nurses' station, and asked the clerk to notify the respiratory therapist of the treatment request.

"Miss? Can you help us?"

Valerie looked up into the face of a tall, thin elderly man. He wore a slight smile, and his blue eyes seemed filled with warmth. He quietly waited.

"Of course, sir. What seems to be the problem?"

He gestured to a gray-haired woman sitting in a wheelchair. "It's my wife, Grace. Grace Gallagher. She's a patient of Dr. Garrett. Dr. Will Garrett. He told us if she had a fever, I was supposed to bring her in to see him, but it's Sunday, and his office isn't open. I hope it was alright that I brought her here." He was very soft-spoken, and Valerie listened very carefully to hear everything he was saying.

"Of course, it's alright, Mr. Gallagher. Your wife is a cancer patient?"

"Yes. Will you be able to call Dr. Garrett? He's a very kind doctor, and my Grace, she adores him." He looked lovingly at his wife.

"Yes, I'll be able to get hold of him. First, let's get your wife into a treatment room." Valerie wheeled Grace into a vacant treatment room and helped her onto an examination bed.

"I'm sorry to be such a bother, Tom," said Grace weakly. She reached out a wrinkled hand toward her husband.

He took her hand and patted it gently. "You're no bother, sweetheart." He lowered his lips to her hand and kissed it. "If anyone's been a bother all these years, it's been me. You've been my angel."

As Valerie quietly took Grace's vital signs, she watched the tender interchange between Grace and Tom. *I hope Will and I are like that when we're old and gray.* She did a quick assessment of Grace's heart and lungs, and then stepped out in the hall to dial Will's number.

After two rings, he answered. "Val? Is everything all right?"

"Good afternoon, Dr. Garrett. Yes, everything is fine." She heard him chuckle on the other end.

"Yes, Nurse Garrett, what can I do for you?"

"Well, actually, Will, this really is a business call. I have a patient of yours here in the ER. Grace Gallagher. She has a fever of 101.4. Her husband brought her in." She heard Will sigh. "He said you told him to come in with any sign of fever."

"Yes, it's not good for anyone to spike a fever when they're on chemo. They're already immunosuppressed, and any infection can be potentially disastrous. I'm upstairs right now. As soon as I'm finished here, I'll be right there."

As Valerie hung up the phone, she glanced back toward treatment room two. An involuntary shiver went through her body, her gaze transfixed on the small form of Grace Gallagher barely visible through the opened door.

"Hello, Mr. Gallagher." Will shook the man's hand and moved near the head of the bed where Grace lay with her eyes closed. He gently closed his hand around Grace's fingers while speaking to her. He spoke softly. "Hi, Grace. It's Dr. Garrett. What's going on with you?"

Grace slowly opened her eyes and managed a weak smile. "Dr. Garrett, I'm sorry to be such a bother, but you know Tom. He insisted we come in. Said you told him I had to come in if I got a fever."

Will nodded. "Yes, I did tell him that, Grace. No point in you staying home when I can give you something to help you feel better. You probably need some antibiotics."

"You're going to stick me with one of those needles, aren't you?"

Will sighed apologetically. "Well, not me, but one of the nurses here will need to. It's the best way to get the medicine into you quickly. Then I'll probably send you home with some pills, okay?"

She chuckled weakly. "Do I really have a choice?"

Will smiled. "Actually, you do, but I'm hoping you'll agree to it."

Grace's slender fingers tightened around Will's hand. "You're a good doctor. I'll do whatever you think is best."

"How's your appetite been, Grace?" He looked over at Mr. Gallagher, who shook his head.

Grace smiled slightly. "Well, Dr. Garrett, I think it's fine. Tom, he thinks I'm starving myself. Always loads my plate up with food. If I ate everything he put on my plate, I'd be as big as a house."

Her husband tapped Will on the shoulder and murmured, "She's taking that liquid protein drink you recommended. Thinks it's a malted milk shake."

Will nodded approvingly. "That's good. Faith still coming by to check on you both?"

"Yes, she's a fine granddaughter. She's getting married in a week or so." He lowered his voice once more and continued.

"I'm hoping Grace will be well enough to go to the wedding. It'd mean so much to both of them... and me, too."

"Well, Mr. Gallagher, I'm going to do everything I can to get Grace to that wedding. Let's get those antibiotics in her and see how she does. If all goes well, she can go home tonight."

Will turned to Grace. "I'm going to send the nurse in to start the IV, and then we'll give you that medicine, okay? You just lie back and get some rest, Grace." He made some notations in the chart as he left the room. He saw Valerie stretching to reach some bags of intravenous fluids from the top shelf of a very tall portable cart.

He walked over, easily reached the bags, and pulled them off the shelf. "Need a hand, sweetheart?"

She smiled at him. "You're always rescuing me! Thanks." She took the bags, set them on a lower shelf, and then turned back to Will. He was opening Grace's chart.

"Can you start an IV in Mrs. Gallagher? I wrote an order for one dose of IV antibiotics and some oral meds to follow. Also, I'd like blood cultures times three. Hopefully, they'll come back negative, but if not, at least I'll know what I'm up against."

"Of course." Valerie hesitated before asking, "Is she terminal?"

Will looked at his wife with compassion in his dark eyes. "There's not much more I can do for her except keep her as comfortable as possible."

Valerie's eyes lowered slightly, and she nodded. "I'll go start that IV. Want me to call you after the antibiotic is in?"

He thought for a moment. "No need. I'll probably be back down soon. I want to see how she's doing and answer any questions she or her husband might have. Page me though if either one of them needs me before I get back, okay?'

"You know, you're quite an amazing doctor." There was admiration in Valerie's voice.

"I think you're a bit prejudiced, don't you think?" He signed his name to the orders and handed the chart to Valerie.

She shook her head. "Nope. I call it like I see it. See you later, Dr. Garrett." She blew him a kiss as she walked into Grace's room.

Quickly gathering her supplies from a nearby cabinet, Valerie turned and set them on the bedside table. She pulled on a pair of latex gloves and reached for Grace's hand. "Mrs. Gallagher?"

Grace's eyes fluttered open. "Hello, Nurse."

"Dr. Garrett wants an IV started, so I'm here to do that, okay?"

"Sure. I must tell you, I have terrible veins. At least that's what the chemo nurses tell me."

"They call her 'pin cushion,'" laughed Mr. Gallagher.

Valerie looked up at him. "Really? Well, I hope I can call you 'one-stick Grace' tonight, okay?"

Grace chuckled. "Sure, sweetie. You're a pretty young thing. Married?"

"Yes, I am." She gently lifted Grace's hand, searching for a patent vein.

"Is he good to you?"

"Couldn't be better, Mrs. Gallagher." She ran her fingers over the paper-thin skin and palpated a suitable vein. As she applied a small tourniquet, Valerie asked, "Can you make a fist for me?" She felt once again for the site and then expertly inserted the small needle. She felt it penetrate the vein wall and saw the bright red flashback in the tubing. As she released the tourniquet, she said, "Your veins were very cooperative tonight. You can relax your hand." Quickly connecting the needle to the IV tubing, she slowly adjusted the drip of saline. Securing the line with tape, she set Grace's hand down on a pillow.

"Thank you, Lord," whispered Mr. Gallagher. "for blessing us with such a good nurse." His voice was barely audible, but Valerie heard him.

She glanced up at Tom's face. His eyes were closed. She hesitated for a moment before turning her attention back to her patient.

"I'll put in a good word for you with our doctor," promised Grace, weakly smiling.

"Thank you, Mrs. Gallagher." Valerie quickly tidied up her things and then threaded the IV line into the machine that would automatically regulate the flow of fluid into the vein. "I'll be back as soon as the antibiotic gets here from the pharmacy. Meanwhile, if you need anything, anything at all, just press this button."

Once outside of the room, Valerie stopped and turned her head back toward the Gallaghers. *How can they be so peaceful when they're facing terminal cancer. I don't get it.*

CHAPTER ELEVEN

The weeks passed quickly, and Valerie tolerated her radiation treatments well. Maggie sat across from her on the patio sipping a glass of raspberry iced tea. The sun was high in the sky, its warmth spilling out on a bed of wildflowers whose opened blossoms seemed to reach upward toward the beckoning sunlight.

Maggie smiled when Valerie sat down opposite her. "I'm so proud of you."

"Why? What did I do?"

The physician looked at the nurse with compassion. "You've been such a trooper through this whole cancer ordeal." Maggie hesitated for a moment. "I know you were so scared… we all were, but you've done so well, and I'm just so proud of how you've been handling everything."

Valerie's cheeks reddened slightly, and she flashed a meek smile to Maggie. "I couldn't have done it without you and Will."

"We make a good team, the three of us." Maggie took another sip of tea. "You know, Val, this is not supposed to be a cancer meeting for us; I have something much more important to talk about."

Valerie looked at Maggie, a puzzled expression on her face.

"I have something to show you," said Maggie as she placed her left hand on the table in front of Valerie. A single solitaire diamond encircled by ten smaller versions of the main stone adorned her ring finger. The platinum band was a ropelike pattern of tiny diamonds twisting around Maggie's finger. It glittered in the sunlight.

Valerie gasped. "Oh, Maggie!" She held Maggie's hand up a bit and inspected the ring. "This is the most beautiful ring I've ever seen."

"The center stone belonged to his mother," Maggie said quietly. She held her hand up and stared at the sparkling engagement ring.

"I can't believe you haven't shown this to me before now!"

"It's a little 'blingy' for work, so I leave it at home."

"Have you picked out a dress yet? What are your colors? Is he going to sing to you? This wedding is going to be beautiful!" Valerie's eyes twinkled.

Maggie smiled to herself. This was the Valerie she knew and loved. Celebrating with her, enjoying their time together, and anticipating the wedding to come… that was Valerie.

"No, I haven't picked out a dress yet. I thought I'd need some help, so I wanted to wait until you felt up to shopping with me," explained Maggie.

"Is this going to be a shopping day?"

"I was hoping it would be," admitted Maggie. "Are you up to it?"

"Am I up to it? You've got to be kidding!" Valerie's eyes sparkled and her grin broadened. "I am one hundred percent up to it!"

"It's so good to see you smiling again, Val!"

"It's so wonderful to be able to smile again, Mags. And to be able to enjoy life again. I feel like the worst is over, even though I know there's still a long road ahead of me. Just to have that tumor out of my body is such a huge burden lifted," Valerie confessed. "And now, with only one more week of radiation therapy, well, I just feel like I'm really going to be okay." Valerie's tone changed as she continued. "But I do want to ask you something, Mags, as a doctor. I mean, Will's been terrific, but I kind of wanted a second opinion."

Maggie eyed her sister-in-law warily as she waited for Valerie to continue.

"I know that the usual treatment for lumpectomies doesn't include chemotherapy, but I was thinking that maybe I ought to have it. Renee said it was up to me at this point."

Maggie's brow furrowed. "Up to you? What do you mean? Why do you want to do the chemo, Val?"

"Mags, if I don't do the chemo, and the cancer recurs, I don't think I could ever forgive myself. If I do everything I can possibly do now, and then it recurs, well, that's the way it goes. But if I don't do everything, and it comes back, I don't know how I'd live with myself for taking the easy way out."

Maggie nodded her head. "I think I understand, but for the record, I don't think you're taking the 'easy way out' if you don't opt for chemo. I'm not really sure there is an 'easy way out.'"

Valerie thought for a moment. "I suppose not, but you know what I mean, right?"

"Yes, I do, and if you and Will think this is best, I'm all for it, too."

"Thanks, Mags, but..." Valerie hesitated. "I haven't told Will about my thoughts on chemo yet."

Maggie stared at Valerie, her mouth agape. "You haven't? Why not?"

Valerie hesitated. "I don't know. I think I'm kind of afraid he'll be against it. I get the impression that maybe neither he nor Renee really think it's the way I should go."

"Has he said that?"

"No, not in so many words. It's just... Oh, I don't know." Valerie shrugged her shoulders and stared off into her garden.

"You need to talk with him, Val. He's your husband, but he's also an oncologist. He's not going to let you make a decision that's going to be detrimental to your well-being. You need to discuss this with him."

Valerie sighed deeply. "I know, but I don't want him to not agree with me."

A deep, familiar voice joined their conversation. "Not agree with you about what?"

Both women turned their heads toward the sliding door to the kitchen. It was open, and Will stepped through. He pulled out a chair and sat down next to Valerie.

"Don't look so shocked," he said as he leaned over to kiss Valerie. "I thought I'd come home for lunch, but I didn't know I'd be having it with my *two* favorite women! So, what am I not agreeing with?"

Valerie glanced over at Maggie and mouthed, "What do I say?"

Will looked at his wife and then at his sister. His eyes narrowed. "Okay, what's going on?"

Maggie waited for Valerie to respond, but she remained silent. Maggie reluctantly turned toward her brother. "Will, Valerie and I were discussing the possibility of chemotherapy after the radiation treatments."

Will reached out for his wife's hand, but kept his eyes on his sister. "Chemo? What brought that up?" He turned a puzzled gaze toward his wife. "I thought you said you didn't want to do chemo."

Valerie smiled weakly at her husband. "I know. I've been thinking that maybe it would be better if I had it. You know, so I would know that I did everything I possibly could to avoid a recurrence."

Will rested his arms on the table and clasped his hands. He thought for a moment before speaking, and when he did, he looked directly at Valerie. "If that's what you're thinking of doing, then let's talk to Renee about it. Chemo is not easy, Val. You know that, and it's important that you are one hundred percent comfortable with the treatment plan you choose." He paused for a moment. "And why wouldn't I agree with that?"

Valerie averted her gaze from him. "I don't know. I just thought that…"

"Valerie, tell me what you're thinking." Will's fingers closed around her hand once more.

She took a deep breath, then turned to look into Will's concerned eyes. "I want to be sure I've done everything I possibly can to keep this from coming back. If I don't do the chemo, and the cancer recurs, I don't know if I could ever forgive myself. On the other hand, if I do the chemo, and the cancer does come back, I'll know it wasn't a mistake on my part." She sighed deeply, then looked away from her husband. "I suppose that doesn't make the most sense, does it?"

"It makes perfect sense, sweetheart. If you want to have the chemotherapy, I'll support you, one hundred percent."

Valerie lifted her eyes now brimming with tears, and smiled gratefully at Will.

"How did I ever get so lucky to have you in my life?"

Will lifted her hand to his lips and gently kissed the back of it. "I'm pretty sure I got the better end of the deal."

Maggie rolled her eyes in mock disgust. "Oh, please, you two. You're making me nauseous with all this."

"You're just jealous," laughed Will as he winked at Maggie. He released Val's hand and stood up. "How about I fix us all some of my famous grilled cheese sandwiches?" He bowed with a dramatic flair before retreating into the kitchen.

Maggie glanced at Valerie whose gaze was fixed on the spot where Will had disappeared into the house. "That wasn't so hard, was it?"

"No. No, it wasn't. I never should have doubted him. He is so good to me, Maggie. I don't know what I'd do without him," sighed Valerie, her eyes still on the now-closed sliding door.

CHAPTER TWELVE

The weekend began with an offshore breeze that ushered in a brief respite to the usual summer heat of southern California. Finishing a conversation, Valerie stuck her cell phone in her back pants pocket and poured herself a glass of iced tea while grabbing an apple from the fruit bowl that sat in the center of her kitchen table. She walked into the living room.

"Who was that?" asked Will drowsily, sitting up on the sofa. "What time is it?"

Valerie plopped down on the couch next to him and bit into an apple. "It was Maggie, and it's about three."

"Three? Good grief! The whole day is shot!" he complained. Kissing his wife on her forehead, he snatched the apple out of her hand and took a big bite before giving it back to her.

"I figured you needed the rest, you apple thief!" she joked.

"What did Maggie want?" he asked as he leaned back on the cushions.

"She invited us to church again."

Will frowned. "Again?"

"I take it you don't want to go?" Valerie laid her head on his shoulder.

"Not really, but I will if you want to," he answered truthfully. "You know I don't see things the same way she does, Val. She talks about how much God loves us and all, but then He lets something like this happen. That's not love. I mean, you're the sweetest, most caring person I know, and I'm not just saying that because you're my wife. You have a great outlook on life; you're good to people, and you have the biggest heart of anyone I know. Why did God give you cancer?"

"I don't know, honey, but it could be a lot worse," commented Valerie softly.

"Oh, I know that, but I don't particularly want to worship some deity who allows something like this to happen to you," stated Will defiantly. "It's wrong."

Valerie nestled in the crook of Will's arm. The disappointment was clear in her voice as she attempted to change the subject. "Maggie said Colin flew in this weekend. Do you think we could have them over for dinner even if we don't go to church?"

Will played with a tendril of Valerie's hair. "Of course, sweetheart. Just because I don't agree with them when it comes to religion doesn't mean I don't love them, or that I don't want to spend time with them. They're family, and I love them both dearly." He hesitated for a moment and then took a deep breath. "I tell you what. Let's go ahead and go to church with them. Maybe afterwards, we can go somewhere and have lunch together and maybe even dinner, okay?"

Valerie's eyes brightened, and she sat up. "Oh, Will, that sounds perfect! Thank you!" She kissed him and gave him a big hug. "I love you so much!" She pulled out her cell phone and punched in Maggie's number. She stood and walked toward the kitchen as she began to talk with Will's sister.

Will could only hear his wife's half of the conversation, but the joy in her voice was unmistakable. He observed her as she turned back toward him. Her laughter delighted his heart, and the animation in her conversation with his sister convinced him that his decision to go to church was the right thing to do. He sighed to himself as he continued to listen to her chatter excitedly on the phone. *Church... not exactly what I had in mind for my day off, but if it makes her happy...*

"She is really glad we're coming," reported Valerie as she set her phone on the coffee table. She sat on the arm of the sofa and faced Will. "I told her we'd be there for the eleven o'clock service." She smiled at him knowingly. "I told her that Sunday school would be asking a bit much of you."

Will grinned. "You know me so well, my dear." He paused for a moment and then asked, "Have I told you lately that I love you?"

"I believe you have, but I never get tired of hearing it," smiled Valerie as she stood. "I'm going to head out to the garden. I need a fresh bouquet for the table. Care to join me?"

"Can't think of anything else I'd rather do." He stood, swept her into his arms, spun her around, and then kissed her.

"Will Garrett, what are you doing?" She squealed in delight, and her arms went around his neck.

"Just kissing my beautiful wife." He stopped, set her down, and looked into her eyes, keeping her in his arms. He didn't say a word for a moment, and when he started to speak, he tilted her head up and looked deep into her hazel eyes. "You know, you're the best thing that ever happened to me. I love you so much."

Valerie smiled as she stood on her tiptoes and kissed him tenderly. "I don't know what I'd do without you, Will. You are my strength and my life."

Maggie nervously glanced at her watch. Ten more minutes until the worship service would begin. *Please come...*

She surveyed the last few cars pulling into the church's parking lot and then smiled when she recognized Will's lunar blue Mercedes. She watched them exit the car, smiling warmly at the two of them as they approached the entrance to the sanctuary. "I'm so glad you both came!" Maggie embraced her sister-in-law.

"Me too!" Valerie's eyes twinkled happily.

Maggie looked up at her brother, who stood behind his wife. She mouthed 'thank you,' and he nodded with a slight smile.

"I suppose you've got us right up front?" teased Will as he put his arm around Valerie and followed his sister.

"Almost, but really it's because Colin is singing," admitted Maggie. "We're only in the third row. It's not that bad."

Will rolled his eyes and then grinned at his sister. The anxiety in Maggie began to dissipate, and she smiled at her brother. *Thank you, Will. I know you don't want to be here, but I am so glad you came!*

"Hey, good to see you, Will!"

Will turned to see Colin offer his hand. Shaking it firmly, Will responded with a smile. "How've you been, Colin? When did you get here?"

"Friday evening. I've got a couple of weeks off, so I thought I'd come for a short visit. Val's looking good," he noted.

"Yeah, she's tolerating the radiation well. Now that the initial shock has worn off, I think both of us are coping better."

Maggie listened to the exchange between the two men before turning her attention to Valerie. "I am so thrilled you two came, and with Colin here, it… well, it's just wonderful having everyone here."

"I'm glad we got to come. I wasn't sure Will wanted to, but he did, and I'm glad," admitted Valerie.

They took their places in the pew as Jesse McClellan, the pastor of the church, walked up the aisle, shaking hands with those he passed. When Jesse took his place on the platform, the music director rose and stood facing the choir. He motioned for them to stand as the pianist began to play the introduction to their first song.

Their collective voices sang about the grace of God, and how it could sustain someone in times of trouble. Maggie thought about how much the Lord had brought her through and prayed silently that He would use the songs and message to touch the hearts of her brother and his wife. Lost in thought, she came back to the present when the congregation was invited to stand after the opening prayer and sing a few more songs. At the conclusion of the singing, Jesse walked up to the pulpit. As the people sat, their attention turned to their pastor.

"Good morning. It is so good to see you all here today. As many of you know, my boyhood friend, Colin Grant, has visited with us frequently over the last year or so. I asked him to share his testimony with us today and then sing a song. I know you'll be blessed by both." He motioned for Colin to come forward.

Colin sat on the piano bench and adjusted the boom microphone. He turned to face the congregation. "I grew up in a small town on the eastern coast of England. My Mum and Dad were killed in a car accident when I was a young lad, and my two older brothers had the daunting task of raising a somewhat stubborn teen. I had gone to church with my parents and even accepted Christ as my Savior when I was a young boy. After they died, I drifted away from church and went my own way. Many of you know that I started my career as a pop singer. I was greatly blessed with success, but something was missing, and even with all the fame and success, I felt... well, I guess I felt empty inside.

"When I was twenty-six, I took a brief sabbatical from music and went home. You could say I was searching, but I didn't really know what I was searching for. I ended up at my parents' church one day and met the pastor. We talked for a bit, and he invited me to church the following Sunday. I decided to go, and it was, in a sense, like coming home.

"After a few weeks, I realized that what I was missing was a *personal* relationship with Christ. I knew I was saved, but it stopped there. My life was not the living sacrifice that it speaks of in Romans 12. My life was my own. It didn't reflect that I was a Christian. I had no works demonstrating my faith in God.

Therefore, my faith was, in essence, dead. The Bible tells us in James 2:17 that 'Even so faith, if it hath not works, is dead, being alone.' After several meetings with the pastor, I finally understood what was missing. I needed to surrender my life completely – not just in word, but in deed as well." His voice was strong and sure, and Maggie listened intently despite the fact that she had heard his testimony many times before.

"I knew that if my life was going to change, it had to be completely and in every aspect, which included my career. The decision to switch my music from pop to gospel was extremely difficult for me, but I had to take that step of faith and really trust the Lord with my life. Thankfully, He has been faithful in allowing me to continue in a career I love and to share the gospel at the same time. I had felt so empty and lost for such a long time, but His love lifted me and gave me new life."

His fingers danced over the keyboard, and he began to sing softly.

"I was sinking deep in sin far from the peaceful shore,
Very deeply stained within, sinking to rise no more,
But the Master of the sea heard my despairing cry,
From the waters lifted me, now safe am I
Love lifted me, love lifted me, when nothing else could help,
Love lifted me.
Love lifted me, love lifted me, when nothing else could help,
Love lifted me.

Colin finished the hymn and walked back to his seat as Jesse returned to the pulpit. Slipping in beside Maggie, Colin reached for her hand, lacing his fingers with hers.

"Thank you so much for that, Colin. Isn't it wonderful to know that no matter what the circumstances, God's love can touch and heal us. Whether it be salvation, financial problems, sickness... it is the love of God that saves us from them all." Jesse paused for a moment as he opened his Bible.

"Please open your Bibles to Genesis 28, verse ten. This passage begins with Jacob, the son of Isaac, being sent away from home to avoid his brother Esau's anger after stealing his birthright. Here we find Jacob in the wilderness, tired, and probably a bit frightened. His older brother is threatening to kill him, and he has basically been banished from his home. He makes a bed on the ground, and his pillow is composed of rocks. Scripture tells us that while he sleeps, Jacob dreams of a ladder reaching into heaven on which angels are ascending and descending. Please read with me." He read from verse ten to verse twenty-two.

Maggie quickly stole a glance at her brother and his wife. She couldn't tell if they were really listening, but she fervently prayed that the Spirit of God would touch their hearts.

Lord, please help them understand how much You really do love them.

"I'd like to call your attention to the first of many promises regarding God's constant presence to those who trust Him. Verse fifteen states 'And, behold, I am with thee, and will keep thee in all places whither thou goest, and will bring thee again into this land; for I will not leave thee, until I have done that which I have spoken to thee of.' In this passage, God is promising Jacob that He will be his protector. As we study the life of Jacob, we see that God was with him through all situations. But Jacob is not the only one God protected.

"He promised Joshua, in Joshua chapter one, verse five, that He would be with him and would never fail or forsake him. Remember Jericho? God led Joshua and the children of Israel to victory when the odds were insurmountable against them as they moved into the Promised Land. The Bible is full of promises that God has given to those who trust in Him."

Jesse continued to expound on different individuals who received promises from God. He spoke about Abraham and the promise of a son, Noah and the promise of salvation from the great flood, and David and the promise of an eternal kingdom. Finally, he instructed the congregation to open their Bibles to the third chapter of the book of John.

"The most precious promise God gives us, as New Testament believers, is in the book of John. It is here that God promises eternal life with Him if we trust His Son, Jesus, as our Savior. John 3:16 says 'For God so loved the world that He gave His only begotten Son that whosoever believeth in Him should not perish, but have everlasting life.' When we trust Christ to forgive our sins, we are born again into the family of God, and we are promised an eternal life in heaven. Once saved, all the wonderful promises that God gives us in His Word are ours to claim.

"The Bible goes on to tell us in I Corinthians 2:9 'But as it is written, eye had not seen, nor ear heard, neither have entered into the heart of man, the things which God hath prepared for them that love Him.'

"Sometimes it is difficult to see beyond the circumstances of the moment, whether they be physical problems, financial woes, family issues, or a myriad of other trials and tribulations that come our way. It is easy to become discouraged and disheartened by things in this world, but I encourage you to remember the promises in God's Word and take hope in them. God promises us that no matter what we face in this life, if we are saved, we never walk alone. The Lord Jesus said He would never leave us nor forsake us.

"Jesus also tells us in John 14:1-3, 'Let not your hearts be troubled: ye believe in God, believe also in Me. In my Father's house are many mansions: if it were not so, I would have told you. I go to prepare a place for you. And if I go and prepare a place for you, I will come again, and receive you unto Myself; that where I am, there ye may be also.'

"We cannot fully comprehend what He has prepared for us, for those who love Him and await His return, but we can be assured that God keeps His promises and in due time our eyes will see, our ears will hear, and our hearts will fully comprehend the enormity of God's love through His Son, Jesus Christ."

Maggie glanced at Valerie and saw that she sat without moving, her gaze fixated upon the pastor. *Please Lord, open her heart...* She quickly looked beyond Valerie to see her brother. Will was sitting back, one arm resting on the pew behind his wife. Although he was looking at Jesse, his face had a slight scowl; his eyes were narrowed. Maggie took a deep breath and sighed. Colin looked over at her. She managed a meager smile and nodded slightly toward Valerie and Will. Colin squeezed her hand in acknowledgement, then turned back to the pastor.

Jesse continued as he stepped out from behind the pulpit. "I want to close with a comment that was shared with me. A woman once came to me and complained that when hard times came, a Christian friend recited Romans 8:28 to her. This woman said she felt that that particular verse had become trite and meaningless, especially since she could see no good coming from her situation. I tell you today that nothing could be farther from the truth. As Christians, we have the assurance, the *promise* that everything works toward good for God. We may not see it; we may not comprehend it, but Romans 8:28 tells us that 'All things work together for good to them that love God, to them who are the called according to His purpose.' Without a true relationship with the Lord, tragedies that befall us are incomprehensible and often generate fear and anger, but with God, we have hope and confidence knowing that He is in complete control, and all things *are* promised to work to the good for God."

Maggie noticed that both Will and Valerie were now looking intently at the pastor. She felt another squeeze on her hand and turned toward Colin. Her eyes met his, and she knew that their thoughts were united. He gave her a small smile and squeezed her hand once more before returning his gaze to his boyhood friend at the pulpit.

Thank you, Lord, for Colin. His faith is such an encouragement to me. Help me to trust You like He does. And please... please help Will and Valerie learn to trust You as well.

Jesse concluded his message with Romans 8:39, reminding his congregation that nothing "*shall be able to separate us from the love of God, which is in Christ Jesus our Lord,"* and an invitation to come forward if anyone felt led by God's Holy Spirit to do so. Several people walked forward and knelt at the altar to pray silently while the pianist played softly. After a few minutes, Jesse prayed and the service concluded.

After talking a few minutes with the pastor, Maggie and Colin walked with Will and Valerie to the parking lot.

"Do we want to get lunch somewhere?" asked Valerie hopefully.

"Sounds good to me," responded Colin. "How 'bout it, Maggie? Are you hungry?"

"Starved. Will?" She turned to look at her brother.

"I can always eat," grinned Will. An animated discussion ensued about where they would go, and finally they decided on a well-known seafood restaurant overlooking the Pacific Ocean.

Their booth was somewhat secluded, but it had an expansive view of the ocean waves crashing against the rocky shoreline. The four of them easily slid into the bench seats and began perusing the menus.

"I love this place," commented Valerie closing her menu. She gazed out toward the choppy sea. "It's so beautiful. Will brought me here for my birthday last year."

Will smiled at his wife, put his arm around her shoulders, and sipped his iced tea. The nearness of Valerie comforted him, and he found it difficult to believe the vibrant young woman sitting next to him was actually embattled with a disease that could possibly end her life. It consumed most of his thinking when he wasn't preoccupied with work. Even today in church, Will had found it hard to concentrate on the message delivered from the pulpit. His mind was constantly going over the plethora of available treatment plans, side effects, medications, and prognoses for stage one breast cancer patients. He knew he would do whatever he had to do to make sure Valerie had the best medical care, but he secretly feared it might not give her more than the five to ten year life expectancy.

I can't live without her. She is my life. I will not let her die.

"And for you, sir?"

Will glanced up at the waitress awaiting his order. "I'm sorry." He quickly scanned the menu once more. "I'll have the... uh, grilled halibut."

Valerie looked into the eyes of her husband. "A penny for your thoughts."

Will smiled. "I'm sorry. Just thinking." He kissed her forehead. "See any dolphins?"

Valerie laughed softly. "Not yet, but I'll keep on looking!" She relaxed and rested against his side. "So, any more wedding plans, you two?"

Maggie took a swallow of her coffee. "Not really."

"I can't get her to commit to anything," said Colin, sipping his tea. He leaned back, placing his arm on the top of the bench seat behind Maggie.

Maggie tilted her head and stared directly at him. "Well, actually, Valerie and I have been talking about our headpieces. I think we may have come to a decision, right Val?" She started to giggle, and Valerie joined her as they erupted in a fit of muffled laughter that brought tears to their eyes.

"What's so funny?" asked Will. He looked at Colin, who just shrugged his shoulders and shook his head.

Valerie's eyes sparkled playfully. "We thought the wedding should be postponed until we know for sure if I'm going to have chemo. If I do, Mags and I thought we could all shave our heads for the wedding!"

Will's mouth dropped open, but no sound came out.

Colin simply stared at Maggie for a moment. "You're kidding, right?"

"Colin, you've got to get used to the morbid sense of humor we medical professionals have," admonished Maggie with an impish grin.

Will shook his head. "If I'm not used to it, how is he supposed to get used to it? You two should be ashamed of yourselves."

"Oh, we are, Will. We really are," giggled Valerie as she took a bite out of a breadstick.

Their meal was delicious, and the conversation was lighthearted and peppered with laughter. As they prepared to leave, the waitress came up and stood by their table, seemingly hesitant to speak.

"I'm sorry," she began, "but I was wondering if... I mean..." She looked directly at Colin. "You are Colin Grant, right?"

Maggie, Will, and Valerie simultaneously turned their heads toward Colin.

"Yes, I am." He nodded expectantly at the waitress.

"I was wondering if you would mind if... uh... could I have your autograph? I'm a really big fan." She hesitantly held out her order pad and a pen.

Colin grinned, and the waitress smiled shyly. "I don't mind at all," he replied, taking the paper and pen from her. "What's your name?"

"Cheryl... with a 'C'."

He wrote quickly and then handed the pad and pen back to her.

"Thank you so much, Mr. Grant. I really love your music, even the religious stuff."

"Thanks, I appreciate that very much."

She scurried off, and Colin returned his attention to the group. The three of them had their eyes focused on him. No one spoke.

"What?" He looked at them quizzically. "Don't people ever ask doctors for their autographs?" He raised an eyebrow as he sipped his tea.

Maggie's widened eyes finally blinked. "I've never actually been with you when someone has asked you for an autograph."

"That was so awesome!" exclaimed Valerie. "I can't wait until you're officially my brother-in-law! You're like... like... a celebrity!"

"Sweetheart, he *is* a celebrity," Will said, laughing softly at his wife.

Valerie's cheeks warmed. "I know that, but I mean... like people know him... and... they come up to him... oh, this is so awesome!"

"You want me to sign *your* napkin?" Colin chuckled and then he winked at Valerie.

CHAPTER THIRTEEN

"The decision is yours, Valerie. There are pros and cons to undergoing chemotherapy. I'm sure you and Will have discussed this at length, but this is the time to ask any questions you may still have," stated Dr. Sommers.

Valerie sat quietly opposite her oncologist, still contemplating her options.

"I never want to have to say 'Why didn't I do it?' If this cancer comes back, I want to know... I *need* to know that I did everything possible to fight it," admitted Valerie. She clasped her hands in her lap. "I guess chemo just seems so drastic, and maybe I don't really need it."

"Chemotherapy does take a toll on your body, but as to whether or not you need it... I can't really answer that one. If you opt for the chemotherapy, it will consist of only four treatments at this time. One of the reasons is that there is a lifetime limit on how much chemo you can have, and if it should recur, we need to be sure we still have options available to us. Another reason is that your tumor was just under the limit where chemo usually is recommended, but it is borderline, which makes chemo optional. So, the choice really is yours," informed the doctor.

"I know I will lose my hair, right?"

"Yes, you will. About fourteen days after your first treatment, you can expect that to happen. You may experience some nausea, probably fatigue. It'll be different from the radiation. Remember, just like the radiation, chemotherapy attacks healthy cells as well as the cancerous ones, except chemo is system-wide. It has the potential to affect any part of your body. You may get mouth ulcers, joint pain, and your immune system will be compromised greatly. You can still work, but if anything infectious comes in, someone else will have to handle that," said the physician, matter-of-factly.

Valerie sat quietly, contemplating the impact of chemotherapy. Finally, she asked, "When would it start?"

"I can set it up for tomorrow, next week, or next month. We'll decide that once we know what you want to do."

As Valerie looked into the warm eyes of the doctor, her body shivered involuntarily.

"I really want to do it, Dr. Sommers, but part of me is frightened about it. I mean, everything is okay now, but if I do the chemo, everything will change. I'll be sick again, and... and my hair... I know that sounds vain, but..." Valerie couldn't go on.

"I understand, Valerie. Body image is very important to some people, but it's not permanent. Have you and Will talked about this? About how you feel?"

Valerie nodded.

"And what did he say?"

"He was amazingly supportive. He wanted to be here today, but I told him he needed to go to work. I wanted to... I needed to prove to myself that I was strong enough to handle this. I guess I just keep second-guessing myself. Should I or shouldn't I? I told Will I wanted to do it, and as of this morning, I was very confident. Now that I'm sitting here, well, it seems all my confidence has flown out the window. I don't want it to impact my work, but it will, and that worries me. Well, actually, it makes me kind of mad. I love my job, and I don't want to just stay home. I guess I'm worried about that, too."

"Valerie, these are all legitimate concerns. I can't predict exactly how the chemo will affect you, but there's a good chance, you'll be able to continue just as you are now. You may have to make some temporary concessions. You need to remember that it's not forever. In about four months, this will be behind you. Do you want to go home and think about it? Talk a bit more with Will?"

"No." She shook her head and sighed deeply. "I think I need to do the chemotherapy. I just have to know I did everything I possibly could to fight this." Valerie sat back in her chair and sighed one more time. "And I'd like to start as soon as possible. Maybe in a few days or so?"

"That'll work. How about Monday? That will be in four days. Is that soon enough?"

Valerie tilted her head and bit her lower lip before speaking. Her brow furrowed as she narrowed her eyes in thought, but her voice was strong and determined when she finally said, "Yes. Yes, Monday will be fine."

"Monday, it is then. Do you have any other questions or concerns you'd like to share with me?"

"No." Valerie shook her head. "I actually feel some relief now that the decision has been made. Thank you so much."

She left Dr. Sommer's office and strode purposefully toward the building that housed many of the doctors' offices. It only took her a few minutes to reach the door to Will's private office. She gingerly knocked on it. When it opened, Will's eyes widened upon seeing his wife standing there.

"Val? Is everything all right? Did your appointment go okay?" He quickly ushered her into his office and closed the door.

Her eyes sparkled triumphantly. "Yes! Yes, it did."

He led her to a chocolate brown leather sofa and then sat down beside her. Taking her hands in his, he looked directly into her shimmering eyes.

"Tell me about it."

"I just came from Dr. Sommers. I told her..." She hesitated for a moment and then took a deep breath. "I told her that I wanted to do the chemotherapy, and we agreed that Monday would be a good day for the first treatment. How does that sound to you?"

The concerned look on Will's face vanished, and he reached for Valerie. He pulled her to him and hugged her tightly. "Sounds like you did great."

She pulled back slightly and looked at his face. "I'll lose my hair," she stated with a hint of distress in her barely audible voice.

Will smiled at her and nodded. "Yes, you will, but it'll grow back. Moreover, your beauty comes from your heart, Valerie, not from your hair. If you think I won't love you when you lose your hair, then I've been a pretty neglectful husband." He kissed her fully on the lips. "I love you, Valerie Garrett. Nothing, and I mean nothing, will change that... ever."

Valerie abruptly threw herself into his arms. She hugged him fiercely, and his hold tightened around her.

"What would I ever do without you, Will?"

"You'll never know the answer to that one, Valerie, because I will always be here with you."

Will had told Valerie what to expect from her first chemotherapy treatment, but she was still nervous as she sat in the recliner from which she would receive the medications.

Will sat next to her and held her hand until the oncology nurse came in.

"Hi, Valerie. I'm Monica. I'll be your nurse while you're here. Good morning, Dr. Garrett. Valerie, I have some medications for you to take. These are both for nausea. One is lorazepam, and this one is dexamethasone. I'll need to start an IV in just a few minutes, but before we start, do you have any questions for me?" The nurse waited for Valerie to swallow her medications.

"No." She shook her head. "No, I don't think so."

"I'll be back in a few minutes then."

Valerie turned to Will. "Are you sure you can stay with me?"

"Positive, sweetheart. It's one of the perks of being an oncologist. They allow us in the cancer treatment areas."

Valerie chuckled softly. "That was kind of silly, wasn't it?"

Will squeezed her hand. "I won't leave you. I promise. My entire calendar is cleared for you today."

"I wish I were braver."

"You don't have to be. I'll be brave for both of us."

"Dr. Sommers said it would take a couple of hours or so."

"I know."

"Are you okay?"

"Yes, sweetheart. I'm fine. You?"

Valerie nodded. "Yes, just... just a little--"

"Scared?"

Valerie frowned. "Does it show?"

"A little, but this isn't easy. We'll get through it. The first time is the hardest because you're really facing the unknown."

"I can't even comprehend having stage three or four cancer, like my mom. She must have been so scared, Will."

Monica returned and easily started an intravenous line in Valerie's right arm. She adjusted the fluid to a steady drip that would keep the line open for the administration of the cancer fighting drugs. Valerie watched her secure the line with tape and then prepare the syringe of anti-carcinogenic medications.

"The drugs we're using are called Adriamycin and Cytoxan. We affectionately call it the AC cocktail here. When I inject these meds, you'll feel a coldness creep up your arm. That's normal. It's the medicine. Are you ready?" Monica waited for Valerie to answer.

Valerie looked at Will. When he nodded his head, she turned to Monica.

"Yes, I'm ready." She squeezed Will's hand, and once again felt his grip tighten around hers. Within seconds, she felt the icy tentacles of the cancer fighting drugs make their way up her other arm.

"Oh, Will, I can feel it." Her voice was barely above a whisper.

"You okay?"

"Yes, but it's so cold."

Will didn't leave Valerie's side for the duration of the treatment, and although they didn't speak much to each other, Valerie felt an enormous comfort and security with him there. *I hope I was a comfort to you, Mom, when you needed it. I can't imagine doing this without Will.*

She watched the ruby colored liquid drip through the tubing and imagined an army of red soldiers amassing to fight an enemy. She hoped for victory despite what she feared were impossible odds against it.

CHAPTER FOURTEEN

The morning sun sent its warm rays through the beveled bathroom window, illuminating the small vanity in the corner. It had been two weeks since her first chemotherapy treatment, and Valerie stared at her reflection. *It's hard to believe I had chemo or breast cancer. I feel so good today!* She stepped into the shower and allowed the warm water to run over her head and face. She squirted a dollop of citrus scented shampoo into her hand and began to lather her head.

As she ran her fingers through her wet hair, she felt something in her hands. Opening her eyes, she looked down at her fingers. Stunned, she stood staring at clumps of dark brown hair. She slowly reached up and gently pulled at another lock of her hair. It easily came loose into her fingers. *No! Please, no!* She leaned against the tiled wall of the shower, her mind racing with the reality of what was happening to her body. She sank down to the floor of the shower, sobbing uncontrollably as the water cascaded from the top of her head.

Valerie walked into the salon, resisting the impulse to turn and run.

"May I help you?" The clerk was young, pretty, and had a head full of blonde curls with dark brown highlights. Valerie quickly averted her gaze when she realized she was staring at the young girl's hair.

"Yes. I'd like a haircut." She gave the clerk her name and then sat down in the waiting area. The tables were covered with stacks of hairstyle magazines, but Valerie didn't have a need to look in any of them. She reached into her bag and nervously fingered a soft peach colored scarf.

Upon hearing her name, she stood even though her legs felt numb. She forced herself to walk toward the cosmetologist.

"Hi. I'm Cassidy. How would you like your hair cut today?" Her smile was welcoming; her eyes were bright and cheerful, and her hair was long, black, and beautiful. Its ends curled gently against her alabaster skin. She motioned for Valerie to sit in her beautician's chair.

I'm sure your smile will disappear as soon as I tell you why I'm here. Valerie took a deep breath, willing her voice to remain calm and steady. "I need it all cut off. Actually, I need it buzzed off. All of it."

Cassidy's facial expression changed immediately; her mouth formed a small "o." She pulled up a stool in front of the salon chair. Her wide chocolate brown eyes never left Valerie's face, her voice compassionate, but not pitying.

"Are you a chemotherapy patient?"

Valerie nodded and fought to maintain her composure.

Cassidy thought for a moment before speaking, nodding her head. She stood up, grasped both of Valerie's hands, and pulled the nurse to her feet.

"Okay, Valerie. Not only are we going to cut your hair, but we're also doing a manicure and pedicure, on the house. You may leave here without your hair, but honey, you're going to leave here beautiful. I happen to have a whole box of very attractive knit hats just for chemo patients. You can pick out your favorite and wear it home. We'll pick that out first and then cut your hair and do your nails to match the hat! How about that?" Her bright smile returned as she waited for Valerie's answer.

Valerie couldn't speak, but tears of gratitude welled up in her eyes. She just nodded her agreement and allowed Cassidy to lead her to a room in the back. The young cosmetologist opened a huge box full of colorfully knitted hats and gestured for Valerie to look inside. Each hat was unique in its design. Some were solely solid colors, while others had a design woven through them. A few had scalloped edges, and on several others, there were small pink ribbons, the symbol associated with breast cancer.

"One of my customers went through chemotherapy. When she was finished, she decided to knit these hats for women in similar circumstances. She brings in three or four a month. She said that we had to promise we wouldn't charge for them. Just give them out as needed. She said that God had blessed her by healing her cancer, and now this was her ministry... a way to share God's love with other women fighting cancer. Please look through them and pick out one that you like," encouraged Cassidy. "Then we'll get started!"

Clutching the soft knit cap in her lap, Valerie sat quietly as her beautiful dark brown locks were clipped away. The soft curls fell silently to the floor as tears traced their way down her pale cheeks. *It's really real, isn't it, Mom? I really do have cancer. Oh Mom, I feel so alone, and I'm so scared...*

After completing her task, Cassidy gave Valerie a warm hug before escorting her to the manicurist. "God bless you as you fight this battle, Valerie. Come see me when you're all well and your hair grows back out. I'll style it free of charge!"

Ninety minutes later, Valerie left the salon still unsettled with her new body image. A pale pink crocheted cap with a row of small white daisies around the bottom adorned her head, protecting her from the stares of other patrons in the salon. She avoided the faces of other shoppers as she made her way to her car. As she drove home, she rehearsed what she would say to Will when he returned home from the hospital.

The trip to the salon had exhausted her, and upon arriving home, Valerie had laid down for a short nap before beginning dinner. Now she was scrambling to have everything ready for Will when he came home. The table was set with her fine china, and in the middle of the table, a single candle sat in the center of a ring of freshly cut flowers. She took care in selecting an outfit that matched her new hat, and when she looked at her reflection in the mirror, she was satisfied with the pale pink chiffon dress she had chosen. Pearl earrings adorned her ears, and she accented her outfit with a dainty pearl necklace that had once belonged to her mother. She fingered the necklace lovingly.

Oh, Mom, is this how you felt? Were you as scared as I am? She stared at her image for a few minutes, remembering the battle her mother had valiantly fought, but ultimately lost. The faint aroma of dinner brought her back to the present.

Too tired to cook a fancy meal, she had settled for one of Will's favorite casserole dishes. She peeked into the oven to check it and then reduced the heat to low. Dimming the kitchen lights, she walked into the living room and lit two white pillar candles on the fireplace mantle. Selecting an instrumental CD with some of their favorite songs, she placed it in the player. Its soft melodies filled the house. Now, she just had to wait.

Less than fifteen minutes later, she heard Will's car drive into the attached garage. She took a deep breath, stood up, straightened her dress, made sure her hat was in place, faced the door, and waited. She watched the doorknob turn, and then Will came in.

"Hi, sweet-" He stopped mid-sentence and looked around, first at her, then the table. His gaze returned to Valerie. He hesitated before saying anything. He looked questioningly at his wife.

"Valerie?" His words were slow and deliberate. "Is everything all right?"

"Yes. Everything is fine... well, it will be, I hope. I just needed tonight to be special."

Will set his briefcase down and walked over to his wife. His brow furrowed, and he started to speak, but Valerie put her finger to his lips.

"Wait, please. This is really hard for me, so if I don't do this now, I'm afraid I won't have the courage to do it later." Her tear-brimmed eyes pleaded with him.

He nodded and waited.

Valerie took a deep breath. She very slowly reached her beautifully French manicured fingers to her newly acquired pink hat, and after a moment's hesitation, snatched it from her head.

Will's eyes widened. He didn't move at all; he just stared at his wife.

Valerie stood perfectly still without saying a word. She held her breath.

Finally, he spoke. "You... look... amazing!" His face broke into a broad grin.

Valerie's astonished eyes stared at Will as he took her into his arms and kissed her fully upon her lips. He held her to him as he whispered huskily, "Valerie, I love you so much. Despite all you've said to me, you are the bravest woman I know." He held her away from him and looked into her vulnerable eyes. "You didn't have to do all this." He gestured to the table.

"I wanted to make this night a good memory, not a sad one," she confessed.

He smiled at her again and kissed her on the top of her smooth head.

"Every night with you is good, Val." He hugged her again. "You should have called me."

"I... it just happened so fast, Will. I... had to go while I still had the courage." Her voice trembled, and she fingered the knit cap still in her hands.

"I am so sorry you have to go through this. I wish we could trade places." He paused for a moment and tilted her face up toward his. "So, my beautiful bald wife, what's for dinner?"

"I made your favorite." She sought for approval in his eyes.

"Chicken casserole?" He picked her up and twirled her around. "Did I mention that I love you?"

For the first time, Valerie allowed herself to smile. "I believe you did. Now, let me go get dinner."

He shook his head and pulled out a chair. "No. You sit here. I'll get dinner. After this day, you deserve a little more pampering, and I am just the guy to give it to you!" He gently pushed her in toward the table and then disappeared into the kitchen.

Thank you, Will. Thank you for loving me... for caring about me... for still wanting me...

By the time he had returned with the casserole, Valerie had replaced her hat. It was too new for her to be comfortable without a head covering, and she didn't want to feel self-conscious this evening.

Will scooped out a small helping of casserole on her dish and then put a generous portion on his own plate. "This smells great, Val. You really shouldn't have gone to all this trouble. I could've whipped up something spectacular," he informed her as he took his seat opposite her.

"Like scrambled eggs? Or grilled cheese sandwiches?" Valerie laughed lightly.

Will grinned. "Yeah, or cereal."

During their meal, Valerie had recounted her experiences from the shower to the beauty salon, and Will had listened intently to every detail she shared with him. Now, as they lay next to one another in bed, he was unable to sleep. He glanced over at his sleeping wife.

I should have been there with her. She needed me, and I wasn't there.

His guilt overwhelmed him and in response, he felt an anger rising up against the God he blamed for Valerie's cancer.

How could You let this happen to her? She doesn't deserve this, You know. You're supposed to be such a loving God. Well, this doesn't seem very loving to me. How can You just stand by and let her go through this? What kind of a god does that? She's the kindest, most loving person I know, and You give her cancer. First, You break my sister's heart by letting Scott die, and now You're doing this to Val. Some God, You are.

Valerie stirred in her sleep, and Will glanced over at her. Her breathing was deep and regular, and he knew she was sleeping soundly. He fell into a fitful sleep, tossing and turning until the early hours of the morning. Every now and then, he would waken and look over at Valerie. His heart broke each time he thought about what the future might hold for her, and the possibility that no matter what he did, she still could lose her fight against the deadly disease.

CHAPTER FIFTEEN

Valerie sat on the edge of her bed staring at the clock. It was nearly noon, and she struggled to stay in a sitting position. Her head was swimming, and her stomach was heaving. She flopped back on the bed, her head sinking into the downy pillow. Voices from the outer room floated in, and Valerie reluctantly opened her eyes once more as the sound of footsteps grew closer.

"May I come in?"

Recognizing the voice, Valerie slowly answered, "Come on in, Mags." Her voice faded as she closed her eyes again.

The bed sagged a bit as Maggie sat on its edge and touched Valerie's arm.

"How are you doing?"

Valerie managed a half-smile. "I suppose it could be worse, but I don't know how."

"Are you keeping anything down?"

"No. I'm afraid to eat anything. I feel so sick, Mags. I just want to lay here until the nausea passes," admitted Valerie. "I'm so tired of being sick. I know it'll pass, but it is so hard right now. If I'm not sick from the chemo, I'm so tired, I can hardly move. I thought it'd be so easy since the first treatment went okay. My back hurts from being stuck in this bed, but if I try to sit up, the whole room spins, and I feel like I'm going to lose it all."

Maggie reached around and began to rub Valerie's upper back. "I'm so sorry, Val. I wish I could help make it better."

Valerie weakly smiled at her sister-in-law. "You do make it better, Mags. Just by being here, but don't get mad if I drift off to sleep, okay?" Her voice waned.

"Mad? Never. You go right ahead and nod off, sweetie. I'll be here when you wake up in case you need anything."

Later, when the sun was beginning to arc toward the western horizon, Valerie drowsily opened her eyes. She reached for a glass of water on the nightstand and took a few small sips. Glancing at the clock, she noticed it was nearly four o'clock in the afternoon.

I can't believe I'm still in bed. It's almost been the whole day! Ugh, I feel awful...

Quickly turning over the side of the bed, Valerie grabbed the small plastic lined trashcan and retched. Over and over, she felt the muscles of her stomach revolt against the water she had so meagerly sampled just moments before. It wasn't long before only bile was coming up, and she cried as she vomited. Just when Valerie thought she was not going to be able to survive another bout of vomiting, Maggie was at her side.

"I'm here, Val. It's okay, honey." Maggie took the trash receptacle from Valerie's hands and held it until Valerie had finished heaving. She offered her the glass of water and brushed the hair away from Valerie's face. "Just swish and spit, sweetie." Maggie carried the trashcan into the bathroom and then returned with a wet towel, placing it on Valerie's forehead.

"It's okay, Val. You're going to be okay," consoled Maggie as she held the nurse's hand.

"Oh, Maggie, I'm so tired of being sick." Valerie's voice was weak and shaky.

"I know, honey."

"Is Will home?"

"Not yet."

"I need to get up."

"Val, you're not really up to getting up. Will understands. He won't expect you to be up, not when you're feeling like this."

Tears fell from her eyes, but Valerie's weeping was silent. Her eyes remained closed, and her body shook slightly as she cried soundlessly.

Maggie's heart broke for her sister-in-law, and she hesitated for only a moment before she began to pray softly. "Father, please help Val right now. She's feeling so miserable, and Lord, I don't know what to do to help her feel better. I know You do, though. The Bible says You are the Great Physician, so I know You can touch her right now and give her the strength she needs to get through this moment. Please, ease her nausea and vomiting and give her rest. In Jesus' name, I pray. Amen."

Valerie's eyes weakly fluttered open, and she looked intently at her sister-in-law. "Maggie, do you think… do you really think God hears you?"

Maggie regarded Valerie tenderly and smiled lovingly. "Yes, Val. I do believe God hears me when I pray."

Valerie nodded and closed her eyes. "I was just wondering… does He always answer you?"

"No. Not always."

"I hope He answers you this time."

"Me, too, Val. Me, too."

"She's had a rough day, Will," reported Maggie as she sat down on the sofa. Will took off his jacket and tossed it over the easy chair in the corner of his living room. He sat down next to his sister.

"Thanks for staying with her, Maggie. I really appreciate it. I can focus better on my work when I know you're here with her." Fatigue etched the features of his face; his dark eyes were somber.

"She'll be better tomorrow."

"I know. It's just a very long thirty-six hours."

"I made some spaghetti. It's not like Mom's, but it's as close as I can come to it. It's simmering on the stove, and the noodles just need to be reheated in the microwave." Maggie reached over to Will and held his hand. "Call me if you need me, okay? I'm not on until tomorrow morning."

"Thanks, Sis. I really do appreciate it."

"I know, and I mean it. Call me anytime." She rose to leave.

"I will. I promise." He stood and kissed her on the cheek. As Maggie closed the front door behind her, Will walked into his bedroom.

"Val?" His voice was low and soft. The shadows of the night were already creeping into the room, and he turned on the lamp on the nightstand.

"Hi, honey." She managed a small smile; her voice sounded drained.

Will sat down gingerly beside her. "Rough day?"

"A little."

"What can I get you? Water? Crackers?"

Shaking her head slightly, she reached for Will's hand. "Nothing. Just having you here is all I need right now." She closed her eyes, and within a few minutes, she was asleep. Her hold on him lessened, and Will slipped his hand from hers. Leaning over, he kissed her gently on the forehead and then quietly tucked the blankets around her. He cast one more look at his wife before turning off the light and going to prepare his dinner.

CHAPTER SIXTEEN

Valerie's toughest days were the third and fourth days after her chemotherapy treatments. Fatigue and nausea usually kept her in the bed for those days, but she quickly regained her strength by day five after chemo, and she usually was able to work two to three days per week without too much difficulty. Careful to handle cases that dealt with injuries instead of contagions that could compromise her own health, she felt a sense of victory with every shift she completed.

Today, she sported a bright green knit cap that matched her scrubs, and her energy level was up as were her spirits. Sitting behind the nurses' station, she looked up quickly when a young man ran in carrying a limp child in his arms.

"My son's not breathing! Somebody help me!"

Valerie moved swiftly to take the child from him. "What happened?" Receiving no answer, she shouted at the father when he failed to answer the first time. "Tell me what happened!" She rushed into treatment room one and placed the young boy on an examination table.

"I found him tangled in an electric cord in the garage. He must have got shocked. I was cutting some wood, and I only turned away for a moment. Please help him!"

"Has he been sick?" Receiving no answer from the father, her voice rose in intensity. "Has he been sick?"

"No. No, I don't think so. I only get him every other weekend, but he hasn't seemed sick. Please help him."

Valerie put a stethoscope to the child's chest. *Nothing.* There were no breath sounds and no pulse. Knowing that precious minutes were ticking off and not knowing how long the boy had been without oxygen, she became the heart and lungs for the child.

"Need some help in here!" she called out between breaths. She reached for the code button and punched it. Immediately, ER personnel filled the room. Ben Shepherd donned a pair of gloves before realizing that Valerie was performing CPR.

"Toby, take over for Valerie," he ordered.

Valerie looked up in surprise, but she did not question the physician. She stepped back, and another nurse picked up the resuscitative efforts.

"Can you get an IV in for me, Val?" His eyes met hers, and she nodded, quickly moving to get an intravenous line established in the child's arm.

Within seconds, Valerie had started the IV. "Line's in," stated Valerie as she adjusted the normal saline drip.

Ben put his stethoscope on the chest of the small boy while simultaneously feeling for a carotid pulse. "Stop compressions."

Everyone ceased activity, but remained poised to continue on Ben's command.

"Got a pulse, but no breathing. Continue bagging him," ordered the doctor. "Where's the dad? What happened to this kid? Get him on the monitor."

"Father states the kid got shocked on an electric cord," came the reply.

Ben quickly inspected the hands of the boy. The left hand had a full thickness burn in the palm. He quickly checked the feet and found no exit wound. He proceeded to remove the boy's jeans and found a small area of dry parchment-like skin on the left knee indicating an exit site for the electrical current.

"He's breathing on his own, Dr. Shepherd."

Ben glanced up at the cardiac monitor and then resumed inspecting the young boy's body. "Here's the exit wound," he said to his team. "See if Mark Denton's in house. Let's get a bed in the PICU, and get me the pediatrician on call. Get a Foley in; we've got to monitor his fluid status. I need a CBC, chest x-ray, urinalysis, and EKG. For now, let's do the standard wound care for his hand and knee until Denton gets here."

"BP's stable."

"Good. Let's get him upstairs as soon as possible." He tossed his gloves into the waste receptacle. "I'm going to speak with the father. Call me if there's any change at all."

Twenty minutes later, Valerie sat in the nurses' station writing her notes on the patient's chart. Dr. Mark Denton was on his way, and she was just waiting for an available bed in the pediatric intensive care unit. She didn't notice Ben Shepherd arrive at the nurses' station until he sat down beside her.

"Val, I need to talk with you about... about what happened in there."

She looked up, her perceptive gaze meeting his concerned eyes. "I know what you're going to say, Ben, but I asked the dad before I started doing anything. This was a clear case of injury, not illness."

Ben nodded and smiled. "Good, Valerie. I'll admit, you scared me in there. I thought... well, never mind what I thought. I just need you to remember that you're immune-compromised right now. You know that chemotherapy lowers your body's ability to fight off infection. Delivering mouth-to-mouth resuscitation really shouldn't be part of your job description right now."

She looked up at him through her lashes and defended her actions. "I didn't know how long he'd been nonresponsive. What if he was out for more than four minutes? He could end up with permanent brain damage... or worse. What was I supposed to do? Let him die? I couldn't just wait." Valerie's voice was strong and determined, yet respectful in her justification. "No one else was here. I had to do something." She sighed deeply. "And I *was* careful, Ben. I *did* ask."

"I understand, Val, just please be careful. Your health is important, too."

"I know, but –"

Ben locked eyes with Valerie. "You know as well as I that we're in a hospital. Help is available in seconds. All you need to do is call. You've got to be sensible, Val. Things are different for you right now. Adapting your work has to be a priority."

Valerie reluctantly nodded just as the boy's lab results and chest x-ray films arrived. She picked up the lab sheet while Ben held up the x-ray film. She heard him sigh and looked over at him.

"Problem?"

"What's his WBC count?"

Valerie looked at the lab sheet. "White blood cells are thirteen-five. Isn't that normal for burns?"

"Yes, but his x-ray shows infiltrates." Ben scowled. "That's definitely not good, Val... for him or you. There's a good possibility that this kid has pneumonia."

Valerie walked slowly into the staff lounge. She sank down into the worn beige sofa, rested her elbows on her knees, and dropped her head into her hands.

What was I supposed to do? He wasn't breathing. I couldn't just let him die. I couldn't bag him and do compressions at the same time. I hit the code button. I did exactly what I was supposed to do. Besides, he was a burn victim, not a pneumonia case. I did everything right.

"Oh, I hate this!" Valerie pounded her fists on her knees, never hearing the door to the lounge open and close.

"Valerie? What's wrong?"

She looked up into the concerned eyes of her sister-in-law.

Valerie tightened her lips but couldn't control her outburst. "Oh, Mags, I hate this cancer! It's robbing me of everything! I'm tired all the time. I can't work like I did before. I might as well not even be here if I can't do my whole job. What's the point?"

Maggie sat down on the sofa beside Valerie, putting one hand on the nurse's shoulder. "What happened, Val?"

Valerie recounted the entire episode for Maggie, culminating with the elevated white blood count and Ben's report of the chest x-ray. She took some tissues from Maggie before speaking again.

"I'm so tired of being sick, Mags. Sick and scared. I'm scared for me; I'm scared for Will. I'm just so tired of living my life in fear," lamented the nurse.

"Valerie," Maggie began slowly. "You don't have to be scared all the time, you know."

The nurse looked at Maggie through wet lashes. "How can you say that, Mags? If I cough, I worry about pneumonia. If I'm tired, I worry about infection. If I feel the tiniest lump, I worry the cancer is back. How can I live like that? I feel like I'm fighting a battle I can't win. My life seems so out of control."

Maggie took a deep breath and then spoke softly. "You can't control it, Val." She hesitated for a moment and then quietly added, "But God can."

Valerie shook her head vehemently. "No, Maggie. I'm not a hypocrite, and that's exactly what I would be. I've lived my whole life without religion, and now that I'm sick, you're telling me I'm supposed to turn to God? That's just not right." She spoke intensely, her voice determined.

"It's not about religion, Val. It's about a relationship. God doesn't care about the reason you come to Him. He just loves you, and He wants to have a relationship with you."

Valerie frowned. "A relationship? With God? What's that supposed to mean, Maggie?"

Maggie closed her eyes briefly. *Help me, Lord, please.* She thought for a moment before continuing. "A relationship with God means that you trust Him and depend on Him for everything."

"You mean become a Christian?"

"Well, yes. When I surrendered my life to Christ, things took on a different perspective. Those things I tried so hard to control, but couldn't, I realized God *could* control. That included my life." Maggie paused and looked around. The lounge was empty, and she decided to continue.

"Val, I finally understood that God really did love me. He loved me so much more than anyone else ever could. He actually sent His Son, Jesus, to die on a cross for me, so I could have forgiveness for my sins. He did this so I could have a relationship with Him and someday be with Him forever. I don't have all the answers, Val, but I do know that after I accepted Christ as my Savior, something in me changed. I'm learning to trust God in all aspects of my life now, personal and professional."

"Well, it's different for you."

"How is it different? Because I don't have cancer?"

Valerie sighed deeply and shook her head. "No, I didn't mean... Oh, Mags, why did God let this happen to me?"

"I don't know, Val, no more than I know why God allowed Scott to die." Maggie faltered for a moment. She was referring to the fateful day in Santa Molina when a massive earthquake had taken her husband's life during their honeymoon. She squeezed her eyes tightly before reopening them and focusing on Valerie. "But I do know that God can help you... if you let Him."

Valerie looked at Maggie; her eyes filled with doubt. "It's kind of hard to think that God really cares about me." Her voice was barely audible.

"But He does, Valerie. He cares for you more than anyone else could. More than Will, more than me, more than anyone."

"Then why did He do this to me, Maggie? I keep trying to figure out what I did that was so bad."

Maggie intuitively reached for Valerie's hand. "You didn't do anything bad. You didn't do something that made God give you cancer, Val. It's just something that happens to people, good or bad. It's not a punishment from God."

"Then what is it, Maggie, if not that?" Her shoulders shook as she wept.

Maggie's eyes misted over. The anguish in her heart was great as she struggled for an answer to Valerie's question. *Please God, help me. I don't know what to say.* She tried to remember what Colin had shared with her before her own salvation, but nothing came to mind. She tried to recall the verses she had so often read in the Bible and now chastised herself for not memorizing more than just John 3:16. She could only speak from her heart.

"Val, do you know why Jesus came to Earth?"

Valerie dabbed at her eyes with a tissue. "To die on a cross, right?"

"Well, yes. That's *what* He did, but do you know *why*?"

"Not really. Something about forgiving our sins, isn't that what you said?"

Maggie nodded. "Yes. God loves us all very much. He made us; we're His children, and He wants to have a relationship with us, but He can't. He can't because of sin. You know, all the wrong things we do."

"But I really haven't done a lot of bad stuff, Maggie. I'm a pretty good person. I haven't killed anyone or cheated on my taxes or anything like that, plus I help save lives," Valerie protested.

"It doesn't matter how good we are, Val. We can't ever be as good as God's holiness requires. We're all sinners. There's a verse about that in the Bible. It says that everyone is a sinner. And it's the sin that keeps us from having a relationship with God at all. In order for us to be able to have a relationship with Him, our sins have to be forgiven. That's what Jesus did. As God's Son, He took the punishment for our sins on the cross. And then after He died, He rose from the grave, which proved that He was God, and that He really did have the ability to forgive sins."

Valerie's gaze never left Maggie's face, but she shook her head fiercely. "It just doesn't seem right, Maggie. I've never needed God before. And now? To go to Him now seems so wrong. I don't know how to even start making things right between Him and me."

"*You* can't make things right, Val. None of us can. If there was another way to have this relationship with us, God wouldn't have sacrificed His only Son. Think about it, would a loving father subject his own son to such suffering if he didn't have to? If there really was another way? God loves us so much He sent Jesus because that *was* the only way to save us."

Maggie swallowed hard and continued. "If you ask Jesus to forgive you, He will." She paused for a moment, remembering her own struggle with finding Christ and then spoke unreservedly from her heart.

"When I was in Santa Molina, I just couldn't understand why I didn't have the same relationship with God that Colin and Scott had. I mean, I believed in God, but I was really missing something. Then one night, I realized that accepting Christ was like a vaccine. I can believe a vaccine will keep me safe from a disease, but until I actually accept that vaccine into my system, it's useless. That's like Christ. I could believe in Him all I wanted to, but until I asked Him to forgive me and accepted His work on the cross as my only way to heaven, my belief in Him was pretty useless.

"That night, I finally got it. I finally understood what it meant to have salvation... to be saved. I prayed and asked Him to forgive all my doubts, my fears, and my sins, and then I asked Him to be my Savior-- to take control of every part of my life." Maggie's voice was calm and strong.

"This incredible sense of peace came over me, Val. Not some mystical experience, but I just knew everything was going to be okay. It was as if God came into my heart and gave me this amazing confirmation through the peace I felt. I know that sounds strange, but... it's true. I know that no matter what happens to me, He is the One in control. Am I ever afraid? Yes, lots of times, but I've got Someone I can talk to now, and I know He can handle anything that comes my way... no matter how bad it seems."

Valerie sat very still, looking at her hands now clasped in her lap.

"Val?"

Valerie raised her head. "You're saying it's like having cancer and knowing the chemo drugs can save me, but if I don't agree to have the chemo, I'll die."

Maggie stared at Valerie and nodded. "Yes. Without Christ, we all die in our sins, but with Him, we have everlasting life in heaven with God. You just have to pray and ask Him to forgive you and be your Savior."

"Just like that?"

"Just like that."

"What if God doesn't want me?"

"Why wouldn't He want you, Val? He loves you. He died for you."

"I never reached out to Him before, and now... now, if I do, maybe He won't want me." She shook her head hopelessly. "When everything was wonderful, I never gave Him a second thought. And now when I'm scared and fighting cancer, I come to Him? What does that make me?"

Maggie silently prayed. *Please God, I don't know what to say to her.* She sat quietly and willed herself to trust the work of the Holy Spirit of God.

An image came to her mind. She saw it as vividly as if she'd painted it on a canvas.

"Val, do you remember when Jesus was on the cross?"

Valerie blotted at her eyes again. She nodded her head and whispered, "Yes."

"There were these two thieves there with Him, remember? One on each side of Him. One of the thieves made fun of Jesus and challenged Him to get off the cross. The other thief tried to explain to the first one that Jesus didn't do anything wrong. That second one believed Jesus was who He said He was. The second one knew that as thieves, they both deserved to die, but he also believed that Jesus didn't deserve the punishment He was getting because He had done nothing wrong. Well, Jesus looked at that second thief and forgave him -- right on the spot! He told that thief that he would be with Him and God in heaven that very day.

"That thief didn't need to do anything more than accept Jesus's gift of salvation to be saved. It didn't matter that he had lived his whole life for himself. Jesus didn't care about that. He just cared that the thief finally accepted Him. That thief didn't have to work for salvation... in fact, we can't work for it. I know the Bible says something about salvation being a gift from God; we can't do anything to earn it.

"All you have to do is ask, Valerie. You might still have some fear, but I promise you, you'll never be alone, and there is nothing that God and you cannot handle together, and that's the first step to getting rid of that fear."

Valerie's voice was just a whisper, but Maggie heard her clearly. "Are you sure, Maggie? Why would God do that for me?"

"Because He loves you, Valerie."

The silence of the room was broken only by Valerie's occasional sniffling. Maggie closed her eyes and silently prayed for her sister-in-law. The waiting seemed interminable.

Finally, Valerie spoke quietly. "So, what do I need to do?"

Maggie stared at her sister-in-law for a moment as the realization of what Valerie was asking became very clear to her. *Don't let me mess this up, Lord, please!* She took a deep breath and slowly exhaled. "Just talk to God, Val. Just like you're talking to me. That's what I did. I told Him I was sorry for everything, and I asked Him to forgive me and be my Savior."

"You're sure He'll want me?"

"I'm very sure."

Valerie bowed her head and hesitantly began to pray. The longing she had for peace in her soul overcame her fear of rejection from God, and she humbly begged His Son to save her from her sins. As she petitioned Jesus for His forgiveness, she timidly opened her heart to the Savior and His gift of salvation. When she was finished, she opened her eyes and looked at Maggie. Although her face was tear-stained, she managed a weak smile for her sister-in-law. She blew her nose into a tissue and then took a deep breath. "That's it?"

"That's it." Maggie's eyes brimmed with tears, and she beamed at Valerie.

"So, I'm officially a Christian? I still feel the same."

"Colin told me that Christianity isn't based on a feeling. It's based on fact. The facts of the Bible. That means it doesn't matter how you feel; the fact is you're saved. Believe me, there will be times when you won't feel saved, but that's when you turn to the Bible and the verses about salvation. The ones that promise your place in God's kingdom is secure." Maggie's tears fell unhindered, and a broad smile covered her face.

The tears in Valerie's eyes sparkled; her smile was radiant. "Maggie, I'm a Christian! I can't believe it! I'm a Christian!" She embraced her sister-in-law as her tears fell unashamedly.

"So, what do I do next?" The elation in her voice was impossible to miss.

"Nothing, really. I mean, there are no rules that I know of," said Maggie. "Do you have a Bible?"

"I think so. I'm not sure where it is," admitted Valerie sheepishly. She wiped her nose with another tissue.

"We'll have to get you one, and you should start going to church when you can. That way you can learn more about God, and what it means to be a Christian." She hesitated and then added, "You can always come with me if you'd like."

"Okay..." The jubilation in her voice abruptly changed to apprehension.

"What's wrong?"

"Just wondering what Will is going to say when I tell him. I'm not sure *how* to tell him," confessed Valerie. Her lips formed a thin line. "He's not exactly a fan of God right now."

"I know. He's angry and scared, but I'm praying for him. God is still in the miracle business." She paused for a moment. "Want to practice?" Maggie had a twinkle in her eye. "I know someone who would love to hear that you're saved." She pulled out her cell phone.

"I don't know..." Uncertainty gripped Valerie as she shook her head slightly.

"He'd love to hear it from you. It's number two on speed dial." As Maggie punched the number, she held out her phone to Valerie.

Taking the phone from Maggie, Valerie put it to her ear. It rang a few times before being answered.

"Hello, love. How's my favorite doctor?" There was no mistaking the British accent of Maggie's fiancé. His voice sounded cheerful, but sluggish.

"Um...sorry, it's not Maggie, Colin. It's me, Valerie." She made a face at Maggie, who shrugged her shoulders and mouthed "Sorry."

"Val? Is something wrong?" He now sounded completely awake.

"Um... no... I just... uh... I wanted to tell you something." Valerie looked at Maggie as if she needed help from her.

Maggie gestured for her to tell him.

"Valerie?"

"I'm here, Colin. Maggie's with me. Everything's fine. I just wanted to tell you that... that I just... I just asked Christ to save me..." Her voice broke, and she stopped talking.

"What? Really? That's fabulous! Tell me about it!" His enthusiasm was the catalyst needed to coax Valerie into telling him her salvation story. She shyly shared the details with him before handing the phone to Maggie. As Valerie wiped away her joyous tears, she excused herself and left Maggie alone in the lounge.

Hearing his voice on the line made Maggie yearn to see him, and she fought to keep from begging him to fly to California. "I'm just so amazed at it all! I wasn't sure what to say, but I remembered so much of what you told me. However, as for actual Bible verses, well, I can certainly see why you stress the importance of memorizing them," confessed Maggie.

Colin chuckled. "Well, you obviously did a fabulous job of sharing the gospel, love. I'm very proud of you for yielding yourself to God's Spirit."

His words touched Maggie's heart and encouraged her greatly.

"I'm sorry we woke you, but I thought you'd want to know."

"No apology needed. You know you can call me any time. And you're right, I do want to know when things like this happen. I can sleep any time, but this is a time for rejoicing. Are you going to take her to church with you?"

"I hope so. It depends on how she feels, and if Will lets her go. Sundays are rough days for her right after chemo, but her off weeks should be okay if she's not scheduled to work. Who knows, maybe Will will come with her," said Maggie hopefully.

"I'll pray for that."

"I knew you would."

"Ah, you know me so well."

"Go back to sleep. I'll call you later. I love you, Colin."

"I love you, too, Maggie."

They said their goodbyes, and she disconnected the call. She held the phone to her and closed her eyes. *Lord, I miss him so much. Please keep him safe and bring him to me soon, and thank You so much for Valerie's salvation.*

The door to the lounge opened, and Claire stuck her head in.

"Dr. D, we need you in two."

"I'll be right there." *Interesting...no one came in the whole time that Val and I were talking. God sure does work in mysterious and wonderful ways!*

CHAPTER SEVENTEEN

Will sat quietly listening to Valerie tell about her salvation experience. He took time to think about what she was saying, and when he spoke, he chose his words very carefully so as not to hurt her feelings or put a damper on her high spirits.

"And then we called Colin and told him. Maggie thought he'd like to know," stated Valerie as she cuddled next to Will. The fireplace illuminated the room with a flickering pale orange light, and soft music played in the background.

She felt Will take a deep breath. "Are you okay?" She looked up at him.

He kissed the top of her head. "Yes, sweetheart. I'm fine. Just thinking about what you said."

"It just made so much sense to me after Maggie explained it. I never understood how much God loved me. I'm still a little scared with the cancer and all, but nothing like before. Now God is the One in control, and He promised He'd take care of me!" She watched the dancing flames for a few moments as Will gently caressed the back of her neck.

"Will?"

"Hmm?"

"I'd like to go to church next Sunday if that's okay with you."

He hesitated for a few seconds before replying. "Of course, it's okay with me. I'll even come with you if you'd like." He reached to pick up his coffee.

Valerie turned her head to look at Will. "Really? I would love for you to come with me!"

He took a sip from his cup. "Then it's a date, Mrs. Garrett." Although he smiled at his wife, his voice was unemotional, and his response lacked enthusiasm. As he stretched his legs out and propped his feet up on the coffee table, his pager went off. Picking it up off the end table, he frowned when he saw the number.

"It's the service," he said as he picked up the phone. He punched in the number and waited for his answering service to pick up the call.

It was a request to call the hospital. He dialed the number for Eastmont and waited again. "This is Dr. Garrett. Yes. When? What's her current status? Yes, 5 milligrams to start. Let me know if that doesn't help with the pain. I'm on my way." He hung up the phone.

Valerie sat up and faced her husband. "You have to go to the hospital?"

"Yes. It's Grace. The lady you met in the ER. I need to be there, sweetheart," he started. "I hate to leave you--"

"You go." Valerie kissed him on the forehead. "She needs you more than I do right now. I'll be fine. I'll wait up for you."

Will grinned at her. "Like that's gonna happen! You'll probably be asleep before I get the car out of the garage. Call me if you need me. I can be home in no time, okay?"

She nodded. "I will, but don't worry. I'll be fine, Will. Now go!" She kissed him once more and shooed him out the door.

Will hurried to the nurses' station on the oncology floor. He was met by the second shift charge nurse, Theresa Howard.

"Hi, Dr. Garrett. I'm sorry we had to call you, but she's asking for you. She's febrile and having some signs of respiratory distress. She's still on oxygen." She handed the patient's chart to him.

"Thanks, Terri." He looked over her recent vital signs and frowned when he saw the temperature. *102.4. That's not good. I thought I had this under control.* He set the chart down and headed for his patient's room.

As he entered, he saw that she was not alone. Her husband and granddaughter were by her bedside. Will shook the man's hand.

"Mr. Gallagher. Faith." He nodded at the young woman in the chair. Her eyes were reddened, and she dabbed at them with a tissue as she smiled faintly at him.

The gray-haired man grasped Will's hand. "Dr. Garrett, thank you so much for coming in. Grace... she's not doing so well since you admitted her this afternoon. She's been wanting to see you, but we didn't want to bother you--"

"You're no bother, Mr. Gallagher. Let's see what going on." Will perused the chart one more time. "She's got a fever. That's not good, but she's had fevers before, and we've been able to treat them quite successfully. We're going to do whatever we can to make sure she's comfortable," explained Will. "I'd like to do a quick exam. You're welcome to stay if you want."

Mr. Gallagher cast a quick glance at his granddaughter. "I think we'll wait right outside, Doctor." He took Faith's hand and led her out of the room. Will did not miss the tears that trickled down Faith's cheeks. He turned to his patient.

"Grace? It's Dr. Garrett. How are you feeling?" He leaned over and spoke near her ear while taking her hand in his. It was evident to him that the frail body was struggling to fight against the invasive disease. Her hand was very warm, and Will knew her fever had not abated.

"Grace?"

The old woman weakly opened her eyes. "Dr. Garrett... so good of you... to come in to... see me." Her breathing was shallow and labored.

Will smiled at the old lady. Grace always had a special place in his heart. He recalled the day he had to tell her and her husband that she had cancer. Grace had not cried. In fact, she didn't even seem fazed by the diagnosis. She simply told him that her God was in control, and she trusted Him to help Will determine the best course of treatment. As the months had progressed, and the cancer spread, Will had expected her faith to wane, but it never did.

At her last scheduled appointment, he had gently informed her there was really nothing more he could do except keep her comfortable. Grace had smiled and patted his hand, thanking him for being a wonderful doctor. She told him that she always thanked God for bringing him into her life.

This is how You treat those who say they love You?

As if reading his mind, Grace opened her eyes once more and reached out a feeble hand. He took it.

"Sit down beside me, Dr. Garrett, just for a moment before you check me over."

He obediently sat down and waited for her to speak.

"I've been praying for you, Dr. Garrett." She turned her head to look at him. "I want you to know that you don't need to feel bad when I'm gone. You did the best you could do, but the Lord, well, I think He's about ready for me to come home." Her speech was clear and unlabored.

Will shifted in the chair, uncomfortable with her comments, but he listened nevertheless, without interrupting her.

"You know, everything's in God's hands," continued Grace. "He's the One who's in control. My God, well, He can still heal me if He wants, but if He doesn't, I can accept that. He's still my God, and He wants to be your God."

"Grace, I don't—"

"Now, now, you don't need to say anything. You're a gifted doctor, there's no question about that, but you need to know something." She inhaled deeply, and her chest had a slight rattle.

"Grace, you really--"

"Let an old woman speak, Doctor, please. I need to ask your forgiveness."

"*My* forgiveness? For what, Grace?"

"How long have we known each other, Doctor?"

"A little more than two years."

"Two years. Two years and I never sat down and shared the gospel with you, and for that, I'm asking your forgiveness. I am so ashamed of myself for never sharing God's love with you, so now I need to talk to you before the Lord takes me home." She smiled at Will, and he couldn't help but return a smile to this dear woman who often brought homemade cookies to his office staff or sent him cards of encouragement for no particular reason.

"Well, I forgive you, but there's really no need for it."

"No, that's where you're wrong, Dr. Garrett. Pretty soon, I'm going to be standing in the presence of my Savior, and when He asks me if I told you about Him, I want to be able to say 'yes' without any doubt. Do you know about Him? And how much He loves you?" she asked pointedly.

What am I supposed to say to that? The truth would just upset her. Will thought carefully before responding. It was rare for him to share personal details of his own life with his patients, but tonight was an exception. He felt compelled to open his heart to Grace. He sighed deeply.

"As a matter of fact, Grace, I do know a little about that. My sister's a Christian, and my wife just... uh... just became a Christian today," admitted Will. "And she told me all about it."

"And what about you, Dr. Garrett?"

Will's cheeks reddened, and he looked away from the old woman. "Well, honestly, Grace, I'm not.

"What's holding you back?"

"I... uh... haven't found the need to... become one." He found it difficult to look Grace in the eyes.

"The need, Dr. Garrett, is your sin," she stated bluntly.

"My sin?" Will looked skeptically at his patient. He folded his arms across his chest.

Grace responded with a loving nod. "Yes, we're all sinners, and we all deserve death because of our sins. That's what the Bible says, but Jesus loved us so much that He chose to take the punishment for our sins by dying on the cross, and now when we ask Him to forgive us and save us from those sins, He does. Then He gives us the gift of eternal life with Him in heaven.

"So you see, Dr. Garrett, God really does love you," continued the old woman, "and He wants to have a personal relationship with you. He wants it so badly that He'll wait for as long as it takes for you to come to Him."

It's going to be a very long time, Grace.

Grace looked at Will, her eyes clear and seemingly peering into the debts of his soul. Will shifted his weight in the chair and averted his eyes from her gaze.

"I know you don't think that He cares right now, but one day, you'll come to understand it. I heard that your wife has cancer, too. Is that correct?"

Will just nodded. His discomfort was growing.

"Is that why you're angry with God?"

Will looked up in surprise. "What makes you say that?"

She continued as if she hadn't heard him. "You know, God didn't give your wife cancer, but He's the One who can get her through it. I suspect many of your patients believe in the Lord, but they still die. Am I right? If I was a cancer doctor, that'd probably make me doubt there's a loving God out there. I mean, why would He allow so many people to suffer and die? It's got to be hard on a doctor... seeing all that sickness and death.

"That's a result of sin, Dr. Garrett. It's not God's fault. It's that ol' devil's fault and sin. If you want to be mad at someone, be mad at him. God loves you, Dr. Garrett, and He loves your wife."

"I respect your beliefs, Grace, but I don't think there's anything He can do that I can't do."

"Jesus can forgive my sins and wash me white as snow, Dr. Garrett. Can you do that? Jesus can prepare a place for me in heaven to dwell with Him for all eternity. Can you do that? He can love me with an everlasting love, and Dr. Garrett, He'll do the same for you, if you let Him," informed Grace.

Will nervously shifted in the chair.

"Contrary to your thinking, God is still in the healing business. Sometimes it's the body, but most of the time, Dr. Garrett, it's the soul. When the time comes, and you realize that you need Him, you remember how much Jesus loves you, and you call on His name. He'll lift you up, save you from your sins, and free you from bondage, Dr. Garrett.

"You remember that. When those dark days come, and they will, remember that God still loves you both. He is in complete control, and no matter what you face, joy will come in the morning." Grace started coughing, and Will stood up abruptly to help her sit upright until the spasm passed.

"You... can do your... examination... now," panted Grace. She relaxed into her pillow.

Will slowly put his stethoscope in place. *What is going on? She talks without a problem for ten solid minutes, and now she can barely catch her breath?* He listened to her heart's slow, irregular rhythm and the struggle of her lungs to move air in and out. Grace was quietly laying back, eyes closed, not saying a word to him. He finished his exam automatically, still pondering her words when he went to get her husband and granddaughter.

"She's not doing very well right now," stated Will honestly. "She's on oxygen, and I'd like to start her on some IV antibiotics and get a chest x-ray."

Mr. Gallagher nodded. "Grace said she didn't want anything heroic done, especially if it was close to her home-going."

"Home-going?"

Faith stepped in. "Close to her passing and going home, Dr. Garrett – to heaven."

"Oh, I see. Well, I can't tell you when that will be, but the antibiotics and oxygen are not really extraordinary measures. I have her advanced directive on file, and I will honor that, but for now, the antibiotics and oxygen will help with any respiratory infection and make it easier for her to breathe."

"You will make sure she isn't in any pain?" asked Mr. Gallagher.

"Of course."

"You've done so much for us, Dr. Garrett. We are so grateful. The Lord gave us the best doctor possible for Grace. You have no idea what a blessing you've been to us." Mr. Gallagher shook Will's hand one more time.

"My grandmother adores you, Dr. Garrett. We can't thank you enough for all you've done through her illness," commented Faith.

Will felt his cheeks warm in response to their praises.

"I'll be here for a while tonight, so if you need anything, just ask. If I'm not right here, the nurses can page me," he said as he motioned for them to enter the room.

He walked over to the nurses' station and reopened up Grace's chart. He made a few notations, wrote a few orders, and then sat down. Grace's words still echoed in his mind.

When those dark days come, and they will, remember that God still loves you both. He is in complete control, and no matter what you face, joy will come in the morning.

Valerie curled her feet underneath her as she sat on the sofa watching the fire. She held a mug of hot cocoa in her hands and inhaled the chocolate aroma. She had searched for her old Bible and finally found it tucked away on a shelf with a thick layer of dust on its top pages. She had wiped away the dust and carried it back to the living room before making her cocoa. Now, she was ready to open it up.

She took a final sip of the hot chocolate, set the cup on the end table, and picked up the Bible. Not knowing where to look, she flipped through the pages, and stopped in the book of Psalms. She scanned a page and began to read aloud.

"Because thou hast made the LORD, which is my refuge, even the most High, thy habitation; there shall no evil befall thee, neither shall any plague come nigh thy dwelling. For he shall give his angels charge over thee, to keep thee in all thy ways. They shall bear thee up in their hands, lest thou dash thy foot against a stone."

She looked around her living room.

"Are your angels here with me?" Her voice was a reverent whisper. "Will you really keep the cancer away? I know that everyone is saying it's a good kind of cancer, but it seems to me there isn't any kind of cancer that's good." She raised her eyes toward the ceiling. "I know that mine's not very advanced, at least not that I know of, but it's still cancer, and it still scares me. I don't really know how not to be scared, but God, I don't want to die. Please help me through this. Please help me not end up like my mother." Valerie struggled to maintain her composure as she completed her prayer, but tears still fell as she prayed.

Can I really ask You for anything? Do You really hear me? Do You really care? She closed the Bible and held it against her chest. Within minutes, she fell into a deep, peaceful slumber.

CHAPTER EIGHTEEN

Maggie was placing the last stitch in a minor laceration when she heard the hospital loudspeaker paging her brother. She glanced at her watch.

It's awfully late for him to be here. That's never a good sign.

She turned to her patient, a young man in his early twenties. "Okay, you need to see your primary physician in about a week to remove those stitches. I'll give you a prescription for an antibiotic, and I think you'll be just fine. Any questions for me?"

"No, Doctor. Thanks again."

"You're very welcome. Take care." She left the room and walked over to the nurses' station. She wrote a few notes, scribbled a prescription, and then gave the chart to the clerk, who prepared to discharge the patient.

"Hey, Maggie!"

She turned around to see her brother hanging up a phone. "Hey, Will. I heard them page you. What are you doing here so late?"

"Seeing one of my patients upstairs. Got a minute?"

"Sure, it's quiet tonight. Let's grab a cup of coffee. Everything okay with Valerie?" They entered the staff lounge, and Maggie poured two cups of coffee, handing one to Will.

"Thanks. Yeah, everything's fine." He took a sip of the strong liquid. "Wow! That'll keep me up all night!"

Maggie chuckled. "It's supposed to do that. That's why we brew it strong here."

Will pulled a chair out from the table so Maggie could sit down and then sat opposite her.

"Valerie told me what happened today."

Maggie took a sip of her coffee and then set her cup on the table.

This could get ugly real quick. What am I supposed to say? She resigned herself to a verbal confrontation and mentally prepared to spar with her brother.

"Will, she--"

Will leaned back in his chair and a small smile appeared. "You worried I might bite your head off? You know, I'm not anti-God; I just don't need Him like you do."

Maggie frowned but remained silent. She eyed Will carefully, and although his words seemed light, tension was evident on his face.

"What's really wrong, Will?"

Their bond had always been close, and over the years, they had shared their innermost secrets with one another, never violating that confidence, always loving unconditionally, and always supporting one another.

"Up until now, Valerie and I have been on the same page. Now we're not, and I don't understand why she thinks she needs God. I mean, I know she's fighting cancer, but I am an oncologist *and* her husband. What can God give her that I can't? This is my job. I know what I'm doing. That should be enough for her."

Maggie shifted slightly in the chair. *Lord, I know I've been asking for Your help a lot lately, but if You wouldn't mind one more time.*

"Will," began Maggie cautiously, "no matter what you think, there's no way we have all the answers. Valerie is going through something that neither you nor I can fully understand. We know the clinical aspects of cancer, and we know the ramifications of it, but we don't know... really know... what it's like to actually have the disease and face the possibility of not winning the battle against it. It's got to be awful to bear that kind of burden."

"I'm her husband, Maggie. Husbands and wives are supposed to share their burdens with one another." He held his hands up in apparent frustration.

Maggie struggled to find the right words to say to her brother. "Valerie's decision to make Christ her Savior doesn't exclude you from her life, Will. God doesn't take your place. And it may not necessarily be about the cancer. While it's true that the disease may have been the catalyst, Valerie decided she wanted a relationship with God. She made the choice to trust Him with her life... and soul. No matter what people say about doctors, we're not God. He's the One who really is in control of things."

Will sat without speaking, his gaze on his now interlocked fingers. "Really, Maggie? How can she put her trust in God when He's the One who gave her cancer to begin with? It doesn't make any sense to me!" He ran his fingers through his thick black hair. "I mean, she's a smart woman, Maggie, why doesn't she see this?"

"Will, God didn't *give* cancer to Valerie. You can't tell me that you believe God's given every one of your patients cancer, can you? Things happen. It's a natural course of events. You know that as well as I do. Cells mutate. Something in their genetic makeup goes haywire, and bam! you've got cancer, but I can tell you one thing, God's the only One who can completely cure it.

"You can give all the drugs you want, but you never really know if the cancer's gone, do you? The only one who can truly eradicate that disgusting disease is God. Not you, not any pharmaceutical company, not anyone, but God! You know that's true."

Will stared as his sister and shook his head. He crossed his arms in front of his chest. "That's a fine stand for a doctor to take."

Maggie's eyes narrowed and focused on Will. Her voice was clear and purposeful. "I don't know why God allowed Valerie to have cancer. I don't like this any more than you do, but sometimes, I just have to trust God and go with it. And I'll tell you one thing I do know. He's never wrong, and He's always in control. He loves Valerie more than I love her and more than you do. Whatever He decides is best for her, He'll do. I know it. I've seen Him work before, and I know He'll take care of her. He promised. He has to." She grabbed her coffee cup, stood up, and moved toward the counter, her back to her brother.

"He hasn't done a very good job so far." The sarcasm in Will's voice was impossible to miss.

Maggie spun around; her eyes flashed in anger. "How dare you, Will! How dare you say that! Valerie's cancer could be stage four. It could have spread throughout her entire body. She could be nonresponsive to treatment. Who do you think is responsible for the fact that she has a pretty good chance of survival? You? I don't think so. So, don't tell me that God hasn't done a good job taking care of her. I'd say He's done a better job than any of us could have ever done!"

"Really? The same way He took care of Scott?"

Maggie stood speechless for a moment. She stared hard at Will as her eyes bore into him. She spoke each word with emphasis. "Get out, Will. Now."

Will swallowed hard, regretting his words. "Maggie, I'm sorry. I didn't mean to upset you."

"Really, Will? You insult my God, and you don't think it's going to upset me? You just don't get it. God loves you. He sent His Son to die for you, and you just spit in His face. I feel sorry for you."

"Sorry for me?" Will's look of remorse abruptly changed into one of defiance, and with that look, he challenged Maggie. "Why? Because I don't need a crutch to get through life?"

Maggie glared at Will. "Please tell me you didn't just say that I need a crutch to get through life. After all I've been through, you have the audacity to tell me I need a crutch?"

Will's eyes immediately became apologetic once more as he realized the depth of hurt he had inflicted upon his sister. "Maggie, I--" His pager began to vibrate.

Maggie turned away from him and shook her head. She held her hands up as if dismissing him. "Just go, Will. Your patient needs you."

"Maggie, please --"

"Not now, Will." Her voice was unyielding; each word articulated sternly.

"Maggie... I'm sorry." He stood up and waited for Maggie to respond. When she didn't, he signed in resignation and left, leaving her alone in the lounge.

She didn't know how long she had been standing at the counter when the door reopened, and a nurse entered the lounge.

"Dr. Devereaux, I'm sorry to bother you, but you're needed in one."

"Thanks. I'll be right there." She willed the trembling in her hands to stop. Her anger slowly began to subside, gradually replaced with immense sorrow and oppressive regret. Her heart weighed heavy as she retrieved Will's cup from the table, and set it, along with her own, in the sink. She sighed deeply, wiped away a tear, and exited the lounge.

"So that's how it ended," reported Maggie as she sat at her kitchen table balancing the phone on her shoulder. She tore a croissant in pieces and popped a small fragment into her mouth. A steaming cup of black coffee sat in front of her.

"Have you spoken with him since then?"

Colin's voice calmed her down a bit, but she still felt great remorse at her lack of self-control the night before.

"No. Not yet. I don't know what to say."

"Have you prayed about it?"

A long pause intensified her awkwardness in confessing her lack of seeking God's help through prayer.

"No."

"Hmm... Do you think you should?"

"You know I should."

"Yes, I know it, but do you?"

Despite what could have been perceived as a chastisement, Maggie knew that Colin was trying to help her find the solution to her problem herself. She sighed audibly and then heard him chuckle. "You find this funny?"

"No, love. Not the situation, just your exasperation with me."

"I'm not... well, maybe I am. I just want you to tell me what to do, but you're not going to do that, are you?"

"No."

"Is this what life with you is going to be like?"

"Most definitely."

She heard him laugh again and found herself smiling. "You amaze me."

"Really? How so?"

"You haven't given me any concrete advice, and yet, I'm feeling much better than when I first called, despite the fact that you haven't really done one single thing."

"I'll be happy to pray with you."

She sipped her coffee. "I think I would like that. Yes, I would like that a lot." She closed her eyes and waited for him to begin.

"Father, You are an awesome God, and we love You. We come to You seeking Your wisdom and help. The burden we carry for Will is so great. He needs You, Lord. Open his heart and help him understand his need for salvation. Please give Maggie the courage and wisdom she needs to speak to him again. Help them both have forgiving hearts for one another and mend the rift from their earlier disagreement. May Your perfect will be accomplished, and may You be glorified in all that is done in her family. In Jesus' name, I pray. Amen."

"Amen," Maggie echoed. "Thank you so much, Colin. You always know exactly what to say."

"Maggie, you need to remember Proverbs 3:5 and 6," reminded Colin, "and then wait on the Lord."

"Trust in the Lord with all thine heart and lean not unto thine own understanding. In all thy ways acknowledge Him, and He shall direct thy paths," recited Maggie. "It's just so hard to wait."

"Believe me, I know all about that."

Maggie smiled to herself. "I guess you do, don't you?" She thought about the ups and downs of the journey that had brought them from a doctor-patient relationship to one that now saw them as a betrothed couple. Colin had been extraordinarily patient, waiting on the Lord and His direction before actively pursuing Maggie, and even then, he had jumped several hurdles before Maggie was ready for another relationship in her life. But the wait had paid off. She held her left hand out in front of her and studied the ring Colin had presented her when she accepted his proposal. The diamonds glittered brightly as she maneuvered her hand to catch a stream of sunlight coming in through the kitchen window.

He interrupted her thoughts. "Well worth it, I might add. So, what's your plan?"

"No plan, I guess. Just wait on the Lord, as one very wise man has advised me."

Colin chuckled once more. "You'll keep me posted?"

"I will. I promise. Keep praying, okay?"

"Always, love."

After a few more minutes of conversation, Maggie ended the call, sat back in her chair, and took another sip of her coffee. *If this is what Colin went through with me, I should be apologizing to him as well as to Will!*

CHAPTER NINETEEN

It was half past six in the morning when Will walked into Grace's room on the oncology floor. His eyes widened, and his mouth fell open slightly when he saw Grace sitting up in her bed reading her Bible. She looked up and smiled when he entered the room.

"Dr. Garrett, how are you?" She reached out to grasp his hand.

Amazed at her status, Will smiled unbelievingly at his patient and gently took her hand in his. "I'm doing well, Grace. How are you feeling this morning?"

She chuckled. "Better'n last night. You sure do know your doctoring." A cough interrupted her. "I've been reading about how good the Lord is. Listen to this… 'Hast thou not known? Hast thou not heard that the everlasting God, the Lord, the Creator of the ends of the earth, fainteth not, neither is weary? There is no searching of His understanding. He giveth power to the faint; and to them that have no might He increaseth strength. Even the youths shall faint and be weary, and the young men shall utterly fall: But they that wait upon the Lord shall renew their strength; they shall mount up with wings as eagles; they shall run and not be weary; and they shall walk and not faint.' Isn't that just grand, Dr. Garrett? Here I've been waiting to go home and be with my Lord, and He renews my strength. I guess my work for Him here isn't finished yet."

"I guess it isn't, Grace." Will pulled his stethoscope out of his lab coat pocket.

"I'm praying I'll be around long enough to see someone very dear to me find his way home... to the Savior," stated Grace. She patted Will's hand.

Will smiled faintly at his patient and placed his stethoscope over Grace's heart. "Now, who would that be?"

Grace's eyes twinkled as she met Will's gaze. "I think we both know the answer to that one, Dr. Garrett."

Will could not find it in him to be irritated or offended by Grace's concern for his soul. He moved to the other side of her bed to have easier access to hearing her lungs. "Take a few deep breaths for me, Grace, if you would."

She complied with his request, and when he finished his exam, he pulled up a chair next to her bedside.

"You still have some crackles in your lungs, Grace, but they sound a lot better than last night."

"Like I said, Dr. Garrett, you're the best. Between you and my Lord, I wouldn't be surprised if I beat this cancer."

Will thought for a moment before speaking. "Grace, what happens if God doesn't heal you? I mean, you've prayed for that, right?"

"Of course, but God may have other plans."

Her candor caught Will off guard. "And you're okay with that?" He leaned forward in the chair, awaiting her reply.

Grace smiled compassionately at the doctor. "I don't have much choice when it comes to my healing, Dr. Garrett. It's all in God's hands. I've prayed for Him to heal me, but I've also prayed for His will to be done in my life. If He chooses to heal me, well, that would be wonderful. I'll continue to serve Him to the best of my ability and have a little more time with my Tom, but if He doesn't, well, either way, He's still my God. He knows what is best for me, and I can accept that. There's a story in the Bible about some boys who thought the same thing. They were told to bow down to a foreign king, and when they refused, the king sentenced them to death. Tossed the three of them into this fiery furnace. The king demanded to know if their God would save them. They told him that it didn't matter if they were saved from the fire or not, that no matter what happened, they would continue to worship the one true and living God.

"As the king looked into the furnace, he saw not three, but four men in the fire. The king realized it was God Himself protecting the boys. That's the way I feel, Dr. Garrett. If God does heal me, so be it, but even if He doesn't, He's still my God, and I'll always love Him."

Grace reached out a frail hand and pointed a finger at Will. "I know that's hard for you to understand, Dr. Garrett, being a doctor and all. You want everyone to get well, but that doesn't happen now, does it?"

"No, it doesn't, Grace." His voice was sober as he continued. "Don't you feel let down by God when He doesn't answer your prayers?"

"Not let down, Dr. Garrett. Maybe a wee bit disappointed, you know, not getting my way and all, but I get over that. I know He only does what is best for me. I don't always understand it, but I believe it. It's written in His Word."

"Not all Christians think like that, Grace."

"No, I suppose they don't, Dr. Garrett. But Job, he went through some pretty terrible times. Lost his wife, his kids, and he was awful sick. Even his friends thought it'd be best if he just turned his back on God, but he didn't. Job believed in God, and he believed that whatever God allowed to happen to him was the Lord's divine will. No matter what happened, Job was not going to reject God. He chose to trust Him. That's what I'm doing. You see, Dr. Garrett, whatever happens to me is a win-win situation. If the Lord chooses to heal me, I'll have a little bit longer here with Tom and the rest of my family. If He doesn't, I'll be ushered into His presence. There's no way I can lose, Dr. Garrett. No way at all."

Will smiled at his patient. "You're an amazing woman, Grace."

Her pale cheeks pinked up. "Wouldn't that be something if you were the reason He's keeping me here, Dr. Garrett?"

Will's eyes widened. "Me? What do you mean?"

"Maybe God's going to let me live until I see you surrender your life to Christ. You know you're not the only stubborn human being God's ever faced." She paused for a moment and winked at the doctor.

"Stubborn?"

Grace giggled. "Do you have a better word for it?"

Will opened his mouth to respond, but Grace interrupted him. "I imagine you're working real hard trying to understand things in this world that can't be understood without God, and you're too stubborn to let Him into your life to help you."

Will crossed his arms. "I don't think—"

"That you're stubborn? I don't know what else to call it." She raised an eyebrow as she continued. "But we've known each other for a long time, Dr. Garrett, and I do know one thing. You need Jesus. He's the only One who can give you the peace you're seeking. He's the only One who can answer those questions you've been asking."

"What questions?"

"Questions like 'Why do people have to suffer?' or 'Why can't we cure cancer?' or..." She paused for a moment and added softly, "'Why is my wife sick?'"

Will squirmed in his chair, glancing away from Grace. He swallowed hard but said nothing.

"Dr. Garrett, I don't always understand why God allows things to happen, but I do trust Him to do what is best."

Will hesitated before asking, "Even if that means suffering and... possibly dying?"

Grace looked at the doctor with a deep understanding in her eyes. "Yes, even if it means suffering and death. That's what trust is about. I don't have to understand God to trust Him. He promised to take care of me, and I believe Him. No matter what happens, He is my God and Savior."

"It doesn't sound very fair."

"It's not."

Will's questioning gaze was fixed on Grace's face.

Her eyes misted over as she explained, her voice choked with emotion. "It's not fair that my Lord had to leave the splendor of heaven to die on an old rugged cross so my sins could be forgiven. It's not fair that I don't have to pay the penalty for my own transgressions, but that Jesus had to do that with His own precious blood. It's not fair that when I deserve death, He gives me eternal life. It's not fair that in spite of my sin, He loves me more than I can comprehend. You're right, Dr. Garrett. It's not fair. It's love."

Will took a deep breath, exhaled slowly, and shook his head. "Love? I might disagree with you on that one, Grace. It seems to me that if God really loved you, He'd heal you."

Grace wiped a tear from her eye. "Oh, I don't know about that. If He did that, you'd be out of a job. Maybe He loves you a bit more than He loves me!" She laughed softly at herself, but then became serious. "It's going to work out exactly as God wants it to. I'm not worried—"

"How can you not worry?"

Grace studied Will's puzzled look, then recited, "'Thou wilt keep him in perfect peace whose mind is stayed on Thee: because he trusteth in Thee.' I trust in God, Dr. Garrett, and because of that, I am at peace. You'll understand that one day."

Will smirked, and his skepticism amused Grace. She patted his hand. "If you weren't such a gentleman, you'd tell this old woman to hush up, wouldn't you? But you won't, will you?" She cocked her head and beamed at Will.

He gave her a one-sided grin and shook his head. "No. No, I won't. You're something else, Grace."

"What I am, Dr. Garrett, is a sinner saved by grace."

Will sighed and smiled at her as he stood. "I suppose you'll be up and dancing a jig tomorrow?"

She laughed lightly. "Only if He calls me home tonight!" She paused for a moment. "Dr. Garrett?"

"Yes, Grace?"

"I want to give you something to look up and read when you're ready. It's some advice that was given a long time ago to another man who was pondering some rather difficult questions like you. May I borrow your pen?"

Will handed Grace his pen and watched as she scribbled a note on the back of one of his blank prescription pads. When she handed it to him, he tore off the page, glanced at it, folded it, and put it in his jacket pocket.

"Now don't you lose that, Dr. Garrett." Grace smiled mischievously at Will.

He patted the pocket and grinned. "I won't, Grace. I promise."

CHAPTER TWENTY

"Oh, Maggie! Look at these! They're beautiful!" Valerie exclaimed as they entered one of the local bridal shops. She immediately held up an elaborately beaded wedding gown with layers of satin and lace.

Maggie's eyes widened. "I don't know about that one, Val. It's awfully fancy." She walked over to the rack and inspected several other gowns. "Hmm... what about this one?" She held up a white empire gown with a lace overlay and a poufy hem.

Valerie put her hands on her hips, shook her head, and frowned. "Oh no, it reminds me of an upside down ice cream cone. Let's keep looking."

Maggie laughed as she replaced the dress on the rack. "How do you really feel about it, Val?"

Valerie scrunched up her face and stuck out her tongue. "Don't you dare pick that one! Besides, we should look at a bunch before deciding, don't you think?"

Maggie grinned. "I suppose so. After all, we've got plenty of time, so no need to rush."

Valerie nodded. "This is so much fun, Mags! Maybe God will direct you to the perfect dress! Let the hunt begin!" Her eyes had the familiar sparkle that Maggie had only seen sporadically since Valerie's diagnosis.

"I think that's the best idea I've heard so far!" Maggie decided to keep her altercation with Will to herself and assumed he had done the same since Valerie didn't mention it. Despite the fact that she had been unable to let go of the hurt from their argument, Maggie chose to put it out of her mind today and focus on her wedding.

Together, they perused racks of dresses, refusing the assistance of a store clerk due to the joy they had on their own quest for the perfect gown.

"What about this one, Val?"

Maggie held a satin A-line gown with short sleeves, scoop neckline, and a scalloped lace hem. The antique white dress had a delicately embroidered bodice with a lace overlay on the satin skirt. She held the dress up in front of her.

"Oh, Maggie..." Valerie's voice was almost awestruck. "It's beautiful!" She walked over to her and gingerly touched the embroidery on the bodice. "You've got to try this one on."

They continued to shop until, armed with several selections, they sought out a sales associate to help direct them to the fitting area.

Forty minutes and three dresses later, Maggie, wearing the first dress they had chosen, stood before Valerie on a small platform in front of several full-length mirrors.

Valerie sat speechless, her hands up to her mouth. Her eyes were moist with tears as she stared at Maggie. "Oh, Mags... you're beautiful!"

Maggie turned slowly and drew her breath in sharply. She stared at her reflection. The multiple mirrored images provided varied angles of view of the elegant gown. She gingerly ran her fingers over the delicate material.

This dress is beautiful! It's perfect! This is the one I want to wear when I marry Colin.

She turned back around to face Valerie, who sat looking intently at Maggie.

"Think this is the one?"

Valerie blinked her tears away and nodded enthusiastically. "Without a doubt, Maggie! Colin will absolutely love it!" She whipped out her cell phone from her purse and snapped a picture of the future bride. "I want to send this to Will."

Maggie ran her hands over the lace once more. She gazed at herself in the mirror. "It is beautiful, isn't it?"

"It's gorgeous, and it's you! Now, what about a veil?" Valerie asked.

Maggie shook her head. "No, I don't want a veil. I'm actually thinking about maybe tiny flowers or pearls... something like that. What do you think?"

"I think that would be perfect for this dress!"

"Well, now that we know what I'm going to wear, let's find something for you," stated Maggie as she stepped down from the platform. "I'll go change, and then we'll shop for your dress!"

They spent another half hour or so selecting dresses for Valerie to model, but couldn't decide on one until Valerie came out in a rose pink gown. Like Maggie's wedding dress, it had a scoop neckline and short sleeves, but the waistline was swept to one side and held in place by an intricate embroidered design. The satin skirt was a narrow A-line with tiny faux diamonds that glittered in the light.

Maggie's mouth dropped when Valerie stepped up on the modeling block. "I thought a lighter pastel color would be the way to go, but Val... that dress is amazing on you! You look like a princess!"

"You think so?" She tilted her head to one side as she studied her reflection. "Isn't it a bit too dark for a springtime wedding?"

"I don't know. Are there rules about that?"

Valerie turned to look at Maggie. "I don't know. Are you okay with the color?"

Maggie thought for a moment. "Yes, I think it's perfect! What do you think?"

Valerie returned to her reflection and then announced, "I love it!"

"Then that's the one!"

They ordered their dresses and then headed for a quick lunch at a Japanese restaurant. Sitting down in a small booth, they quickly scanned the menu.

"Everything looks so good," commented Valerie. "I think I'm going to get the teriyaki chicken lunch."

"Me, too. Want to split a California roll?"

"That sounds wonderful!" Valerie sipped her green tea. "So, what about flowers and stuff?"

Maggie shrugged her shoulders. "I'm really not sure what to do, Val. We haven't decided if we want to get married here or in England."

"England?" Valerie's eyes registered shock. "You'd really get married in England? What about all your friends and family here?"

"Well, I was thinking about maybe getting married in England and then having a reception here after the honeymoon," explained Maggie.

Valerie grimaced. "Seriously? I know he has family there and all, but you have family here, too, you know!"

"I know." Maggie sighed. "It's just that Colin is away from home so much, and I know how much he loves it there. I know he'd get married here if I asked him, but honestly I just haven't made a decision."

"Has he told you what he wants?" asked Valerie thoughtfully.

"He says he wants what I want."

"Men are so helpful," chuckled Valerie as she took a bite of sushi. "Well, I vote for California. Make sure you tell him that our weather is so much better than England's. No fog." She picked up a sliver of pickled radish with her chopsticks. "Have you decided on the date yet?"

Maggie shook her head. "No. We're thinking about maybe next spring." She bit into her chicken.

"Why so long?"

Without looking up, she responded, "Gotta wait until my matron of honor has hair again. Can't stick flowers on her head with glue."

Valerie stopped with her chopsticks midway to her mouth. She stared at Maggie for a second and then burst out laughing. Maggie joined her, and they laughed until tears came.

"I didn't think about that. On behalf of your matron of honor, I thank you for taking that into consideration!" They started giggling again.

Valerie picked up her napkin, sneezed once, and wiped her mouth. "Are you having any other attendants?"

"I don't think so, but Colin has two brothers, so if he decides to use them both, I'll be off by one. I don't know who else I would ask. I know lots of people at work and church, but no one I would actually think of having stand up for me at my wedding. Do you think it matters if we're a bit lopsided?"

"Maybe if we can exchange my dress for that poufy ice cream looking one, I'll look like two attendants!" Valerie began to giggle once more, and Maggie joined her.

It feels so good to laugh together again!

By the end of the day, they were exhausted from their shopping spree. Dresses and shoes had been purchased, plans had been laid for the wedding, and they were both very satisfied with the results of their efforts.

Maggie eased her car into Valerie's driveway and slowed it to a stop.

"I had a great time today, Val. Thanks for coming with me." Maggie reached over and squeezed Valerie's hand.

"Me, too, Mags. I haven't laughed so hard or so much in a long time. I'll see you tomorrow. Love you."

Maggie smiled and waved as she watched Valerie enter her house and close the door. *Take care of her, Lord.*

CHAPTER TWENTY-ONE

Valerie's energy level had steadily declined in the last two days. She had felt a growing fatigue since bridal shopping with Maggie, and now she couldn't shake the weariness that seemed to envelope her. She hesitantly picked up the telephone and dialed the nursing supervisor. There was no way she could manage a twelve-hour shift in the emergency room today.

She thought back to earlier in the morning when she had sent Will off to work. He had asked her if she was all right when she had remained in bed, and she had told him she was fine. She had forced a smile and told him that all she needed was a shower and her morning cup of coffee. Now, she noticed a small twinge of pain every so often when she took a deep breath and a deeper hurt when she coughed.

As she waited for someone to answer her call, Valerie took shallow breaths to prevent a coughing fit. The nursing supervisor's answering machine came on, and Valerie left a message requesting the day off due to illness. She hung up quickly, just as an episode of coughing ensued. She crawled deeper beneath the quilting on her bed, closed her eyes, and fell into a restless sleep interrupted by several bouts of coughing.

Later that evening, when Maggie came out of treatment room two, she saw Will standing by the staff lounge. His eyes were closed, and he leaned against the wall, his arms crossed against his chest.

"Will?"

His eyes opened immediately, and he stood straight. He cleared his throat. "Maggie. You busy?"

"No more than usual." Her reply was cool. "Problem?"

"I hope not. I came down here to see if my sister was still speaking to me."

Maggie pulled him into the staff lounge and then closed the door behind them. She turned to face Will, her hands on her hips. "Yes, I'm speaking to you. Of course, I'm speaking to you. You're my brother. I love you."

"Maggie, I'm sorry. I shouldn't have said those things."

"No, you shouldn't have." Her eyes were glued to Will's face. Her lips set in a firm line.

"You're not going to make this easy for me, are you?"

"Should I?"

Will held his hands out for a moment before dropping them to his sides. He sighed deeply. "What do you want me to say, Maggie? I don't want it to be like this between us. I'll admit I don't understand why you or Val need God in your life so badly, but I do know she's happier since her... her... conversion or salvation, or whatever you call it, and I won't deny her that. I promise."

"Thank you for that." *Cut him some slack, Maggie. He did come down here.* She sighed deeply and reached for his hand. As she gave it a squeeze, her voice apologetically added, "I'm sorry, too, Will. Not a very good way of winning you over, is it?"

Will smiled half-heartedly. "Well, it's probably not what the Church recommends when trying to get converts, but I won't hold it against you, okay?"

Maggie nodded and managed a small smile. "Please Will, don't let me be the reason you don't give God a chance."

"Maggie, please... can we leave Him out of it for right now? I don't have the strength to fight you and deal with this, too."

"Deal with what? What's going on Will?" Maggie searched his eyes for the meaning behind his comment.

"I came to find you because I wanted to tell you that Val's here. She's got a fever, and Renee thought it best to bring her here now for a chest x-ray. Apparently, she's had a slight cough for a few days now. She didn't want to worry me, and I... I should've caught it, but... she's in three. Will you see her, Maggie?"

"Of course. How's she doing right now?" She quickly moved to the door, held it open for him, and they walked into the corridor.

He shook his head. "Not too good. She's pretty upset. She was crying when I brought her in. I think... I think maybe she's got pneumonia." He walked beside Maggie without looking up; his shoulders were sagging. "I should have picked up on it sooner."

Maggie moved closer to her brother as they walked toward Valerie's treatment room. "You look worn out."

He smiled weakly. "I'm okay, Maggie. Just worried about Val. I shouldn't have missed this."

"It's not your fault, Will. We'll take care of her... you and I together. I promise."

As she entered the room, Maggie grabbed a pair of latex gloves. She slipped them on and quickly glanced up at the cardiac monitor. Heart rate and rhythm appeared slightly elevated but not grossly abnormal. The oxygen saturation was acceptable, and Valerie's blood pressure was within normal limits.

Maggie stood for a moment and looked at the still form on the bed. The quiet hiss of oxygen flow through the nasal cannula was the only sound in the room. Valerie's eyes were closed, but when Maggie moved near the bedside, they fluttered open.

"Mags?" Valerie's voice was weak, and her eyes had the glassy look of fever.

Maggie smiled at her sister-in-law. "Hey, Val. How are you feeling?"

"I guess I've been better." Valerie managed a feeble smile. "Will said it might be pneumonia." A coughing spasm interrupted her, and she held a tissue over her mouth until the coughing stopped. She reached for a second tissue and dabbed her reddened eyes. The frown on her face quivered when she looked up at Maggie.

"Oh, Mags. I don't want to be here." Her breathing was rapid and shallow. "It hurts to breathe. Everything feels so tight. I should've told Will sooner, but--" She took several short breaths. "I wanted it to be nothing. I didn't want to worry him. I just didn't want to be sick anymore..." Her voice trailed off as she tried to catch her breath.

Maggie glanced at a student nurse standing on the other side of the bed. "Let's get her on a mask. She's breathing through her mouth. The tubing's not going to do any good for her." Maggie then moved closer and held Valerie's hand. "Dry those tears, Val. We'll take care of you. Do you mind if I listen to your heart and lungs?" She placed her stethoscope on Valerie's chest and listened to the rhythmic pulsations. Nothing seemed abnormal with the heart, but when she assessed the lungs, the breath sounds were definitely atypical.

Through the stethoscope, she heard faint crackles in the lower left lobe. As Valerie inhaled, the air movement irritated the bronchial tubes and another coughing fit ensued. Maggie slung her stethoscope around her neck and stood up. She frowned slightly. "I'll need a chest x-ray. You have some faint rales in your left lung. I need to rule out pneumonia."

Valerie shook her head. Her lips were tight and drawn as she reached for Will. His strong hand enveloped hers, and she clung to it. "If it's pneumonia, what then?" Her frightened eyes darted from Maggie to Will.

He reached out to gently touch his wife's cheek. "Well, it's really not up to me, sweetheart. I'd give you some antibiotics, but Maggie and Dr. Sommers have to make that call. They're your doctors, Val, not me."

"As soon as I see the films, I'll call Renee and see what she wants me to do," stated Maggie.

"I don't want to stay here, Will, please..." begged Valerie.

Will looked at Maggie, his anguished eyes locking with hers. Maggie hesitated for a moment before responding to Valerie's plea. "Val, you need to remember that whatever is decided, it'll be in your best interest. Normally, I could give a patient some antibiotics, send them home, and have them follow-up with their own physician, but with you, well, your immune system is compromised from the chemotherapy. No one wants to take any chances with that."

Closing her eyes tightly, Valerie pressed her lips together and swallowed hard. "Maggie, I'm trying not be afraid, but it's so hard. Will you pray for me? I tried, but I couldn't. I didn't know what to say."

Maggie faltered. *Now?* Her unsure eyes moved quickly from Valerie to Will, and then back to Valerie.

Valerie held tightly to the sleeve of Maggie's lab coat. "Please, Maggie. God listens to you."

"Oh, Val, honey, God listens to you. Just talk to Him. Just like you talk to me. He's always waiting, ready to hear His children's voices. There's no special way to pray." Maggie glanced up at Will. He didn't smile, but gave her a small nod.

What do I say, Lord? She took a deep breath and exhaled slowly. She turned back to look at Valerie, and an unexpected serenity overcame her spirit. She paused for just a moment, and then she prayed. "O God, thank You so much for loving us as much as You do, and thank You for hearing us when we pray. Please be with Valerie right now and comfort her as only You can do. Touch her body and help it to heal. Give us wisdom as we diagnose and treat her. Give Valerie the strength she needs to get through this without getting discouraged. Help Will, too, Lord. Give him the comfort and strength he needs as he supports Valerie. In Jesus name, I pray. Amen."

Will's eyes were fixed on Maggie when she stood up. She avoided his look and smoothed her lab coat. "I'm going to go order the blood work and the chest x-ray. I'll be right back." She felt Will's eyes follow her as she left the room.

That was so out of my comfort zone.

Twenty minutes later, Maggie had the chest film in her hands when she reentered the treatment room. Will stood up, and after handing him the x-ray, she turned to speak directly to Valerie.

"Val, the x-ray shows a very small pneumonia in the lower lobe of your left lung. The good news is that we caught it nice and early. I talked with Renee, and she wants me to start you on a broad-spectrum antibiotic. I'll need a sputum sample to help determine what we're dealing with, and of course, some more blood work. She also wants to postpone your next treatment until the pneumonia is resolved."

Dejection was evident in Valerie's voice. "I was hoping this would be all over by next weekend."

This time Maggie looked at Will for support. He stood by the edge of the bed and spoke quietly. "It will be over very soon, Valerie. You've just hit a bump in the road. It happens to lots of my patients."

"Really?"

"Really. None of them are happy about it, but if you had a chemo treatment right now, the pneumonia would be very difficult to control. That could be disastrous. So, we have to make sure it's gone before your next treatment. Meanwhile, you need to allow Maggie and Renee to do what they do best, and that's making you well enough to finish fighting the cancer, okay?"

"Oh, Will, I'm so sorry. I don't know why I'm so emotional. I feel so stupid. Of course, I'll do whatever you say. Will I have to stay?"

"You're not stupid, Val. You need to understand how difficult this whole thing is. It's never easy being sick, and it sure isn't easy facing something that takes a long time to get over. You're doing fine, sweetheart, just fine. Believe me, I've had some pretty difficult patients. You're doing great," reassured Will. "But you will probably need to be admitted at least for a day or two."

Maggie listened quietly to the tender conversation between Valerie and Will. She saw the way he gently caressed her hand while he talked with her. His words were encouraging, yet truthful. His tone was calming and soothing.

You're something else, dear brother. No wonder your patients adore you.

By the time Valerie was admitted to the medical floor a few hours later, Maggie was exhausted. Sitting at the nurses' station, she stared at the chart opened in front of her, but wrote nothing. A cup of hot coffee slid on the table into her range of vision, and she blinked her eyes when she caught sight of it. She turned her head toward its origin.

"Thought you might need this."

Maggie looked into the thoughtful eyes of Ben Shepherd.

"There's a reason why we don't treat our own family members, Maggie. It takes quite a toll on us, plus sometimes it's difficult to remain objective, and without objectivity we aren't always as efficient as we could be."

Maggie took a deep breath. "I know. You're right, Ben, but Will asked me to see her. I couldn't say no to him. Not this time."

Ben didn't ask her any questions, but simply sat beside her drinking his own cup of coffee. "It looks like it's going to be quiet for a while. You want to get some rest? I'll call if anything comes in."

"You don't mind?"

"Of course not. There's no need for both of us to be sitting here when one of us could be resting." He nodded toward the room set aside for ER physicians.

"Thanks." She picked up her cup of coffee and headed for the sleep room.

Maggie entered the room and closed the door behind her. She made herself comfortable on the narrow bed. She grabbed a thin blanket, pulled it up around her shoulders, and laid her head on the small pillow at the head of the bed. Visions of Valerie's tearful face compelled Maggie to pray fervently for God's touch upon her sister-in-law and brother.

Please, Lord, help Valerie get well. Please help her beat this...

Twenty minutes later, Maggie heard a faint knock on the door. Although sleep had evaded her, the opportunity to lie down had renewed her energy, and she quickly sat up.

"Come in."

"Sorry, Dr. D., but Dr. Shepherd is busy, and we need a doctor in four."

Maggie stifled a yawn. "No problem," she stated as she stretched her arms and stood up. "I'll be right there."

"Belinda Cauldwell?" Maggie read the name off the chart as she entered the treatment room. She looked up at a six-year-old girl sitting on the exam table. Her light brown hair framed a tear-stained oval face. Her left arm was in a makeshift sling. Next to her was a young woman wearing a worried expression on her face. Maggie extended her hand and said, "I'm Dr. Devereaux. What happened?"

"She slipped in the shower and hit her arm on the floor. My neighbor said it might be broken. She's a nurse, so she put it in the sling and told me to bring her in."

"Are you her mother?" Maggie scribbled a few notes on the chart.

"Yes, yes I am. I was just on the other side of the bathroom door when I heard her fall, and then she started crying." The mother's distress was evident on her face. "I can't believe this happened to her. I'm always so careful."

Maggie smiled reassuringly at the mother. "Accidents happen even to the most careful of moms. You did the right thing by bringing her in." She then turned to Belinda. "Hi, Belinda. Can you tell me what happened?"

Big blue eyes stared up at Maggie, but the little girl said nothing. She cradled her arm protectively.

"It's okay, Belinda. You need to tell the doctor what happened, honey," coaxed the mother.

"I fell and hit my arm." Belinda's voice was barely discernible, and her lower lip trembled.

Maggie stooped down and looked directly at the little girl. "Will it be okay if I take this sling off if I promise to be very careful?"

Belinda looked up at her mother and then back to Maggie. The tears in the little girl's eyes threatened to spill over as she nodded her consent.

Maggie glanced at Mrs. Cauldwell. "Did she lose consciousness?"

"I don't think so. I heard the thud, and then she was crying almost immediately."

Maggie turned back to her patient. "Let's do this nice and slow, Belinda. It's the only way I can check your arm. You tell me if it hurts you, and I'll stop, okay?"

Fifteen minutes later, Maggie had sent Belinda and her mother down to x-ray while she hurried to treatment room three.

She grabbed a new pair of latex gloves and put them on as she approached her next patient.

"Mary Gladden?" Maggie read the name off the chart.

"Yes, ma'am. That's me."

Maggie looked up at the middle-aged woman sitting on the edge of the examination table, noting beads of perspiration on her brow. As she flipped the chart open, her patient cried out and bent over clutching her abdomen.

"Mary, I need you to lie back on the bed. I've raised the back, so you just need to move your legs up on the bed and then lean back," instructed Maggie. She helped Mary settle back into the bed. "Can you show me where it's hurting you?"

"Everywhere." She cried out again, holding her abdominal area. Her breathing was in short gasps. "It's the worst thing I've ever felt, and I feel so nauseated." She moaned softly as the pain subsided. "I tried to make it until morning, but it hurt too much."

"Sharp?" Maggie placed her stethoscope near Mary's navel, moved it several times, and listened carefully to each quadrant of her abdomen.

"Yes, and -- ohhh ... I think I'm going to be sick."

Maggie grabbed a disposable emesis bag and held it as Mary bent over in bed.

"I've got it, Dr. D."

Maggie looked up at Claire and nodded her gratitude. She allowed the nurse to take the bag just as Mary retched and vomited a small amount of clear liquid into it. Maggie waited for the wave of nausea to pass before resuming her physical examination.

Finally, Mary leaned back against the bed. "It's easing up a bit, but oh, how it hurts when it comes on. It feels like I'm going to die."

"I'm going to press gently. You tell me if it hurts." Maggie carefully palpated Mary's abdomen, expertly assessing the size of liver and spleen, as well as watching her patient's face for any indication of rebound tenderness. She quickly finished her exam, noting no abnormalities in the lungs or heart sounds, just the intermittent abdominal pain.

"Claire, please give her five milligrams of morphine for the pain and 25 milligrams of Phenergan for the nausea. After that I'd like an x-ray of her abdomen, a CBC, and Chem-12 blood panel." The nurse nodded, took the chart from Maggie, and exited the treatment room.

"Do you know what's wrong with me? Will I be all right?" Another muffled groan escaped Mary's lips as soon as she spoke.

"I'm not sure yet, Mary, but I'd like to have a few tests done first, and then I'll have a better idea of what's going on," stated Maggie. "As soon as the test results come back up, I'll be in to talk with you. If you have any problems before I return, make sure you let Claire or one of the other nurses know."

"Okay, Doctor. Thank you... ohh..." cried Mary just as Claire was returning with the prescribed meds.

Half an hour later, Maggie perused the lab results given to her by the floor clerk.

"Hmm.... alkaline phosphatase is elevated. I need an abdominal ultrasound on Mrs. Gladden." She turned to the clerk. "Can you call radiology? I'd like that ultrasound done as soon as possible." She didn't wait for an answer, but headed for her patient's room.

"Mary, how are you doing?"

Managing a small smile, Mary responded, "A little bit better. It still hurts, but the edge is off."

Maggie stood by the bedside. "You mentioned that eating affected the pain, right?" She waited for her patient's response.

Mary thought for a moment. "I think it's worse after I eat. Maybe not every time, but yes, I think eating does makes it hurt more."

Maggie nodded thoughtfully. "I'm ordering an abdominal ultrasound. Your symptoms are very indicative of gallstones—"

"Gallstones?"

"Well, I don't know positively at this point, but the ultrasound will be more definitive for us. If gallstones are the problem, your gallbladder may need to be removed."

"Removed? You mean surgery?" Mary's eyes widened. "I can't have surgery. I'm a teacher. I can't be out of work that long. My students need me."

Maggie reached out and put a hand on Mary's shoulder. "You won't be much good to them doubled over in pain. I promise we won't perform any surgery unless there is no other viable option. Try not to worry about that right now. Let's wait on the ultrasound, okay?"

Although Mary nodded, Maggie didn't miss the tears in her patient's eyes. As she left the room, she made a mental note to check the O.R. schedule for the next day so she would know whether she could admit Mary Gladden directly from the ER or have her return to the hospital in the next day or so for the inevitable surgery.

"Dr. D, I have the x-ray on Cauldwell."

Maggie looked at the film and saw a clear break on the radial head. *No wonder she's complaining of elbow and wrist pain.*

"Claire, I'm going to need ortho on this one. Can you see who's on call for peds?"

"Will do, Dr. D."

Maggie glanced out at the waiting room and noted it was nearly full. *This is going to be one long night.* Sighing, she went to inform Belinda and her mother that a specialist would be coming to assess the little girl's broken arm.

CHAPTER TWENTY-TWO

"Oh, my goodness! It was awful, Colin! I couldn't believe this reporter. He just came right in to the ER and bombarded me with questions about us. Of course, I didn't answer any of them. Then his photographer held up a camera and tried to take a picture of me. Ben had just come around the corner, and he stuck his hand out in front of the lens and asked him to put the camera away. Then they started yapping about freedom of the press. It took all I had to keep from punching that reporter in the face! I finally had security take them out." Maggie cradled her phone against her shoulder as she reclined on her ivory sofa and popped a grape into her mouth. One of Colin's recordings softly played in the background.

"I would have loved to have seen you. I imagine it was close to what I witnessed when I first saw you," chuckled Colin. "You were quite formidable, as I recall."

Maggie laughed. "Was I that bad? I was just doing my job. Anyway, does it get better or worse?"

"What?"

"The photographers and reporters."

"Oh, that. Well, eventually someone else comes along that is more interesting and their attention is diverted to that poor soul. I haven't been approached in quite a while, so I'm kind of surprised anyone would come there. I'm not really a hot commodity in the entertainment world. Not many gospel singers are, unless of course, we do something that tarnishes our image. Then it's headline news. You know how that goes… someone falls from grace, so to speak, and it's all over the six o'clock news. Christians are fodder for those kinds of predators."

"Wow, that doesn't sound like you." Maggie twirled her hair between her fingers.

"Sorry, love. It just irritates me to think they're bothering you, especially at work," Colin explained. "Sometimes folks forget that Christians are humans, too, and that we live normal lives, facing the same kinds of troubles as they do, yet we're expected to handle it perfectly. When something happens, and we don't, it spreads like wildfire."

"I guess that's the only way to discredit God is through His followers," Maggie reflected.

"That's why our unspoken testimony is so important. You may be the only one in whom someone sees the Lord. While it is the Word of God that saves people, it is our personal lives that present the evidence to an unsaved world that God is real. Being in the world, yet not part of it has to be shown in order for people to realize that Jesus is exactly who He said He is. Only the Son of God changes the hearts and souls of men."

"So, I need to be a bit more… umm… compromising when photographers come into the hospital?"

"Not compromising, just remember that you are an ambassador for Christ all the time. Your actions will say more than your words ever will. Maybe your testimony will lead that reporter to Christ one day or some nurse who may be watching you. You never know how the Holy Spirit will use you."

"I need to do the same with Will, don't I?" The remorseful understanding in Maggie's voice was very clear.

"Maggie, don't ever forget how big God is, and that no matter what we do or don't do, there is no way we can thwart God's plans. He's much bigger than that. If our mistakes… our sins… got in the way of God's work here on earth, nothing would ever get done. Instead, God uses every mistake, every problem that arises to help draw us closer to Him and to accomplish His will. It's God's job to save, not ours. God's Holy Spirit will be the One to open Will's heart to Him--"

"But why is He waiting? Will needs God now, Colin! I've prayed and prayed for Will, but he's still as stubborn as--"

"As his sister?"

A cloud of silence enveloped their conversation.

"Maggie?"

"I'm here." She paused for another moment. "Just thinking."

"About what?"

"How hard it must have been for you." She reached for the cup of coffee on the end table and took a sip. "You know exactly what I'm going through, don't you?"

She heard Colin sigh. "Not exactly, but close. Will will always be your brother. You've got a lifetime to witness to him, and I really do believe God will open your brother's eyes one day, but me, if I'd have lost you back then, I'd probably have lost you forever. It was... difficult to wait on the Lord." His honesty touched Maggie's heart.

Her voice was a whisper. "I'm so sorry, Colin." She swung her legs over and sat upright on the sofa. "I didn't know how much--"

"You don't need to apologize to me, Maggie. It was a learning experience for me, too. I'd go through it all again without reservation. It was all worth it. Just be patient with Will and trust in the Lord with all your heart. God's timing is not our own, and although it's difficult, Scripture tells us in Psalms to 'Wait on the Lord and be of good courage, and He shall strengthen thine heart.'"

"You know, you're a very special man, and I am so glad God brought us together. I can't imagine my life without you."

"You're a pretty special lady yourself, love.

Maggie curled her feet under her once more and reclined against the overstuffed cushions on her couch. She savored the aroma of her coffee as Colin continued.

"How's Valerie doing?"

"She's hit a rough patch, but I think she'll be fine. She should be going home today or tomorrow. She's on antibiotics for the pneumonia, but it's the postponement of the last chemo treatment that's really got her down. I wish there was more I could do for her, but I honestly don't know what that could be. I mean, I pray for her and visit her, but beyond that I don't know how to make it easier for her."

"Maybe you can't, Maggie. Just being there with her probably helps her tremendously. How's Will holding up?"

Maggie shifted on the sofa. "He looks exhausted. I can't get him to go home. If he's not working, he's with her. Not that I blame him. If he wasn't there with her, I would be." She heard Colin sigh once more on the other end of the line.

"Hmm... what would you think if I came out and visited Valerie? Think it might cheer her up a bit? After all, I believe she once said that I was her favorite celebrity."

Maggie smiled as she heard his quiet chuckle. "I wish you really could."

"I can, Maggie. I can be there by tomorrow afternoon, if that's okay with you."

"Are you serious? I thought you weren't going to be here until next month?"

"That was the previous plan. Things have changed, and I think... I think that my family needs me. I know I'm not a doctor, but I once was a deputized nurse, so I can probably help with something. And if not as a nurse, I can certainly sing a few songs to help cheer up Valerie."

Maggie thought back to the time in Santa Molina when Colin had helped her deliver a baby. She had needed a hand in the clinic, and Colin had proven to be an ample substitute nurse during the unexpected delivery. His working knowledge of Spanish had helped one of the local women through the birth of her first child, and that experience had been the catalyst for revealing God's will to Colin in regards to his desire to do more for the Lord with his own life. The event had also indirectly led to an intense soul searching night that finally enabled Maggie to understand what it meant to make Jesus the Lord and Savior of her life.

"There is no way I would tell you no, and unfortunately I cannot say it's entirely unselfish of me," admitted Maggie.

"I understand, love. International relationships are not what they're cracked up to be."

"I agree. I hope you're working on a solution to this problem because I can't see spending the rest of my life missing you," stated Maggie bluntly.

"I am, love. I can tell you I am earnestly working on it as we speak. How does buying you your own jet sound?" His laugh thrilled her heart.

"You are completely insane, Colin Grant. How's that for tabloid fodder?" Maggie giggled, then sobered. "You tell John to fly safely, okay?"

"I will, love. I'll see you tomorrow."

I can't wait." She set her cell phone on the table and lay back down on the sofa, finishing the remaining bunch of grapes in her hand. Despite the joy of knowing that Colin would soon be on his way, her countenance remained downcast. She glanced up at a photo on her mantle of Will and her on his wedding day. Her eyes misted over.

Lord, help me to not be a stumbling block to Will.

Maggie bolted upright in bed. The rapid beating of her heart began to subside as her eyes flitted around the room. Realizing it was the phone that woke her, she reached for it. She blinked hard at the clock on her nightstand, and as she put on her glasses, the digital display came into focus. Three thirty in the morning. "Hello?"

"Hey, Maggie. It's Will."

"Will? What's wrong?"

"Maggie..." His voice was shaking. "They're sending Valerie to the ICU. Can you meet me there? She's really having difficulty breathing."

"What? Yes, of course. I'll be right there." Hanging up the phone as she jumped out of bed, Maggie pulled on a pair of sweats.

What time is it in London? Is he on the plane yet? She looked once more at the clock and mentally tried to calculate the time in England. She punched the speed dial. Colin's voice mail came on.

"Colin, Valerie's being admitted to the intensive care unit. If I'm not home, or don't answer the phone, please meet me at the hospital. Will says she's having a hard time breathing." She hesitated for a moment, and even though she knew she didn't have to add it, she said, "Please pray for her." She ended the call, quickly put on her tennis shoes, and pulled her hair back in a ponytail. Grabbing her keys from off the table, she sprinted out the door to her car. In less than ten minutes, Maggie was on the road to Eastmont Hospital.

"What room?" asked Maggie as she neared the ICU nurses' station.

"Two," came the reply. "Dr. Garrett is there with her and so is Dr. Sommers."

Maggie nodded as she passed the clerk. Without hesitation, she entered Valerie's room, nodded to her brother, glanced at Valerie, who was sleeping, and quietly listened as Renee Sommers talked with Will in hushed tones.

"We need to find out what's going on, Will. She'll probably be here a few days. I know that's not what you want to hear, but it's necessary. I'm afraid the antibiotics haven't had enough time to control the pneumonia yet, and since she's still having some difficulties breathing, I'll feel better if she's here where we can keep an eye on her. I'll order another round of blood cultures to make sure it's not a systemic infection we're facing. We'll keep her on oxygen to ease her body's effort to breathe. Do you have any questions for me right now?" Dr. Sommers waited patiently for him to respond.

Will shook his head. His brow was furrowed, and his eyes focused on his wife. "No, I don't have any questions right now. Thanks, Renee."

"I'm going to write the orders, but I'll be back before I leave." She nodded at Maggie as she left the room.

Valerie coughed several times, but did not open her eyes. Her skin was pale, and her breathing, while not terribly labored, seemed shallow. Maggie glanced up at the cardiac monitor, noting the regular, but slightly elevated rate. She looked over at her brother. His face was drawn, and his eyes never left his wife's face. He was gently caressing Valerie's hand.

Maggie stepped up behind Will and put her hand on his shoulder.

He turned to face his sister. "Thanks for coming."

"What happened?"

Will shook his head. "She was really struggling with her breathing, spiked a temp, and her heart rate skyrocketed..."

"It'll be okay, Will."

"Will it, Maggie? Will it really be okay?" The agony on his face pierced Maggie's heart, and her fear intensified as Will admitted softly. "I don't know if she has the strength to fight this."

For the first time, Maggie didn't know if she could definitively say that Valerie would be fine. She believed the cancer was out of her body, but now she feared the chemotherapy had weakened her body so much that it provided the perfect medium for an opportunistic infection, like pneumonia, to thrive.

Valerie's blood work came back as expected, with elevated white blood cells indicating some type of infectious process. Her arterial blood gases were in the low normal range, and results were pending on both blood and sputum cultures. Even without those, the other lab results pointed toward bacterial pneumonia, and Dr. Sommers placed her on a stronger broad-spectrum antibiotic until the cultures came back identifying the responsible organism and the medication to which it would be most susceptible. While her fever did not subside immediately, it was not rising, and Valerie appeared to be resting comfortably.

Maggie and Will stayed with her throughout the night, and early in the morning Maggie reluctantly called Ben Shepherd to ask if he would cover her shift while she stayed with her family. His willingness to work for her eased her mind, and since she wasn't on the ER roster again until two days later, she took comfort knowing she had plenty of time to stay with Will and Valerie.

Now, at the foot of Valerie's bed, Maggie waited for Will to return with coffee for both of them. Her stomach growled as she heard footsteps behind her.

"How's she doing, love?" The voice was just a whisper, but Maggie recognized the British accent immediately. She whirled around and wrapped her arms around Colin's neck.

"You're here!" She held him close for a moment and allowed his strength to be her own. For the first time since Valerie's admission to the ICU, Maggie allowed herself to cry. "Oh, Colin, I'm so glad you're here!" Slowly composing herself, she kissed him hastily, hugged him again, and then pulled him outside the room. She quickly wiped her tears away.

"She's doing okay. Her lab results indicate bacterial pneumonia, which isn't good, but it could be worse. Her chest x-ray shows that the pneumonia has spread a little since the first x-ray, so the antibiotic has been changed. Hopefully, the bacteria will be more sensitive to this one."

"She looks pretty pale," observed Colin as he moved slightly to peer in through the window.

Maggie merely nodded. "Her cough sounds awful, and she's so weak. She tried to eat this morning, but nothing stayed down."

"Is she aware of what's going on?" He kept his voice low.

Maggie nodded once more. "Yes, but she's been sleeping most of the time."

"She'll be all right, won't she?"

Maggie didn't say anything. She turned to her fiancé, her cinnamon-brown eyes brimming with tears. She whispered softly so that only he could hear her words. "I hope so, Colin. I hope so."

As the main doors of the ICU automatically swung open, Maggie and Colin turned their heads. Will stepped through carrying two cups of coffee.

"Colin?" His eyes widened as he quickly walked to them, handed one cup to Maggie, and then extended his free hand to the singer.

"I was planning to come and cheer up Valerie, but that was before I knew she was so sick. How are you holding up?"

Will rubbed his fingers against his chin and managed a weak smile. "Other than needing a shave, I guess I'm not doing too bad."

Colin nodded. "Is there anything I can do for you?"

"No, unless you'd like to make my rounds for me," Will said as he took a swallow of his coffee.

"I think I'll leave that to you two, but I'm good at running errands. If you need anything, let me know."

"Thanks. I appreciate it very much. I really do." As they entered Valerie's room, Will turned toward his wife and gently took her hand. He bent over and kissed her forehead. She opened her eyes briefly and focused on Will's face. He spoke quietly to her as he tenderly brushed her hair away from her forehead. "Got to make my rounds in a bit, but they'll call me if you need me, and I'll be here in no time."

Valerie nodded slightly. "You look awful." Her voice was feeble, but the concern for her husband was quite clear. She reached up lovingly and stroked the stubble on his chin.

"I've just been a little preoccupied. Nothing a quick shower and shave won't fix." He stepped aside slightly. "You've got a visitor, sweetheart."

Colin moved closer to the head of the bed. He leaned over close to Valerie and whispered, "Hi, love. What's this I hear about you being sick?"

Valerie moved her head toward the voice and focused her gaze on the clear blue eyes of the British singer. Her weak smile broadened, and she reached out for his hand. "Colin..." Her voice trailed off.

"Don't try to speak, love. I just wanted you to know that I was here, and I'll be here until you're better and out of this place. I have grand plans for taking my biggest fan out to dinner, okay?"

Her lips parted into a small smile, and then she slowly closed her eyes and nodded, her smile fading from her face as she tried to breathe through a coughing episode.

When she finished, Colin took her hand in his and said, "Maggie told me that you weren't feeling too good, so I thought I'd come by and try and cheer you up. Listen, love, promise me you'll do exactly what the doctors tell you to do, but more importantly, I want you to remember we're praying for you and that God is in complete control..."

Maggie stiffened as Colin continued to speak quietly to Valerie. She looked up slightly at Will through her thick, black lashes. *Please, please don't say anything Will...*

Will crossed his arms, but remained stoic and silent while Colin continued his chat with Valerie. His eyes narrowed as Colin began to pray with her.

Colin's voice was barely above a whisper, but Maggie could hear his words without any difficulty. She closed her eyes and silently agreed with him as he petitioned the Lord on behalf of Valerie.

"Father, we lift Your name on high and give You our praise and worship. Lord, we don't pretend to understand all that You allow in our lives, but we do know that You are the Almighty, the King of kings, and Lord of lords. Father, we come into Your presence asking for Your help. We know You've started the healing process in Valerie, but now she's facing another challenge. We ask for Your restoring touch on her body, particularly her lungs, Lord. Please give the doctors great wisdom as they minister to her physical needs, and give us the same as we tend to her emotional and spiritual needs.

"We ask for Your Holy Spirit to comfort her heart and give her the strength to endure through this difficult time. Be with Maggie and Will as well, and provide for them the encouragement that they need. Your Word tells us that 'all things work together for good to them that love God, to them who are the called according to His purpose.' Work this to Your good, Father. In Jesus' name, I pray. Amen."

Despite her weakened state, Valerie's eyes were radiant when she opened them, and she reached a hand up to caress Colin's cheek. She whispered feebly, "Thank you for praying for me, Colin..." Her voice faded, and her eyes closed, but the slight smile that remained confirmed the encouragement she received from the prayer made on her behalf.

"I think we need to let Val rest."

Surprised at the curtness in the voice, Colin looked up at Will. "Of course." He turned back to Valerie. "I promise I'll come as often as they let me." He stood, took Maggie's hand, and together they walked out of the room while Will remained behind with his wife.

CHAPTER TWENTY-THREE

Maggie and Colin walked down to the hospital cafeteria to grab a bite to eat before returning to the ICU. It was midafternoon, and the tables were empty.

After making their selections, they sat in a secluded corner of the lunchroom, bowed their heads, and prayed for their food and Valerie.

As she unwrapped a turkey club sandwich, Maggie asked, "How long will you be here?"

Colin took a sip of tea. "Indefinitely."

Maggie gave him a puzzled look, her sandwich in mid-bite.

"I told Gary to put things on hold until I get back. I told him there was a family emergency, and I was needed here. I am needed here, right?"

"Of course, you are. I always need you," whispered Maggie. She set the sandwich down without taking a bite. "I'm so much better with you here. Remind me to thank your manager."

"Valerie looks pretty sick." Colin took a bite from his chef salad.

Maggie nodded. "She is, but she should start responding to the treatment. She still has the pneumonia, but her fever's not rising. Hopefully, she'll be out of ICU in a day or so."

"That'll be-"

"Don't ever do that again!" Both of them looked up as Will entered the cafeteria. His eyes were narrowed, and his angry voice shook as he spoke. His eyes bore down on Colin.

Colin raised an eyebrow. "Do what?"

"Don't preach to my wife!"

Stunned, Maggie admonished her brother. "Will!"

"I mean it! If she gets well, it won't be because of her faith in some cold and callous deity or someone's pathetic prayers. It will be because of good sound medical care from her doctors and nurses!" His face reddened as he continued his stifled tirade. "She doesn't need you or your God!"

Maggie's eyes widened in disbelief, and as she opened her mouth to speak, she started to rise, but Colin stood first and motioned for Maggie to remain seated. He faced Will and spoke in a firm voice.

"Will, I don't doubt for a moment that the people caring for Valerie are doing the best they can, but-"

"She's sick, Colin! Why can't you understand that? She doesn't need a preacher; she needs her doctors and nurses. You and Maggie... you just don't get it. Cancer isn't some mystical ailment that can be treated with some spiritual words and magical powers. It's an actual illness with tried and true treatments that are designed to combat the disease in her body. She doesn't need God. She's got-"

"You?" Colin challenged firmly. His sky blue eyes never left the narrowed eyes of Will. "And where exactly has that gotten her? In ICU?" The intensity in his voice slammed into Will.

The oncologist's heated glare drilled into Colin. "Just leave." Will turned abruptly to exit the room.

"That's not going to happen, Will." Colin remained standing quietly by his chair.

Maggie held her breath as she watched the scenario being played out in front of her. Her eyes darted from her fiancé, to her brother, then back to Colin.

Will froze at the threshold of the cafeteria entrance. His breathing was deep and rapid; his fists were clenched at his sides.

Colin walked toward him. "This isn't God's fault, Will." His calm demeanor defused some of Will's rage.

A fleeting moment of despair crossed Will's face, betraying his angry glare. "How can you even say that?" His voice broke.

"Can we go somewhere and talk ... just you and me?"

Maggie watched her brother and Colin disappear into the corridor. She sat, petrified in her seat, and fear began to envelope her. *No! 'What time I am afraid, I will trust in Thee.' Lord, help him... help Colin help Will. Please...* Her tears fell unfettered as she continued to stare at the cafeteria entrance and petition the Lord on behalf of her brother and fiancé.

Colin and Will walked into a nearby waiting room. No one was inside, and Colin silently thanked the Lord for providing a quiet and private place for them to talk.

Will immediately sat down, rested his elbows on his knees, and dropped his head into his hands. His angry tirade was over.

Colin pulled up a chair and sat opposite the tortured doctor.

"Will, I'm not going to pretend I know how you feel because there's no way that I can. However, I do know you're getting angry with the wrong person. God didn't make Valerie sick. He allowed it to happen, that's true, but don't think for one moment that diminishes His love for her."

Will raised tortured eyes to look at Colin. "Love? You're telling me that God loves her when He lets her suffer like this? You can't be serious? She hasn't been able to eat anything without throwing it right back up; she can hardly breathe without being racked by a sickening cough; she's got some kind of pneumonia that we can't get a handle on, Colin, on top of being immune-compromised... that's your idea of love?"

"My idea of love is a God who sacrificed His only Son so that our sins could be forgiven, and we could have eternal life with Him in heaven. Cancer, heart attacks, strokes... those are all a result of sin, not God. He hates it as much as you do, Will. That's why He sent His Son Jesus Christ, the only cure for sin," began Colin.

"Really? Well, Valerie got saved, trusted God, and look what it got her. She didn't get any better, in fact, she got worse. How exactly do you explain that?" His accusatory tone was impossible to miss.

Colin shifted in his seat. *Father, give me wisdom. I need the right words to say to Will.* He took a deep breath and continued. "I won't speculate on the mind of God. I don't know why this is happening, but I know that God is still in control." He paused once more for a moment, and then added. "Even Christians get sick and die, Will."

"She not's going to die! I won't let her!"

"How are you going to do that?" asked Colin. His voice was controlled and strong, yet compassionate. He patiently waited for Will to respond.

Will's clenched fists slowly relaxed. No words came, and he diverted his grief-stricken stare from Colin's eyes.

Colin chose his next words carefully. "I didn't come here to preach to Valerie, or you, for that matter. I came to support you and Valerie and Maggie. If you don't want my support, that's fine. If you forbid me from visiting Valerie, well, I suppose I'll honor that, but I guarantee that I will *not* stop praying for your wife, your sister, or you. Moreover, despite the fact that it looks like God doesn't care about what is happening, I assure you He does. He cares more about Valerie than any of us can."

Will's anguish continued to envelope his rugged facial features. "Why do you keep on? Why can't you just let it rest?" As he exhaled in exasperation, he clenched his fists again.

Colin took his stand and spoke boldly. "Because I know God answers prayer. The Bible tells us that 'We have not because we ask not.' I plan to keep on asking for complete healing for Valerie until He tells me to stop praying."

"Now He *talks* to you?"

Colin sighed and shook his head. "No, God doesn't talk to me, Will, but--"

"But what? You have some secret connection to Him? Some way the two of you communicate with one another?"

"As a matter-of-fact, He does communicate with me." Colin struggled to maintain his composure despite Will's defensive mockery. "Through His Word."

"Of course, He does." Will stood up and walked toward a window. His hands were now in his pants pockets, and his back was to Colin.

The silence in the waiting room settled like a thick fog. Will didn't move. Colin waited and prayed.

When Will finally spoke, his voice was filled with fearful resignation. "I'm an oncologist, Colin. This is my specialty. There isn't anything new in the field of cancer that I haven't researched, and I still don't know what to do to guarantee my wife won't die. I have done everything humanly possible to help her beat this. There is nothing more that anyone, including God, can do."

"You're wrong about that, Will."

Will turned around to face Colin. "What can God possibly do that I haven't already done? Can you tell me that?"

Colin thought carefully for a moment. "He can offer hope."

"Hope?" Will's skepticism penetrated the room, but his eyes never left Colin's face.

"Yes. You've already said you're out of options," reiterated Colin. "But God isn't. He has plenty of options left. He can still heal Valerie, and that's what I'm praying for."

Will shook his head, but said nothing.

Colin continued boldly. "Maybe He'll work through her doctors and nurses; maybe He'll raise her up on His own. I don't know, but I do know that all things *are* possible with God. My hope is in my faith, and I choose to believe that God will heal Valerie in His time. Nothing is going to change my mind on that," affirmed Colin.

Will sighed loudly. "That doesn't surprise me." His shoulders slumped as he walked toward the door. "I need to get back to Valerie." He stopped midway over the threshold. His stoic stance could not mask the sorrow in his voice as he said, "In spite of our inability to see eye-to-eye on this... I do... I do appreciate you being here."

"I wish the circumstances were different."

"Me, too." He moved into the corridor, then paused for a moment, looking back at the singer. "I'm sorry, Colin. I know we don't agree—"

"Forgiven and forgotten." Colin walked toward Will and reached for his hand.

Will hesitated briefly before taking Colin's hand and shaking it. "I know Valerie's glad you're here, and despite what I said earlier, I would never stop you from seeing her."

"Thank you, Will." Colin drew in a deep breath and exhaled slowly as he watched Will head toward the elevators. *Thank You Lord for defusing this situation. Please work in Will's heart. He needs You so badly.* Colin stood there for a moment, hands in his pockets, and offered another silent prayer for his future brother-in-law before turning and heading back to the cafeteria.

Maggie's hopeful eyes noticed the faint smile on Colin's face when he saw her still sitting at the table. She held her breath as he pulled out his chair and sat down. She reached for his hand. "I was praying for you."

"Thank you, love. God's working in his heart, Maggie. I believe that with every fiber of my being. I don't know how much sank in, but at least he listened to me, and by the time we were done, he wasn't angry with me anymore... I think." He took Maggie's hands into his own. "He's scared, Maggie, very scared. Will's scared he's going to lose Valerie."

"Lose her?" Maggie raised an eyebrow and began to speak heatedly. "She's not going to die. She's not terminal, and pneumonia can be treated with medication. She won't die!"

"Hey," Colin reached for Maggie's hand. "Calm down, love."

Maggie's eyes teared up. "Oh, Colin. I don't want her to die."

"No one's said anything about dying."

Maggie closed her eyes tightly for a moment, and then opened them. She fought to regain her composure. "No, but I think that's what's on everyone's mind. Oh, Colin, if I'm this scared, and I'm trying to trust God, how in the world is Will handling it?"

"Not very well, I'm afraid."

"How is he ever going to find God if something does happen to Valerie?"

Colin looked at the woman he loved with compassion in his heart. "Maggie, nothing is impossible with God. It may look completely hopeless to us, but God still is on the throne. He's going to take care of Valerie. And as for Will, remember, God is not willing that any should perish. He loves Will more than you do. Trust God, Maggie, and keep praying."

Maggie nodded, her eyes brimming with unshed tears for her brother. "I'm scared for him, Colin. He's so angry with God right now. What's it going to take for him to realize that God loves him?"

"I don't know, love... but God does."

They sat in silence for a few minutes, holding hands, each lost in their own personal thoughts. Suddenly, the hospital loudspeaker shattered their quiet reverie.

"Code blue, ICU. Code blue, ICU."

Maggie gasped involuntarily. "No! Not Val! It just can't be! Please, Lord, not Val!"

Bolting up, they rushed out of the cafeteria and headed for the elevators. Two minutes later, as they neared the ICU, Colin grabbed Maggie's arm just outside the double doors leading into the unit. He whirled her around to face him.

"Let's pray." Maggie started to pull away from Colin. She looked at him, then the double door entrance to the ICU, and then back again at Colin. His eyes met hers, and he waited, not pulling her, but not releasing her. Maggie exhaled slowly and nodded her head. She allowed him to draw her closer to him, and as he bowed his head, Maggie followed his example.

The sound of his voice had a profound calming effect on Maggie, and she willed herself to fully concentrate on Colin's prayer.

"Father God, please be with the doctors and nurses in the ICU right now fighting to save the life of this patient. Give them wisdom and guidance to do whatever is necessary to save this life. May your perfect will be done. In the name of your Son, Jesus, I pray. Amen."

Maggie drew in a deep breath, squeezed Colin's hand tightly, and together, they entered the ICU. Maggie quickly scanned the unit, and then visibly relaxed when she saw the frenzied activity on the far side of the ICU, away from Valerie's room.

"Thank you, Lord, for it not being Valerie," murmured Colin as they neared Valerie's room. "Where's Will?" His urgent whisper prompted Maggie to scan the unit.

"Probably over there seeing if he can do anything to help with the code," whispered Maggie, nodding her head toward the opposite side of the ICU unit.

"Should you go?"

Maggie tilted her head, narrowed her eyes, and scrutinized the activity in the far-off room. "No, Ben's there, and Will. Plus, I can see another doctor, so they've got enough help."

They quietly entered Valerie's room and walked over to her bedside. She slept soundly, only the rhythmic sounds of the cardiac monitor filled the room.

Fifteen minutes later, Will stepped into Valerie's room. He managed a meager smile for Maggie and Colin before sitting down close to Valerie. He reached for her hand and held it as he spoke softly to the couple. "He didn't make it. Forty-two years old. Left a wife and two kids."

Colin raised an eyebrow and looked up. "From what?"

"Probably pulmonary embolus... blood clot to the lungs. At least that's what his attending thinks. Came in after a car accident. Fractured his left femur... upper leg and a multitude of ribs. Had surgery this morning." Will was downcast. "Everything looked great. Then, just like that--" He snapped his finger. "He was gone."

Maggie's heart ached for her brother. "I'm sorry, Will."

He regarded Maggie for a moment, and then stated grimly, "You just never know, do you?"

Maggie glanced at Colin, then back to her brother. "No, you never do."

Will glanced at his watch. Five minutes to midnight. Things were quiet in the ICU. Only the muted beeping of the cardiac monitors echoing through the halls interrupted the silence. Maggie and Colin had left to get dinner as soon as Will had returned from his evening rounds. He had been sitting beside Valerie's bed since then. He lifted his eyes to the overhead monitor and mentally assessed the numbers on the screen. He watched Valerie's chest rise and fall with each breath she took. Her eyes were closed, and she slept restlessly, her slumber frequently broken by her fits of coughing. Her petite frame seemed lost in the tubings and wires attached to her.

He had jotted the results of her latest lab values on a blank prescription form in his pocket, and he stared at them once more, hoping he had misread them. They showed no improvement. In fact, her white blood cell count had risen, and for the first time Will allowed his mind to wander to the possibility of life without Valerie. He reached for her hand, careful not to disturb the intravenous line by which the potent antibiotics were entering her circulatory system.

"I love you so much, Valerie," whispered Will. His voice broke, and he took a deep breath as he stared at his wife. "I can't live without you." He fought to control his emotions, but his fears overwhelmed him, and hot tears spilled from his dark brown eyes onto the sheets of Valerie's bed. An oppressive despair seemed to grip its icy fingers around his heart.

Finally, Will cast a weary glance upward. He fought to control his fear, but his whispered voice was low and shaky. "Why are You doing this? What kind of a god are You anyway? If You're as great as everyone says You are, prove it. Why don't You just heal her?" He closed his eyes once more, rubbed his forehead, and then resumed his indicting conversation with God. "If You love her, really love her, like Maggie and Colin say You do, why don't You make her well?"

He dropped his head into his hands. "What do You want from me? I've run out of options. Her fever isn't coming down, and the pneumonia's worse. If she doesn't show any signs of improvement, she may have to be intubated and put on a ventilator. Is that what You want?"

The desperation in his voice faded as he leaned back into his chair and stared at the small form of his wife. Hopelessness besieged him, and Will's angst penetrated his husky voice as he pleaded once more, "What do You want from me?"

He closed his eyes, and the sorrow in his heart threatened to engulf him. He stared blankly at the lab results he held in his hand. A few moments passed before he realized he was not looking at numbers, but rather letters. His mind numbly tried to fathom what he was looking at as he read the handwriting.

Job 37:14 - Hearken unto this, O Job: stand still, and consider the wondrous works of God.

"Will?" He recognized the muted voice of his sister.

Will quickly folded the paper and put it in his pocket before turning his head toward the door. Maggie entered the room hesitantly. Colin lingered behind her, stopping just inside the doorway. Will nodded his head to the couple before returning his attention to Valerie.

"No change?"

Will shook his head. "No. Latest lab values don't show any signs of improvement."

Maggie moved behind Will and leaned down to embrace him. "You need to eat something, Will. You've got to stay strong," she whispered.

Again, he nodded his head. "I know. I just can't leave her right now."

"We brought you something." She took a bag of fast food and a cup of coffee that Colin held out for her and set them on the bedside table. "Take a break. Get up and walk around a bit. We'll stay until you come back."

"Thank you, but no. I'm going to stay with her."

Maggie nodded. "Okay. We'll be back in the morning, unless you'd like us to stay with you."

"No. You go on home."

"If there is any change—"

"I'll call you." Will didn't turn around but maintained all of his attention on his wife.

Maggie reluctantly stepped toward the door and looked back at her brother. As she spoke, tears traced down her cheeks. "We'll be praying for her, Will."

His sigh was quite audible. "I know, Maggie, I know. Thanks."

Alternating between periods of sleep and wakefulness, Will decided he needed a cup of coffee. He checked his watch. Four-fifteen in the morning. A hush had descended upon the ICU, and the nurses were noiselessly making their rounds. He stood, stretched, and rubbed the back of his neck. Throughout the night, a nurse had been in and out assessing Valerie's status, but there had been no change. Stifling a yawn, Will walked to the nurses' station.

"Mind if I grab a cup of coffee?" he asked to a nurse writing in a chart.

"Not at all, Dr. Garrett. There should be a fresh pot in there." She motioned to a room off to the side of the nurses' station.

Will walked into the staff lounge and rummaged through a few cabinets until he found a clean Styrofoam cup. He poured a cup of thick black coffee and sampled it.

"This'll keep me up for days," he murmured as he headed back to Valerie's room.

"Dr. Garrett?"

Will stopped and turned toward the nurse.

"I have the latest lab values for Mrs. Garrett. Nothing's really changed, but I thought you might like to see them before I attach them to the chart." She handed Will the preliminary lab results.

"Thanks. I appreciate it." He set the cup down, reached in his pocket, pulled out the folded sheet of paper, and quickly jotted down the numbers below the first set he had written earlier. He hesitated for a moment, and then turned the paper over. He reread the message.

Job 37:14 - Hearken unto this, O Job: stand still, and consider the wondrous works of God.

"Seriously? What are You planning on doing? Walk on water?" Will scowled and shoved the paper into his pocket. He walked into Valerie's room.

He stood by the monitor, mentally interpreting the numbers that flashed across the screen as he sipped his coffee.

"I'd give anything to have some of that coffee."

Will whirled around at the sound of his wife's voice. "Val?"

She raised her eyebrows slightly and managed a weak smile. "Are you expecting someone else?" She reached a hand out. "How about it? One sip?"

Will stared at her for a moment and then shook his head as if to shake off the mantle of disbelief. He struggled to accept what he was hearing and seeing. Moving quickly to hand her his coffee, he helped her bring it to her lips. "Just a little, sweetheart. I'm sure I shouldn't be giving this to you."

"Who's going to argue with *you*?" Valerie smiled softly as she took a small sip. Her brow furrowed as she perused his face. "You don't look so good, Will."

"Me? I'm fine. How do *you* feel?" He took the cup from her and set it on the bedside table. His bewildered eyes studied her serene face.

"Actually, I feel pretty good. It doesn't hurt when I breathe, so that's good, right?" She lifted her eyebrows and met Will's puzzled look with clear hazel eyes.

"Yes, it's very good," he stammered. He pulled his stethoscope out from his jacket pocket. "Let me listen to you. Can you turn on your side for me?" He moved closer, placed his stethoscope on her back, and maneuvered it around while listening intently. Valerie took several deep breaths as Will carefully assessed each lobe of her lungs.

"Well?"

"I don't know how you did it, but your lungs sound clear. We'll need an x-ray to be sure."

Valerie sighed with a smile. "Good doctoring, I guess!" Her eyes twinkled happily, and she reached for Will.

He leaned over her, kissed her tenderly, and spoke lovingly. "I'd like to think so." He stood and brushed her hair from her face. "No relapses, okay?"

"I will do my best." She held tightly to his hand. "I don't suppose I can go home with you?"

Will shook his head. "No, sweetheart. I'm afraid not. You've got to get a clean bill of health from Renee first."

Valerie nodded her understanding. "Can I eat? I'm starved."

"I'll see what I can do. Don't go anywhere, okay?"

Valerie laughed softly. "I promise I'll stay right here."

As Will left her room, he felt the crumpling of paper in his pocket as he put his stethoscope in it. He reached in and pulled out the folded paper on which Valerie's lab results were written. Once again, he carefully unfolded it and turned it over.

Job 37:14 - Hearken unto this, O Job: stand still, and consider the wondrous works of God.

He hesitated for a moment, then quickly crushed the paper in his hand and tossed it into a nearby wastebasket.

CHAPTER TWENTY-FOUR

It was shortly after seven a.m. when Maggie and Colin hurriedly walked into the ICU to find Valerie sitting up in her bed.

"Maggie! Colin! I'm so glad you're here! Sorry, I've been so much trouble." She smiled timidly. "Will says he can't believe the change that has happened overnight! I'm doing so much better! How could I possibly do worse? No fever since about four this morning! I may even be moved to the floor sometime today."

"They're putting her on the floor?" Colin cast a puzzled look at Maggie.

She stifled a snicker. "No. She's being moved out of the ICU and to the *medical* floor."

"Oh," acknowledged Colin as he turned to Valerie. "How are you feeling, love?" He leaned over and kissed her forehead.

"Tired, but it doesn't hurt at all to breathe. I know the oxygen is helping, but I think I really do feel a little better." She smiled warmly at them. "Thank you for your prayers. I really believe God heard you and answered you. And thank you for everything else you've done. Will told me everything."

"*Everything*?" Maggie raised her eyebrows and looked at Colin.

"Yes, I believe he did. He was quite a handful from what he told me. Said he didn't understand how you two could forgive him, but he was glad you did. So am I." Unable to go on, she paused for a moment and took a deep breath. "I love you both so much. You won't give up on him, will you?"

Colin smiled and shook his head. "Absolutely not. We've just agreed to disagree for the time being, but God never gives up on us, Val. It may take some time, but God's will will prevail."

"Doesn't sound like I have much of a chance, does it?"

Colin winced as he turned slowly to face Will. Maggie involuntarily held her breath as she awaited her brother's reaction.

"You eavesdropping, dear?" Valerie chided her husband with a slight smile.

Will reached her bedside in three strides, leaned over, and kissed her soundly on the lips. "Not intentionally, but now that I know you're all plotting against me--"

"Not *against* you, Will. We're definitely not against you." Maggie said defensively as she held tightly to Colin's hand.

Will gestured as if surrendering. "I know, I know. It's only my soul you want, but I'm not going down without a fight," he teased.

"Funny, I think that's what your sister said," remarked Colin.

Maggie's mouth dropped open, and in mock irritation, she elbowed him in his ribs. "If this is your idea of how to win my brother over-"

"Just telling it like it is, love."

Will chuckled. "Don't worry, Maggie. I won't hold it against him. You can still marry him."

Maggie lowered her eyes and whispered to herself, "As if you could stop me." She felt Colin's hand squeeze her own and looked up at his adoring eyes. Her cheeks warmed, and she smiled as she lowered her gaze from his handsome face.

Two weeks later, Valerie was back at work. Although she was only working part time, she felt her strength returning every day and knew it wouldn't be long before she would be back on a full time basis. Today had been slow, and Valerie was preparing to leave when a call came via the paramedic relay station. In response to the call, she had quickly prepped treatment room one and now awaited the arrival of the paramedics with the young boy who had been hit by a car. As soon as they arrived, Valerie fell into step with them as they wheeled the gurney into the emergency room.

"Car versus bicycle. Kid rode out in front of the vehicle from his driveway. Eyewitnesses say he flew about ten feet or so. Nonresponsive at the scene. Multiple abrasions. No obvious injuries. Kid was wearing a helmet. Vitals are stable and within normal limits. Pupils are round and reactive. Mom and Dad followed in their own car. They ought to be here any minute." The paramedic handed Valerie the field chart. "Mind if we restock while we're here?"

"Not at all. Thanks, Josh." She glanced at the chart. "Michael Pennington." She turned her attention to the unconscious child on the examination bed. Valerie attached electrodes to the boy's chest and assessed his respiratory status. As she finished her preliminary exam, Ben Shepherd walked in, glanced at the cardiac monitor, and picked up the boy's chart. Valerie stood at the opposite side of the bed awaiting the doctor's orders.

"Let's get a portable x-ray up here. Keep the cervical collar on until x-rays are back. I want to make sure there's no spinal column damage. I'll also need a CBC, chem-12 panel, and a baseline EKG."

Ben used a penlight to check the boy's pupillary reactions. "Michael? Michael, can you hear me? Sluggish, but reactive.

Let's get a CT scan of the head, too, Val. And we'll need Dr. Sorenson on this."

Ben gently removed some of the boy's clothing to look for further injury. He deftly felt the arms and legs for any indications of fractures. He palpated the boy's skull. *At least he had a helmet on!*

Suddenly, Michael's body began to shake violently. Valerie moved against the bed, preventing the child from falling off the side with the rail down.

Although he was just a child, the strength of the seizure required both of them to protect the child from injury. Then just as quickly as it had begun, the seizure stopped. Ben reassessed Michael's respiratory and cardiac status. Satisfied with the results, he looked up at Valerie. "Can you see if the parents are here? I need to find out about his medical history."

Ben continued to examine the boy. "Michael? Michael? Can you open your eyes, buddy?" The young boy remained nonresponsive.

"Dr. Shepherd?"

Ben looked up to see Valerie with a man and woman. He stood upright. "Mr. and Mrs. Pennington?"

"How is he, Doctor?" Mr. Pennington asked as his wife stood silently by his side wiping her eyes with a tissue.

"He's still unconscious. I've ordered several tests that will give us more information. Dr. Sorenson is on his way down. He's a neurologist. Is Michael on any medications?" Ben waited for their reply.

"I don't believe so." Mr. Pennington looked at his wife. She shook her head. "No," he restated. "Is he going to be okay?"

"We're going to do everything we can for him, I assure you." He paused to allow them time to absorb all that was happening. "Michael had a seizure a few minutes ago. Has he ever had one before?"

The father's eyes opened wide in alarm. "No. Never. Why did he have one?"

"A seizure?" Mrs. Pennington gripped her husband's arm. "Is something wrong with his brain?"

"Seizures are often associated with traumatic head injuries like the one Michael had from this accident. Dr. Sorenson is one of Eastmont's finest neurologists. He'll examine Michael, and then be able to answer some of your questions as well as determine the best course of treatment for your son."

Mr. Pennington put his arm around his wife. "Do you believe in prayer, Doctor?"

Ben looked at Michael's parents and nodded his head. "Yes, I do, Mr. Pennington."

Both parents smiled for the first time. "Then promise us you'll pray for Michael as you treat him. We'll be praying for both of you, Doctor, that God will give you wisdom to help our son, and that His healing touch will restore Michael to perfect health."

Intrigued by the request, Valerie looked into the serene eyes of Michael's mother and listened as Ben promised, "I will, Mrs. Pennington. I assure you I will be praying for Michael." True to his word, Ben whispered a prayer as he reexamined the little boy in treatment room one.

Later, as Valerie watched the orderly wheel Michael to the pediatric intensive care unit under the careful eye of Dr. Sorenson, she whispered her own prayer for Michael before retreating to the staff lounge for a long awaited cup of coffee. Opening the door, she saw Ben holding a steaming cup of coffee and putting the pot back in its place. "Would you mind pouring a second cup?" she asked as she sat down on the sofa.

He turned at her and grinned. "You got it." He poured another cup and walked it over to her. "Thanks for your help, Val." He sat down beside her. "You okay?"

"A little tired, but other than that, I'm fine." She took the cup that Ben held out for her. "Tell me something, Ben."

His eyebrows raised questioningly as he sat next to her. "Yes?"

"Why do you think God allows some of our patients to live and others He lets die?"

Ben sipped his coffee before answering. "I don't think I have the answer for that one, Valerie. It's difficult sometimes to understand why He allows so much suffering and death, but we need to remember that we live in a world of sin, and with that sin came a heavy price. It wasn't God's choice to have a world like this; it was man's decision to go against his Creator."

"But He could stop it."

"Yes, He could. So, that's the part I can't really explain. I do know that everything that He allows to happen somehow brings glory to Him, but we don't always recognize that part. For instance, take our patient just now. Why doesn't God just raise him up? I haven't the faintest idea, but I know that whatever happens, God has a reason, and ultimately, it will be used for the glory of God. Maybe to lead someone to Christ. Only God knows. We're just called to trust Him."

Valerie nodded. "Do you believe prayer makes a difference?"

"Without a doubt." Ben took another sip of coffee. "Prayer makes me a better doctor because I believe the Spirit of God guides me as I make decisions and carry out treatments."

"But sometimes He doesn't answer the prayer." Her voice was solemn, and she leaned back into the cushions of the well-worn couch.

"God always answers prayer, Valerie, but sometimes it's not the way we want Him to," responded Ben.

"What do you mean?"

"Well, God can say yes, no, or maybe. That's the trust part, I think. We have to trust Him to answer in the way that is best for us. We need to remember that He never makes a mistake, and if He says 'No,' there's a divine reason."

"I prayed for that little boy today."

"That's a good thing, Valerie. Don't ever be afraid to pray."

CHAPTER TWENTY-FIVE

"Oh Will, it feels so good to be done! No more chemo, no more radiation! I feel so… so free!" Valerie called out from the kitchen.

"I agree, sweetheart. I don't need to go through that again," confessed Will as he reclined in the living room. He audibly exhaled. *I can't believe it's been almost ten months since that night when Val found the lump.*

"Hey, I really want to go to church this weekend with Maggie. Do you mind?"

"Really?" asked Will, hoping for a negative reply.

Valerie walked out from the kitchen with a glass of orange juice in her hand. "Yes, I do." She took a sip of the juice. "And it's okay with me if you stay home. You don't have to go if you don't want to."

Will frowned. "You'd go without me?"

"It's not a big deal. I've been cleared for everything. Work, driving…" She poked him playfully in the chest. "… everything. So, if you don't want to go with me, I can go to church by myself and then meet you back here afterwards for lunch."

He shook his head. "No. I'll go with you. It's just not my favorite thing to do on my weekend off."

"Well, I think I'd like to show off my curls!" She ran her fingers through the short, soft brown curls beginning to sprout on her head. "You have no idea how liberating it is to not have to wear a hat anymore!" She shook her head several times, but the curls were so short, they refused to bounce.

Will couldn't help but smile at his wife. The decision to forego the last chemo treatment signified her battle with the cancer was complete. Although initially scheduled for four courses of chemotherapy, the pneumonia had created a time interval between the third and fourth treatments that was too great to be of any great benefit in fighting the disease, so Renee Sommers had cancelled the last appointment. Once reassured that omitting the last treatment would not be detrimental to her odds for survival, Valerie embraced life enthusiastically and that included her new life in Christ.

"I know how you feel about this, Will, so that's why I'm not going to ask you to come with me when I go, but I need to go. I can't explain it, but I just have to be there. Of course, I'd love to have you with me, but I understand if you don't want to go to church." Valerie plopped down beside him on the sofa.

Will sighed once more. "I don't want you to go alone. It's not because I don't think you can't drive there. It's because I want to be with you. It's only an hour or so, right?"

Valerie smiled affectionately at her husband. "Yes. It's only an hour or so."

He tilted his head to one side and eyed his wife. "You're really enjoying this, aren't you?"

"What I am enjoying is being married to the sweetest man I know who is so willing to do whatever I want to make me happy." She pulled him to her and kissed him. "And you do make me happy, Will." She jumped up to take her empty glass into the kitchen.

He watched her disappear into the next room, and then remained staring at the empty door space. *I love you so much, Valerie, but I don't understand your need for God. Why can't you be satisfied with just me?*

Sunday came too soon for Will, but he kept his word and accompanied Valerie to church. They arrived just before the morning worship service and met Maggie and Colin in the foyer.

"I love your hair!" exclaimed Maggie as she reached out and touched Valerie's curls.

Will took Colin's extended hand and shook it. His guilt regarding his outburst with Colin refused to dissipate even though the two men had talked about it at length, and Colin had forgiven him without hesitation. The awkwardness was still there on his part, but Will knew that there were no hard feelings between the two of them, so he greeted his future brother-in-law with a smile and walked with him into the sanctuary, following Maggie and Valerie.

Sitting near the front, Will settled in between his wife and sister. He draped his arm on the back of the pew behind Valerie as the choir stood to sing their first song.

> *Years I spent in vanity and pride, caring not my Lord was crucified,*
> *Knowing not it was for me He died at Calvary.*
> *Mercy there was great, and grace was free,*
> *Pardon there was multiplied to me,*
> *There my burdened soul found liberty at Calvary!*

> *Oh, the love the drew salvation's plan, oh, the grace that brought it down to man,*
> *Oh, the mighty gulf that God did span at Calvary.*
> *Mercy there was great, and grace was free,*
> *Pardon there was multiplied to me,*
> *There my burdened soul found liberty at Calvary!*

Will sat with his arm around Val, listening to the lyrics of the song. *Who in his right mind would actually sacrifice his own son? And for what?* His mind wandered as the congregation sang a song, and then the choir director began to pray. Will glanced over at Colin and Maggie whose heads were bowed, and then he cast a furtive look at his wife. Her hands were clasped together in her lap, and she sat very still with her head bowed and eyes closed. *Why is this so important to them? Colin, I can understand, but Maggie and Val?*

His mind came back to the present when Pastor Jesse McClellan moved to the pulpit.

"Good morning!" His smile broadened as he scanned the congregation. "As always it is good to be together in the Lord's house to worship and praise our Lord and Savior, Jesus Christ. You know, it's interesting how the Lord works. I had been preparing a particular message this week, one I fully intended to bring to you this morning, but yesterday, the Lord directed me to a topic completely different from what I was studying. So, I spent the better part of yesterday working on an entirely new message that I believe God's Holy Spirit is leading me to deliver this morning. Before I start, please join me in prayer."

A hush fell over the congregation as heads bowed. "Father, we love You," Jesse began, "and offer You our praise and worship with a humble spirit. We come to You this morning eager for what You have for us. May Your Holy Spirit have free reign here this morning. Lord, these people have come here to hear from You, not me, but I cannot preach Your Word without the sweet anointing of Your blessed Holy Spirit. So, I ask for that anointing now, and I ask that Your Spirit prepare each heart for what You have for us today. May Your will be accomplished in this place, and when all is said and done, may each of us say, 'It was good to be in the house of the Lord today.' In the blessed name of our Savior, Jesus Christ, I pray. Amen."

He looked up as he opened his Bible. "Let's begin today in the book of Joshua, chapter twenty-four, verses fourteen and fifteen. Please read with me as I read these two verses aloud. 'Now therefore fear the LORD, and serve him in sincerity and in truth: and put away the gods, which your fathers served on the other side of the flood, and in Egypt; and serve ye the LORD. And if it seem evil unto you to serve the LORD, choose you this day whom ye will serve; whether the gods which your fathers served that were on the other side of the flood, or the gods of the Amorites, in whose land ye dwell: but as for me and my house, we will serve the LORD.'

"Joshua is challenging the children of Israel to make a decision about whom they will follow. Their choice was to serve either the true and living God of Israel or the false gods of the pagan people around them. Joshua knew this decision would be of vital importance to his people, just as this same decision is to us today. Joshua knew that true salvation for the children of Israel could only be found in Jehovah God. Yet, he knew that God would never force His children to serve Him. It needed to be a willing choice for the Israelites, just as it must be a willing choice from our hearts to serve the Lord today.

"We make many choices in life. Some are major; others are minor. Some affect us only for the moment while others affect us throughout our lives. The right choices can bring us great blessings whereas the wrong choices can easily lead to heartache and grief, and just as it was in the days of Joshua, the choice to serve the Lord is up to each one of us. Let's examine some individuals in the Bible and the choices they made.

"One such individual was Moses. His decision to relinquish his high position in Egypt and unite with the Israelites may have seemed foolish to his Egyptian counterparts, but due to the choices Moses made, he was used by the Lord in a mighty way, and he is recorded in the Bible as being one of God's greatest prophets.

"Another person to consider is Noah. He seemed quite laughable in the eyes of his peers when he chose to obey God, but that saved him and his family. Imagine what would have happened had Noah chosen to disobey the Lord."

Will leaned forward in the pew and focused on the pastor. *Choice? I always thought Christians were more like puppets on a string. Controlled by... well, by God, I guess.* As Jesse continued to describe several other individuals in the Bible who faced difficult choices, Will listened attentively.

"As we study the Word, we see that Scripture also records for us those individuals who made wrong choices. One example is Jonah. God asked him to go to the city of Nineveh and deliver a message of judgment against those that lived there. Instead of choosing to obey the Lord, Jonah rebelled. His ultimate consequence was being thrown off a ship during a storm and ending up in the belly of a great fish. In the end, the Bible tells us that Jonah amended his choice, and made the trip to Nineveh, but not without other troubles along the way.

"Another individual who chose unwisely was Lot, Abraham's nephew. He made a terrible choice when he selected Sodom and Gomorrah as his place of residence. He chose sin over righteousness, and in the end, he lost his home, his wife, and the respect of his daughters."

As Jesse continued, Maggie noticed Will staring intently at the pastor. She tapped Colin's hand, and he turned slightly toward her. She made a very slight motion to her left, and Colin looked beyond her, seeing Will's gaze fixated on the pastor. Colin glanced back at Maggie and smiled, his nod barely perceptible.

Jesse walked out from behind the pulpit and into the aisle of the church. "Perhaps the most amazing choice ever made was the one made by our Savior, the Lord Jesus Christ. Philippians 4:5-8 states, 'Let this mind be in you, which was also in Christ Jesus: Who, being in the form of God, thought it not robbery to be equal with God: but made Himself of no reputation, and took upon Him the form of a servant, and was made in the likeness of men: and being found in fashion as a man, He humbled himself, and became obedient unto death, even the death of the cross.' Jesus *chose* to leave the splendor of heaven knowing His final destination was to be the cross. But, why did He choose to do this?" Jesse paused for a moment.

Will leaned forward in the pew. *Christ chose to die on the cross? Why would He do that?*

Jesse looked out at his congregation and spoke from his heart. "He made that choice because He loves you with an everlasting love. He made that choice so you and I could live forever with Him in heaven one day. He made that choice so He could be your Savior.

"Maybe you're here today, and you've never made a choice to accept Christ as your Savior. You've never asked Him to forgive your sins and become the Lord of your life. That choice is the most important one you'll ever make. Why? Because its consequences are eternal."

He paused for a moment as he moved back to the pulpit. "Romans 3:23 states that 'All have sinned, and come short of the glory of God.' The penalty for our sin is death, or eternal separation from God. Romans 6:23 states 'For the wages of sin is death;' but it continues to tell us that 'the gift of God is eternal life through Jesus Christ our Lord.'

"Furthermore, the Bible tells us in Acts 16:31, 'Believe on the Lord Jesus Christ and thou shalt be saved.' There's the choice. If you should choose Christ to forgive your sins and become your Savior, every promise that God has given His children in the Bible becomes yours. The blessings of salvation are incredible! Imagine being able to call upon the Lord for anything, at any time, knowing He'll hear you and respond! What a Father He is to those who love and trust Him!"

Jesse then read and expounded upon John 3:16. Will shifted his weight in the pew. He leaned back slightly; his brow furrowed as he studied the pastor's face. His gaze did not falter when Valerie took his hand in hers, but instead his narrowed eyes remained focused on Jesse.

"Salvation is a free gift offered by God to you," continued the pastor. "You cannot work to obtain it. Ephesians 2:8 says 'For by grace are ye saved through faith; and that not of yourselves: it is the gift of God,' and that gift is yours if you choose to accept it." He allowed his words to settle in the hearts of the people before continuing.

"If you are a Christian," said Jesse, "you must choose whether or not you're going to live as one, or if you're going to live as a citizen of the world. Think about the choices you've made already. How do you dress? What kind of music do you listen to? What's your language like? As a Christian, your life should be separate from the world. Your choices should reflect that distinction. II Corinthians, chapter 6 clearly instructs us on how we should live our lives... separate from the world. Does your life reflect the Savior to the world? Does it encourage other Christians in their own faith? People should be able to see a holy difference in you. If they don't, perhaps you need to reconsider some of the choices you've already made. Let's pray."

Jesse offered a brief prayer and then an invitation to the altar, and as the pastor prayed, Will felt Valerie's fingers tighten around his own. He glanced over at her, only to see her head bowed and her eyes closed once more. He bowed his own head and fought to untangle the myriad of thoughts rambling through his mind.

I don't even know if I believe there is a God. How am I supposed to find that out?

CHAPTER TWENTY-SIX

"Thank you for taking time to meet with me," stated Will as he shook the hand of Jesse McClellan. He sat down on a padded grey chair opposite the pastor's desk.

"I'm happy to do it, Will. How can I help you?" Jesse's smile was warm and inviting, and the nervousness that Will felt on the way over began to dissipate.

"Your message last Sunday… well, it brought up a lot of questions, and quite frankly, I haven't got the faintest idea where to go for the answers. I'm not a Christian, as you've probably guessed, and my wife and sister, and Colin, have been… uh… urging me to convert." Will squirmed in his chair.

"Are you a follower of any particular religion?" Jesse leaned forward resting his arms on his desk.

Will shook his head. "No, no I'm not. I'm… I don't know what I am. To be honest, I don't even know if I believe in God."

"Oh." Jesse's eyes widened a bit. "Well, let's start there. What is it that makes you think there's no God?"

"I'm not sure. I've been asking myself the same thing. Maybe it's all the sickness and death that I deal with. I just don't see how a loving God would allow all that," Will stated.

"I see. Have you considered the ones that don't die?"

"What do you mean?"

"They don't all die, do they?"

"No. No, they don't."

"Who's responsible for that?"

Will thought for a moment. "I suppose I would say the medical profession, and you would say God."

Jesse smiled. "They could work together, you know."

Will tensed a bit. "I suppose they could. I know Maggie says that God gave me my intellect, and through that I learned my craft, and therefore, He's part of the healing process, but that seems too convenient of an explanation."

Jesse nodded. "I agree."

"You do?" Will looked up in surprise.

"Yes. Let's try not to work with conveniences. Let's see if we can solve this for you."

Will was intrigued. *This is not what I expected from him. Maybe this wasn't such a bad idea coming here, although I don't see how he can have an open mind about this.* Will relaxed a bit and sat back into the chair.

Jesse took a deep breath. "I suppose you've heard plenty of arguments for a God?"

Will frowned and nodded his head. "Lately, I've heard quite a few. I've pretty much lived my life not even thinking about God. Not until Maggie became a Christian and then my wife. Now, with Colin intending to marry my sister, I'm sort of forced to come to grips with where I stand. The three of them are pretty daunting."

Jesse grinned. "I imagine they could be. Okay, let's see… what is one of the most complicated pieces of medical equipment?"

Will thought for a moment. "Just about everything is pretty intricate. Maybe an MRI machine? I don't really know about the machinery itself. I don't build them."

Jesse nodded knowingly. "So, you would you agree that someone had to put that machine together? That it didn't assemble itself?"

Will smiled and nodded. "Of course."

"And the same for something less complex, like a clock. The pieces didn't just haphazardly come together. There had to be a clockmaker in the process, right?"

Again, Will nodded as he suspiciously eyed the pastor. He crossed his arms in front of him.

Jesse sat back in his chair and met Will's gaze. "Have you given any thought to the human body?"

Will raised his eyebrows and shrugged his shoulders. "Medically, all the time. In regard to God? Not really."

"Well, we all start out as one cell, correct? Then that cell begins to divide until there are many identical cells. Something happens, and those cells begin to differentiate. Some become skin cells; some become brain cells; some become blood cells, etc. Eventually, a baby is born, and life outside of the womb begins for each of us. This body of ours performs more functions than I'm aware of, I'm sure, and does so without anyone doing anything. There's no instruction manual, no on-off switch-- in fact, correct me if I'm wrong, we're not really sure how every part of it works." He paused, allowing his words to penetrate Will's intellect.

"True." Will shifted uneasily in the chair.

"It seems to work this way every time a life is conceived. So, is that chance? Or divine creation?" Jesse waited to allow Will to respond, but when he didn't, Jesse continued. "Now, let's take a look around us. This same process occurs in every living thing. Plants, animals, bugs... How does that happen to every organism that ever was? Even the most logical mind should be able to see that if this is all chance--"

"You're talking about evolution?"

"Yes. The haphazard organization of cellular material to become something, and then the random decision of that organism to adapt and change at will to whatever it wishes. How does a cell do that?"

"It doesn't seem to make much sense, does it? Too much opportunity for variance or failure in the processes," Will admitted.

"It makes as much sense as an MRI machine assembling itself into one of the more complex pieces of medical machinery, but I'm not the one who has spent years studying the human body, or working on it for that matter. Does it seem plausible to you?"

Will shook his head. "No. Not really. Not the way you've explained it. But your analysis might be a bit simplistic."

"Can you offer me another explanation?"

Will shook his head again. "Not a viable one."

"Can we agree to the possibility that maybe there is a God, before we go on?"

"Yeah, I guess so. At least for now." Will sighed deeply. "But even if there is, why do I need God? Maybe that's the question. Val, Maggie, Colin, they all believe I need God, but I don't think I really do. I know you're going to think the same way that they do."

"Well, yes, that's my job," grinned Jesse. "But really, Will, it's not important that I, or anyone else thinks you need God. What matters is whether or not *you* think you need God in your life."

Will rubbed the back of his neck and exhaled slowly. "I don't think I do, but... what if I'm wrong? You talked on Sunday about making choices. What if I make the wrong choice? If I'm right and you're wrong, I've lost nothing, but if you're right and I'm wrong... according to you, I've lost everything. Somehow, if what I understand to be true about God is correct, He doesn't really want me on those terms."

"You mean as an insurance policy? A way to keep yourself from hell? No, not really. God loves you, and He wants a personal relationship with you, Will. One that you desire as well, not just as a way to avoid hell. However, God can't have that relationship with you as long as the sin in your life remains unforgiven. You see, sin is like a barrier between us and a holy God. It was because of sin that God had to sacrifice His only Son for us. Jesus took the punishment for our sins on the cross so that me, you, and everyone else in this world could be reconciled with our Creator, God. There is nothing that you or I could do to merit God's forgiveness. Only Jesus' death and resurrection could secure our salvation. If we're going to live with Him for all eternity, our sins have to be gone, and only Christ can eradicate those sins."

Will stood up and walked over to the window. He looked out toward the courtyard of the church. "You're telling me that no matter how many people I've helped in my career, no matter how many lives I've saved, it's no good to God?"

"Think about it, Will. If there was any other way for us to earn our way to heaven, why would God have chosen to send His only Son to the cross? I'd say that would have been pretty foolish, and definitely not what I'd expect from an omnipotent and omniscient God." Jesse waited for Will to respond.

"I suppose not." Will turned around to face Jesse. "You're pretty sure about all this, aren't you?"

"It's all here." He opened the Bible on his desk to the book of John. "This is like my Merck Manual," he said referring to a well-known physician's reference book. Flipping to chapter three, he turned the Bible around so Will could read it. "See? Right here it tells me the reason Jesus came to us." He put his finger on verse seventeen and then read aloud. "'For God sent not his Son into the world to condemn the world; but that the world through Him might be saved.' And then..." He turned the pages to the sixteenth chapter of Acts. "It says here... verse thirty-one, 'Believe on the Lord Jesus Christ, and thou shalt be saved, and thy house.'"

Will turned around and held his hands up in frustration. "I don't know what to do. I want this confusion to end. How can I believe in something... or someone... without proof that it's real?"

Jesse stood up, walked around to the front of his desk, and sat on the edge of it. "There's proof all around you, Will. The cry of a newborn baby, the rising of the sun every morning, the love between a man and a woman. What it takes is faith." He tapped the Bible. "Faith that what God said is true. Faith that He really does love you and wants a relationship with you." He paused for a moment, and then asked, "How did you know Valerie loved you?"

Will studied the pastor carefully and crossed his arms again. "She told me."

"How do you know she told you the truth?"

"She wouldn't lie to me."

"How do you know that?"

"I just know. She wouldn't lie to me."

"So, you took it on faith. Faith that her words were true. Well, that's what God wants from you. Just to take Him at His Word. This Word." He held up the Bible. "God's telling you that He loves you. That He wants a relationship with you so badly that He sacrificed His only Son to have it. If you can accept that on faith, you're halfway there. The rest is just a prayer away."

Will walked over to Jesse and confessed, "I need some time to think about this."

"Of course. You can call me with any questions you have-- night or day."

"Thank you. I appreciate you taking time to talk with me." Will offered his hand.

"Any time, Will." He grasped the doctor's hand and shook it. As Will left the office, Jesse watched him go, and then he sat down in his chair. Elbows on the desk and hands clasped together, he bowed his head and prayed that God would open Will's heart to the truth of Scripture and the saving grace of Jesus Christ.

On the drive home, Will tried to formulate how he was going to explain his visit with Jesse to Valerie. Never keeping anything from her, he struggled with the right approach. *I have to be careful. She'll jump to the conclusion that I want to be a Christian and not understand that I'm just asking some questions.*

He slowly opened the door from the garage into the kitchen and walked in. Tossing his keys on the counter, he inhaled the aroma of a roast and realized he had skipped lunch to meet with the pastor. "Val?"

"In here!"

He walked into the dining area as Valerie set the last fork next to her plate. He slipped his arms around her waist and kissed her on the neck. "How was your day?"

She easily turned around in his hold and her sparkling eyes did little to mask her joy at seeing her husband. "It was wonderful! Now, with you home, it's perfect!" Her arms went around his neck, and she pulled his head down to meet her waiting lips. "I hope you're hungry."

"Starved. I skipped lunch today," he admitted as he released her. "What's this?" He dipped his finger into a creamy orange dip and then brought it to his tongue. "Wow, that's got a kick to it!"

"It's a chipotle dip for the fried zucchini," she called out as she walked into the kitchen. "I thought I'd try something a bit different tonight."

"I hope the roast is normal!"

"It is. I didn't want to risk ruining the main part of dinner." She returned with the zucchini on a large crystal-serving dish. "Would you help me bring the roast out?"

He followed her back into the kitchen and lifted the roast from its baking pan to a platter. He tore a piece of the juicy meat from its side and popped it into his mouth. "Wow, this is good, Val!"

Her eyes lit up at his compliment, and she smiled appreciatively as she dished up the potatoes and carrots from around the roasting pan to the platter. "Thank you, but I think you'd eat anything I served you!"

"Maybe, but I do know good food, and this is good." He pulled another small piece off the roast and quickly put it in his mouth.

"Will Garrett! You stop that! You're going to spoil your dinner!"

"This is my dinner, isn't it?" He chuckled as he carried the roast to the table.

Valerie followed him with two tall glasses of iced tea and sat down in the chair Will had pulled out for her. He sat across from her.

Following her lead, Will bowed his head while Valerie asked the blessing over their meal. He cut two generous slabs of meat, first placing one on Valerie's plate and the other on his own. She scooped up a healthy portion of the steaming vegetables for each of them as well as a few of the fried zucchini slices.

"What did you do all day besides slave over a hot stove?" asked Will as he dipped a zucchini slice into the chipotle sauce.

"Well…" When she didn't continue, Will looked up holding the zucchini in mid-air.

"Well, what?" he said as he ate the crispy vegetable. He picked up his fork and knife to cut a piece of his roast.

Her eyes shied away from his look, and she began to slice her piece of roast into bite-size chunks. "I ran a few errands. I washed a load of clothes. I did a crossword puzzle."

Will cocked his head and peered at his wife. He set his knife and fork on his plate. "What are you not telling me?"

She tentatively raised her eyes. "I wanted to know what you thought about maybe…"

"Maybe what, *Mrs. Garrett*?" He tried to sound as if he was scolding her, but his eyes had a lighthearted look.

"Maybe… trying to have a baby again."

Her hopeful face tugged at Will's heart as his look changed from playful to astonishment. *She can't be serious about this! Has she already forgotten what we went through?* His mind reeled to two years earlier when they both were optimistic about starting a family. The repeated disappointment after months of trying had led to one attempt at in-vitro fertilization, but the heartache of that failure had taken a tremendous emotional toll on Valerie. Will couldn't bear to see her go through that experience again, so they had decided to forego a second try at starting a family.

"Will?"

He looked into her hopeful eyes reflecting the glow of the single candle in the center of their table and knew there was no way he could deny her the opportunity to try for a baby.

"I'm sorry, sweetheart. Just thinking of all you went through before. Are you sure you want to try again?" His voice was soft and low. He reached out to touch her hand.

She nodded. "Yes, I really do. Do you want to?"

Can I ever say 'no' to her? Will sighed and then smiled lovingly at his wife. "Absolutely."

Valerie's face brightened and the twinkle returned to her eyes. "In that case, I have a present for you!"

His brow furrowed a bit, and he watched her curiously as she placed a small box wrapped in silver paper in front of him. A white bow adorned its top. He picked it up and playfully shook it by his ear.

"What is it?"

"Open it!" Valerie's eyes never left Will's face; she followed his every movement. She bit her lower lip nervously as Will began to unwrap the box.

He carefully removed the top and glanced at the white probe inside. "A thermometer?"

Valerie rolled her eyes and shook her head lightly. "Some doctor you are. It's not a thermometer. Look closer."

He returned his attention to the probe and picked it up. His eyes widened immediately as he recognized what he was holding.

"Is this yours?"

Valerie nodded, and she waited expectantly.

"And these two lines mean...?"

Again, she nodded. "It means we're going to have a baby, Will." Her voice barely contained the excitement within her.

He stared at the thick white pregnancy indicator stick in his hand and inspected it carefully one more time, tracing the thin lines with his finger. "Are you sure?" His voice was nearly a whisper.

"As sure as I can be after three tests," confessed Valerie, her eyes still glued to her husband's face.

Will rose slowly from his chair and reached for his wife. She immediately stood and fell into his arms. They said nothing, but clung to each other in a shared moment of unbelievable joy. His tears were hot as they spilled from his eyes onto the top of Valerie's dark brown curls, and he lost the battle of composure. For a moment, it seemed as if time had stopped.

"I love you, Valerie," he said huskily. He clung to her, weeping unashamedly.

"I've been praying for this, Will. I didn't want to say anything to you until I was sure. I didn't want to get your hopes up and then..." She kept her head against his chest as she spoke. "I was a little worried about being pregnant so soon after chemotherapy, but I researched everything online, and I think it should be fine." She raised her head, her lower lip trembling, and searched Will's face. "What do you think?"

He pulled away from her to facilitate looking directly into her eyes. "Online? Valerie Garrett, I can't believe you! You're married to a doctor, your sister-in-law is a doctor, you work in a hospital-- and you go to the Internet for medical information?" He lowered his head to meet her lips and kissed her deeply.

"I didn't want anyone to know until I told you." She lowered her eyes and allowed him to pull her back to him once more. "So, there really wasn't anyone I could ask," she responded, her cheeks warming.

"What am I going to do with you," chided Will tenderly.

"Just love me."

"I'll never stop doing that, sweetheart."

He held her possessively, saying nothing. *I did ask for proof...*

CHAPTER TWENTY-SEVEN

Will and Valerie had agreed to keep the news of their pregnancy quiet until after it had been verified by an obstetrician, but Will knew within him that it would be a viable pregnancy. The jubilation he felt at becoming a father was dampened only by the turmoil he felt from his indecision about God. He had asked for proof, and now believed he had received it, but he still fought against surrendering his life to Christ.

It was early in the morning when he awoke from a fitful sleep. He glanced over at Valerie who remained asleep, her breathing deep and rhythmic. He rose quietly, slipped on a pair of jeans and a t-shirt, and walked into the kitchen. He swept his tousled hair back from his forehead as he leaned against the counter. His gaze wandered to the small wooden table nestled in the kitchen alcove. In its center sat a crystal vase filled with a bouquet of multicolored zinnias. Next to the vase lay Valerie's Bible.

Will stared at it for a moment and then reached for it as he sat down at the table. He read her name embossed at the bottom and gently traced it with his finger. He fanned the pages quickly, opening the Bible to the book of Psalms where Valerie had placed a lace bookmark. Several verses of chapter thirty were highlighted, and Will began to read silently.

I will extol thee, O LORD; for thou hast lifted me up, and hast not made my foes to rejoice over me. O LORD my God, I cried unto thee, and thou hast healed me. O LORD, thou hast brought up my soul from the grave: thou hast kept me alive, that I should not go down to the pit. Sing unto the LORD, O ye saints of his, and give thanks at the remembrance of his holiness. For his anger endureth but a moment...

Suddenly, he stopped at the fifth verse and reread the last part of it.

...in His favour is life: weeping may endure for a night, but joy cometh in the morning.

Wasn't that what Grace had told him? He struggled to recall the words of comfort the old woman had shared with him that night in the emergency room. *Dark times will come, she had said, but never forget that God loves you, and, she continued, joy would come in the morning.*

Will's mind reeled. *In His favour is life... Consider the wondrous works of God... Believe on the Lord Jesus Christ, and thou shalt be saved... Choose you this day whom ye will serve...*

Will felt a cold chill through his body. *Choose you this day whom ye will serve...*The Word of God penetrated deep into his soul. He felt numb, yet awakened to something that troubled him. He continued to read the words that his wife had underlined.

I cried to thee, O LORD; and unto the LORD I made supplication. Thou hast turned for me my mourning into dancing: thou hast put off my sackcloth, and girded me with gladness; to the end that my glory may sing praise to thee, and not be silent. O LORD my God, I will give thanks unto thee forever.

He glanced at the open bedroom door and saw the faint outline of his wife sleeping in their bed. *Valerie...* Abruptly, he retrieved his cell phone and scanned through his contacts. Within seconds, the connection was made, and Will waited.

The phone rang several times before being picked up. "Hello?"

"Colin, it's Will."

"Will? Is something wrong?"

"No, nothing's wrong. Yes, yes, something is wrong- well, not really, but I need to talk with you. I know it's early, but-"

"No problem, Will. I was up. Is Valerie-"

"She's fine. I need to talk to you about... about God."

There was a brief moment of silence on the phone before Colin responded. "Of course. You want me to come over?"

Will glanced over toward his bedroom and his slumbering wife. "I'd really appreciate it. Val's still asleep, and I don't want to wake her to tell her I'm leaving. She'd just worry."

"No problem. I'll be right over."

Relief came over Will as he made a pot of coffee. *It's time to get this settled, once and for all.*

Early morning beach traffic was light, and the drive to the Garrett home took less than twenty minutes. As he pulled into their driveway, Colin offered up a prayer on behalf of Maggie's brother. *Lord, I don't know what I'm walking into, but You do. Please give me wisdom as I talk with Will. Please open his heart to the gospel. In Jesus' name, I pray. Amen.* He grabbed his Bible, stepped out of the car, and walked purposefully toward the front door of the house.

He had only knocked once when Will had the door open.

"Thanks for coming, Colin. I really appreciate it." He shook the singer's hand and motioned for him to enter. The smell of coffee wafted through the house.

"Can I get you a cup of coffee?"

"No, thanks. I'm more of a tea drinker," admitted Colin. "But I'm fine right now. Maybe later." He followed Will into the living room. "So what's going on?"

Will sat on a brown leather loveseat opposite the matching sofa on which Colin took a seat. "I'm not sure where to start."

Colin tilted his head slightly and noticed Will fidgeting in his seat and avoiding eye contact with him. "You said you had some questions?"

Will nodded. "I do. I... I went to talk with your pastor yesterday."

Colin's eyes widened. "Really? About what?" He leaned forward slightly.

"Initially, I had some questions about his sermon, but it ended up with me questioning God's existence. I told him I needed proof about that. Don't get me wrong; I wasn't there to fight with him. I really did have some questions, and he answered a lot of them, but I guess the whole thing got me thinking. Anyway, last night when I got home, Valerie told me something that I believe is the proof I asked for." He paused for a moment, and then looked up to meet Colin's gaze. "I'm going to be a father."

Colin sat stunned for a moment, but quickly recovered. "Congratulations, Will! I had no idea you were planning a family."

"We weren't." He related the previous experiences that he and Valerie had endured in their first attempts to start a family. "I thought it would be easy to continue denying the existence of God, but I can't do that anymore. One of my patients said something to me before Valerie got pneumonia. She said something like 'In the dark times, remember that God loves you, and in the end joy will come in the morning.'

"And this morning, I was flipping through Val's Bible and, well, I was reading some of the verses Valerie had highlighted when this one caught my eye." He reached for her Bible on the end table and set it on the coffee table between them. He pointed out Psalm 30:5.

Colin leaned over and read it aloud. "'For His anger endureth but a moment; in His favour is life: weeping may endure for a night, but joy cometh in the morning.'" He looked up as Will continued.

"There are thousands of verses in the Bible, Colin. It can't be a coincidence that both Grace and Val happen to pick out the same one, right?"

"I personally don't believe in coincidences when it comes to God. He doesn't leave things up to chance," responded Colin.

"So, what does it mean?" It was now Will's turn to wait for a response.

Colin set his Bible on the table and sat up. "Will, things happen in life. Good and bad, regardless of our relationship with God. That's just the natural course of events, but the Bible tells us 'All things work together for good to them that love God, to them who are the called according to His purpose.' That means that God can take any circumstance, even bad ones, and make it a positive thing for Christians and, at the same time, bring glory to Himself. Sometimes we don't see it clearly, but it's a fact. Sometimes Christians go through hard times in life, but in the end, when it's over, somehow it's made us stronger in our faith, and at the same time, brought glory to God. To me, that verse means that no matter what happens to me, the end product will be victory through Christ, which produces unspeakable joy."

Will frowned and shook his head. "I can't see how anything positive came from Val's cancer, or how God received any glory through it."

"Really? I can."

"Enlighten me, please," Will said, leaning back against the sofa, "because I am completely mystified."

"Well, the obvious and most important thing is that Valerie got saved during her battle with cancer. Secondly, Valerie got over the pneumonia. How did that happen?" Colin prodded Will's memory.

Will gave Colin a puzzled look. "The antibiotics." He thought for a moment, then spoke slowly as understanding began to replace confusion. "No, they weren't working." He reflected on Valerie's condition in the ICU prior to her recovery. Abruptly, he looked at Colin. "Consider the wondrous works of God... that's what she wrote."

Colin's eyes widened in astonishment. *Will's quoting Scripture?*

"Grace... my patient," Will explained, "she wrote that on my prescription pad. I found it the night Val got better..." He lifted his eyes to look at Colin. "I... I threw it out. I actually thought it was nonsense because Valerie had improved..." Will became very quiet. His voice was introspective as he recalled that night. "How could I have done that? Why didn't I see that it wasn't what we had done..." He looked up at Colin. "That was God, wasn't it?"

Colin nodded. "I think that would definitely qualify as a 'wondrous work.' What do *you* think?"

Will shrugged his shoulders and slightly shook his head. "I... I don't know what I think at this point. I just know I can't stop thinking about God, and where I stand with Him. I have to understand it if I'm going to make the right choices in my life. I mean, what could be a more wondrous work than this baby?" The sudden awareness of God's interaction hit Will hard. He looked up at Colin seeking confirmation of his new-found awareness.

Colin raised an eyebrow and nodded. "The Bible does say that children are a gift from God."

"I can't believe I've been so blind." Will shook his head in disbelief but then drew a deep breath. "Ok, God's definitely got my attention, what's the next step? How do I fix this mess I've gotten myself into?"

"I don't think I understand what you're asking."

Will grinned. "Boy, for someone who's been circling for the kill, you're kind of slow on the uptake."

"I beg your pardon?"

"I'll be the first to admit I'm a very stubborn man, but I'm not completely ignorant to what's been going on around me. I've seen the changes in Maggie and Valerie, and believe me, I've been watching you like a hawk."

"Me? For what reason?"

"Truthfully?" Will paused for a moment and cleared his throat. "I... uh... was looking for something about you that wasn't genuine. Something that would prove to me that your faith was not as real as you said it was."

Colin sat speechless.

Will continued. "Even when I was outraged with you, you reached out with love and forgiveness. I..." His voice broke. "I will never forget that. I've never met anyone who not only lived his faith, but defended it so vehemently. I kept hoping I'd see some sort of hypocrisy in you, but I didn't. What I saw was someone who loved God."

Colin's stunned eyes met Will's somber ones. "I'm not perfect, Will. I've had my share of failures in life, and for a long time I lived only for myself. Surrendering my life to Christ was the easy part. I had many life changes to make. It's living for the Lord on a daily basis that's been the hardest."

"Really? From my perspective, you're doing a pretty good job of it."

Colin smiled self-consciously. "Well, my walk with Christ isn't always easy, I'll attest to that, but I thank you for the encouragement. Now, let's get back to you."

Will nodded. "I've spent a lifetime being anti-God. How do I make up for that?" His voice wavered. "I mean, why would God want anything to do with me?"

"It's hard to understand the depth of His love for us." Colin explained. "Our understanding of love is so limited, but God... well, God *is* love, and His love for us is boundless. He loved you, Will, from the moment you were formed in your mother's womb. And He knew the path your life would take, but He still loved you with an everlasting love, and He will continue to love you. Nothing will ever change that."

Will uncrossed his legs and leaned forward. His eyes were sharply focused on Colin's face. "Are you telling me that God will accept me just as I am?"

"Well, yes and no. His one requirement is that your sin must be dealt with. Unfortunately, there's nothing you can do to earn the forgiveness of your sins. Since you can't have a relationship with God unless your sins have been forgiven, He provided the way to forgiveness. It's through His Son, Jesus Christ. That's the reason Christ came to us from heaven. He became the ultimate sacrifice on the cross for the sins of the whole world.

"The Bible explains that without the shedding of blood, sin cannot be forgiven. When Jesus died, it was His blood that made forgiveness of sin possible. All you need to do is ask Him to save you from your sins, and He will."

"That's it?"

"Yes. It's all here, in the Bible. I'll be glad to show you if you'd like me to."

Will swallowed hard and nodded. "I think that would be a very good idea."

Colin opened his Bible to the book of Romans and slowly explained each verse of the Romans' Road, a set of verses often used to share the gospel of Christ with people. As he reviewed each verse, he waited until Will affirmed his understanding. Finally, he came to the tenth chapter.

"Lastly, God's Word says 'That if thou shalt confess with thy mouth the Lord Jesus, and shalt believe in thine heart that God hath raised Him from the dead, thou shalt be saved. For with the heart man believeth unto righteousness; and with the mouth confession is made unto salvation.'" He pointed out the ninth and tenth verses to Will, and as the two men sat quietly, Colin silently prayed for God's Word to work in Will's heart.

Will reread the verses and then turned to look briefly toward his bedroom. "God means so much to Valerie... and you and

Maggie. I don't want to be the outsider anymore, but I don't want to turn to God for the wrong reasons. I want to make the right choice for the right reasons."

Colin prompted Will. "If you removed the three of us from the equation, would you still want God's forgiveness?"

Will thought for a moment, then slowly nodded. His voice was quiet but without reservation. "Want it? I think I'd beg for it. How can someone be so blind? Yes. I'd want God to know that I'm sorry for... for everything." He kept his head down, his hands clasped together. "My anger with Him, my rejection of Him, my pride in myself... all of it."

"All you need to do is tell Him, Will. The Bible tells us 'If we confess our sins, He is faithful and just to forgive us our sins and to cleanse us from all unrighteousness.'"

Will cast a questioning glance at Colin. "All I need to do is *ask* Christ to forgive me?"

"Yes. Salvation is a gift from God. It can't be obtained by anything we can do, otherwise, Christ would never have needed to go to the cross."

"That makes sense." Will took another deep breath and exhaled slowly. "Just ask Him, right? Okay. I can do that. You're sure He's listening?"

"I'm sure."

Will bowed his head and hesitantly began to pray. His voice broke several times, yet he continued. From the depths of his heart, he confessed his great need for God's forgiveness and humbly asked Jesus to forgive his sins and become His Savior.

Colin's head was bowed as Will prayed, and neither of them heard Valerie enter the room.

"Will?"

Will turned his tear-filled eyes toward his wife's voice. She held her hand up to her mouth as he slowly rose. She came to him, saying nothing. Wrapping her arms around him, she buried her face in his chest and whispered her thanks to the Lord for her husband's salvation. As she clung to Will, he tightened his hold on her as he struggled to control his own emotions.

Colin fought to keep his own tears from spilling over. *Thank you, Jesus!* He closed his eyes and quietly praised His Savior. The excitement he felt within his own soul was difficult to contain, and he wanted so badly to call Maggie and tell her the good news, but he knew that was something that Will needed to do.

Valerie grabbed a tissue and sat down on the sofa. Before her husband could join her, Colin stood, reached out, and clasped Will's hand. He shook it robustly and then impulsively hugged him. "Welcome to the family, Will!" Unashamedly, he wept tears of joy.

It was difficult for Will to speak, so he just nodded his head as he sat down beside his wife.

"Does Maggie know you're here?" asked Valerie as she reached for Colin's hand. She pulled him down to the sofa on the other side of her.

"No." Colin shook his head. "Will called me, and I came right over. Plus, she's working." He glanced at his watch. "She should be off soon if nothing unforeseen happens."

"Let's invite her over for breakfast and tell her then!" suggested Valerie joyfully. She turned to her husband. "You can't tell her over the phone, Will. It's too important!"

Will smiled lovingly at his wife. "Whatever you want is fine with me, sweetheart." He kissed her forehead, then turned to Colin. "You will stay, right?"

"I wouldn't miss this for anything!"

CHAPTER TWENTY-EIGHT

"Now promise me, no more beans pushed up your nose!" chuckled Maggie, as she removed her latex gloves and tossed them into the wastebasket.

The five-year-old girl blinked her big brown eyes at the doctor and looked at her mother quickly before answering. "I promise!"

Maggie turned to the mother. "Mrs. Solomon, I think Shelby will be just fine."

"Thank you so much, Dr. Devereaux. I was so worried about her."

"You're welcome. The nurse will be here in just a moment with your aftercare instructions. Have a good day."

Maggie left the room, ready to go home and relax. She walked over to the nurses' station and scanned the treatment board. No new additions and a near empty waiting area made the way clear for Maggie to leave. She headed for the staff lounge to drop off her lab coat and stethoscope in her locker.

"Dr. Devereaux?"

Maggie turned toward the voice.

"I've got a message for you from Valerie." Maggie took the slip of paper from the clerk.

She read the note inviting her to breakfast. Initially inclined to refuse, she changed her mind when she read the part about

Colin joining them. As she left the hospital, she found herself looking forward to the morning visit.

The drive was short to Will's house, and Maggie was met at the door by Colin. She kissed him lightly on the lips. "I was so ready for a relaxing bath and a few hours of sleep, but this isn't a bad exchange."

He raised his eyebrows. "Is that so? It's nice to know that I win out over a bath and a nap." His smile warmed her heart, and she involuntarily reached for his hand.

"I love you," she whispered as he led her to the couch in the living room.

He sat beside her, crossing his legs and leaning back. He stretched his arm out behind her. "How was your shift?"

"Pretty quiet, but steady."

"Need a cup of coffee, Mags?" Will called out from the kitchen.

"Sounds good, Will." She turned back to Colin. "This is a very pleasant surprise."

"That's an understatement," Colin murmured.

"What?"

Will walked in and handed Maggie a cup of coffee while Valerie placed a tray of muffins on the table between them. They both sat down on the loveseat, and Maggie noticed their red eyes.

"What's going on? What's wrong?" She straightened up in alarm.

"Nothing, Maggie. Really. You can relax. It's just that we have some news for you." Will looked at Valerie, then back at his sister. "Valerie and I, well, we... uh... we're going to have a baby," Will stammered as he interlocked his fingers with Valerie's.

Maggie's mouth dropped open. "Seriously? I'm going to be an aunt?" A broad smile spread across her face. She leaped up and rushed to hug both of them. Amid the hugs, tears, and congratulatory kisses, she turned toward Colin. "You knew, didn't you?"

He just shrugged his shoulders and smiled, enjoying the scene before him.

"There's more, Mags, but I want you to sit down before I say anything," Will stated.

Maggie cast an anxious look at Colin as Will cleared his throat.

"Maggie, I... uh... boy, I thought this would be easy!" He clasped his hands together and rested his forearms on his knees. He looked at the floor.

"You can do it, Will," encouraged Valerie.

"Tell me!" Maggie demanded, her lips set in a firm line.

Will looked up at her and nodded. "Be patient with me. This isn't quite going like I rehearsed it." He slowly began by explaining his visit with Jesse McClellan. He left nothing out, including the confusion he felt when he had found the same verses Grace had shared with him underlined by Valerie in her Bible. He finished by recounting his morning conversation with Colin. "And then, I... uh... I... asked Christ to forgive me. I--" He had no opportunity to finish his sentence before Maggie sprang up, threw her arms around him once more, and cried happily.

"Oh, Will, tell me... tell me everything!" begged Maggie as she stepped back to look her brother directly in his dark brown eyes.

"I asked Christ to forgive me for everything... my stubbornness, my reluctance to accept Him, and, well, He did. And now, I... uh... I'm saved."

She cast a quick glance at Colin. He simply gave her a slight smile and nodded. She returned her astounded gaze to Will. "Oh, Will…I can't tell you how happy I am for you… for us!" She moved to Valerie and embraced her once more. As Maggie tried to speak, her voice broke, and all she could do was hug her sister-in-law.

　　Later, as she sat at the breakfast table listening to the chatter going on around her, Maggie silently thanked the Lord for His amazing love. It had healed her sister-in-law's cancer and now her brother's soul. As her gaze settled on Colin, she knew their future could have no better foundation than that laid by their united faith in Christ, and she rejoiced in the knowledge that God would guide them and walk with them each step of the way.

EPILOGUE

Will stood silently by the granite stone marker before quietly walking to a newer stone. This gravesite, still surrounded by massive floral arrangements, was fresh from the burial a few days earlier.

"You'll never know how much you meant to me." He spoke softly, closed his eyes, and reflected upon the last time he saw her. She had lost so much weight and looked so tiny and frail in the hospital bed. Despite all his efforts, she had died, and Will's heart had nearly broken when she drew her last breath.

"I wish I could have saved you, but I guess God needed you more in heaven than I did here on earth. You were right. In everything you told me, you were right." He allowed himself to feel the heartache of emptiness.

"Will?"

He turned around to see his sister approaching. He self-consciously wiped away a tear.

Maggie stopped behind him and clasped his arm. "Are you okay? It's time for the service to start."

Will nodded. "It's kind of odd finding out they're buried in the same place."

"Yes. I suppose you can visit both Mom and Grace now."

"You know, just before she died, Grace told me that she was ready to go home… to be with Christ. Said her work was finished…" Will's voice faltered.

"She's rejoicing with her Father now, Will. And we'll see her again one day."

Will nodded. "I know. I just wish she were here today. She'll never know how much she meant to me."

Maggie looked tenderly at her brother. "You'll tell her one day, Will. When we all get to heaven, you'll just have to tell her."

Will smiled, and together, he and Maggie entered the church. They walked up the aisle taking their places near the front of the church.

"Everything okay?" Valerie whispered as Will scooted next to her. She held tightly to a small, blanketed bundle in her arms and looked up into Will's dark brown eyes. He reached over, moved the edge of the blanket, and ran his finger down the smooth cheek of the sleeping baby.

"Couldn't be better."

As the service progressed, Will listened with a grateful heart, and when the pastor asked the Garretts to come forward for the dedication of their daughter, Will rose without hesitation, proudly escorting his wife and daughter to stand next to their pastor in front of the congregation.

"Will and Valerie are here today with their daughter, Joy, to dedicate her to the Lord…"

As the pastor continued speaking to the congregation, Will gazed out toward the crowd. Each familiar face touched his heart with a depth of emotion that caught him off guard. He nodded slightly at Ben Shepherd, smiled at Claire Donnelly, and fought back tears when his gaze fell upon Tom Gallagher and his granddaughter, Faith, and her husband. When he saw Colin, an immense gratitude filled his heart, and his smile broadened. A mentor in his new walk with Christ, Colin had Will's utmost admiration. Finally, his eyes met those of his sister's. Maggie beamed at him, and it delighted his soul. He saw her tears fall as he winked at her.

Placing his arm around Valerie, Will bowed his head as a prayer was said for his daughter and offered his own prayer of gratitude to the Lord. *Thank You, Father, for all You've given me. My beautiful wife, my precious daughter, my loving family, and friends. Mostly, thank You for saving me from myself and giving me this wonderful new life through Your Son, Jesus Christ.*

As Will guided Valerie back to her seat, he scanned the congregation once more before sitting beside her. He knew he had been through the darkest nights of his life in the past year and a half, but now, as he turned back to his daughter and wife, he knew in his heart that God's Word was undeniably true. His future held the bright promise that only comes from the unspeakable joy of God's healing love and saving grace.